GUNRUNNER

A Brock and Poole Mystery

Graham Ison

severn House

This first world edition published 2011
in Great Britain and in the USA by
SEVERN HOUSE PUBLISHERS LTD of
9–15 High Street, Sutton, Surrey, England, SM1 1DF.
Trade paperback edition first published
in Great Britain and the USA 2012 by
SEVERN HOUSE PUBLISHERS LTD

British Library Cataloguing in Publication Data

Ison, Graham.
  Gunrunner.
  1. Brock, Harry (Fictitious character: Ison)–Fiction.
  2. Poole, Dave (Fictitious character)–Fiction.
  3. Police–England–London–Fiction. 4. Smuggling–
  Investigation–Fiction. 5. Detective and mystery stories.
  I. Title
  823.9'14-dc22

ISBN-13: 978-0-7278-8095-6 (cased)
ISBN-13: 978-1-84751-383-0 (trade paper)

All Severn House titles are printed on acid-free paper.

Severn House Publishers support The Forest Stewardship Council [FSC],
the leading international forest certification organisation. All our titles that
are printed on Greenpeace-approved FSC-certified paper carry the FSC logo.

Typeset by Palimpsest Book Production Ltd.,
Falkirk, Stirlingshire, Scotland.
Printed and bound in Great Britain by
MPG Books Ltd., Bodmin, Cornwall.

ONE

I t was ten o'clock in the morning of Christmas Day when twenty-five-year-old Peter Shaw entered the car park at Heathrow Airport, hunched his shoulders and gazed around at the rows of parked vehicles. There were family cars in profusion, a number of four-by-fours, a fair number of Jaguars and a couple of Rolls Royce limousines. Not for the first time, he wished that he had gone where the owners of those cars had gone. But on the pay he was getting, there wasn't much chance of that.

Anywhere would do. A sunny beach with a gorgeous girl, or a luxury cruise around the Caribbean; anywhere to get away from the cold of an English winter and this mind-numbing job. He didn't really know why he carried on doing it; he wasn't married and his on-off relationship with a girl who worked in one of the shops in Terminal Three was about to become permanently off.

With a sigh, he began his patrol. On five out of every seven days or nights, year in and year out, apart from his annual two weeks holiday, Shaw had walked this same car park at London's Heathrow Airport. His mundane task was to check cars that had been there longer than they should have been, and to make sure that none had been broken into or vandalized. Occasionally, he had found unlocked vehicles containing quite valuable property that the owners had carelessly left behind.

The only bit of excitement was likely to be the sighting of a suspicious character loitering near the cars. Then he would call his control room and they would send for the police.

At first, he had passed the indigo blue Jaguar XJ, but then he stopped, realizing that there was someone in the driving seat. He retraced his steps, moved closer to the car and tapped on the window. Receiving no response, he tried the door and found it unlocked. He pulled it open, and the body of a woman fell towards him. She was an elegantly dressed blonde in a smart grey trouser suit. Her jacket was undone, and Shaw could not fail to see that the front of her stylish silk blouse was soaked in blood.

'Bloody hell!' exclaimed Shaw. Shaking almost uncontrollably, he took an involuntary step back. For a moment he stared transfixed at the body, now lying half out of the car, head almost touching the ground. In a grotesque image of death, the woman's eyes were open, and her long blonde hair was hanging down.

Moving well away from the car, Shaw unclipped the personal radio from his waterproof jacket. 'Hello, control,' he said, and then muttered, almost incoherently, 'I've just found a dead woman in a car.'

The operator at the control room asked for details, and Shaw, agitated by what he had found, eventually managed, somewhat disjointedly, to explain the circumstances of the grisly scene he had chanced upon.

'Stay with it, Pete,' said the operator. 'I'll call the police. Meanwhile, don't let anyone near it.'

'Yeah, right, mate.' Shaw looked around, but the car park was deserted. There was no one to go near the body, just rows of silent vehicles, a dead woman and him. He moved as far away as possible and sat on one of the metal barriers.

Christmas should be a time of joy and understanding and Christian charity, or so we are told. It is a season of goodwill, of good things to all men, and all that sort of claptrap. So how come that there's nearly always a murder on Christmas Day? Where, I ask you, is the goodwill in that?

Well, if there is to be a murder, fate being what it is, the investigation is bound to fall to Detective Chief Inspector Harry Brock of Homicide and Serious Crime Command. I know this because I *am* the said Harry Brock and I'm assigned to HSCC West, a Scotland Yard unit that takes in that segment of London that stretches, wedge-shaped, from Chelsea out to Hillingdon, and all the hotbeds of villainy in between. Unfortunately, it also includes Heathrow Airport, otherwise know to us of the CID as Thiefrow.

My girlfriend Gail Sutton and I had decided to spend this particular Christmas Day at her town house in Kingston. Although in a relationship for a number of years now, we had agreed not to get married, probably because we'd both been married before. And each of those marriages had ended with a measure of bitterness all round.

In my case, I had been married to Helga Büchner, a German girl who, at the time, was a physiotherapist at Westminster Hospital. She had pummelled my wrenched shoulder back to mobility following a somewhat violent disagreement with a group of yobs in Whitehall when I was a uniformed PC. It had been a whirlwind courtship, followed by a marriage that my colleagues at the nick said wouldn't last, even though it had taken sixteen years for them to be proved right in their forecast.

It had effectively come to an end when our four-year-old son Robert had drowned in a pond. Helga had insisted on continuing to work after he was born, and had left the boy with a neighbour, as she had often done.

It had not been a happy marriage, but that tragedy had signalled an end to it. Adultery on both sides became the norm, followed inevitably by divorce when Helga announced that she wanted to marry a doctor at the hospital where she worked, and with whom she'd been having an affair for several months. The only advantage for me that had accrued from the match was that I'd learned to speak German fluently. On reflection it would have been better and cheaper had I gone to night school.

Matters improved significantly when I met Gail Sutton. Gail is an actress when she's not resting, as thespians call unemployment in 'the profession'. Her marriage had endured for far shorter a period than mine, but had ended for a similar reason. Her former husband, Gerald Andrews, was a theatre director. One day Gail, feeling unwell after the matinee, arrived home early and unexpectedly from the playhouse where she was appearing, to find her husband in the marital bed with a nude dancer. That was the end of the marriage, and Gail reverted to her maiden name of Sutton.

Andrews, however, had held an unreasonable and spiteful grudge against Gail, as though that unsavoury incident had been her fault rather than his, and he did his best to prevent her getting any decent parts thereafter. When I'd met her at the Granville theatre, she was hoofing it in the chorus line of a second-rate review called *Scatterbrain*, and I was investigating the murder of one of her colleagues.

Not that Gail has to work. Her father George is a rich property developer who lives in Nottingham with his wife Sally, herself a former dancer. George's two obsessions are Formula One motor racing and the land speed record, both of which he talks about incessantly. Until his wife tells him to shut up. But he gives his daughter a substantial allowance, and that is why Gail doesn't have to work. But, loving Gail as I do, I'm willing to listen to his land speed stories for as long as he's prepared to bore me with them.

On this particular Christmas morning George was in full flow. He and Sally had arrived the previous day to enjoy Christmas dinner with Gail and me. Gail and Sally were in the kitchen preparing the meal, and my only chore was to keep their glasses constantly topped up with champagne, and George's with whisky.

Gail had decorated the sitting room tastefully, but minimally. There was none of the paper chains that my late father favoured. I still remember spending hours as a child sticking the damned things together before my father strung them from each corner of the room to the central light fitting. But Gail had put up just a few sprigs of holly, a number of bells and, of course, the obligatory Christmas tree.

Under the tree were parcels of varying sizes in colourful paper, including my gift to Gail and her gift to me. There was one from me to George, two bottles of malt whisky, and another from me to Gail's mother. Being useless when it came to selecting gifts for ladies of mature years, I'd left that one to Gail, and she'd purchased 'something suitable' on my behalf. It would've been a doubly difficult choice on my part because Sally didn't look much older than her daughter, was vivacious and always stylishly dressed.

My reverie on the subject of Christmas decorations and gifts was interrupted by George banging on about men in fast cars.

'And one of the finest drivers ever to attempt the land speed record, Harry,' he continued, sipping at his Scotch, 'was Frank Lockhart, an American engineer.'

'Really?' I said, realizing that I had missed the first, and probably most important, part of his monologue.

'He had a wonderful car called the Stutz Black Hawk Special with a three-eighty horsepower engine. In test runs at Daytona Beach in Florida, he got over two hundred miles an hour out of her. And that was back in nineteen twenty-eight.' An expression of admiration crossed George's face, and he shook his head in wonderment.

'Did he break the record, though?' I asked, feigning interest.

'No, he broke his bloody neck,' said George mournfully. 'He did three runs, all at over two hundred. But then he burst a tyre and skidded for a couple of hundred yards before the car leaped into the air and turned upside down. Lockhart was thrown clear, but died instantly. He was only twenty-five.' He held up his empty glass. 'Any more Scotch, Harry?'

I refilled his glass and mine with Laphroaig malt and settled down expecting the next instalment. But then George threw me a question that came in right under my guard.

'Are you going to marry my girl, Harry?'

'Well, I, er . . .' But at that moment my mobile rang. I glanced at the little window and saw that it was my office calling. It was probably the first time I'd ever been pleased to get a call from work. 'Brock,' I said.

'It's Don Keegan at the incident room, sir.' Detective Sergeant Keegan was one of the skippers in my team who was standing in as incident room manager for Colin Wilberforce, the permanent manager, who was on leave.

'What is it, Don?'

'A murder, sir, at Heathrow Airport. DCS Cleaver's acting commander, and directs that you take it on.'

'What's the SP?' I asked. SP is racing terminology for 'starting price', but when a CID officer uses it, he means he wants the full story.

'One of the security staff was doing a routine patrol of a car park when he came across the body of a woman in a Jag, sir. First reports are that she'd been stabbed.'

'Terrific! What have you done so far?'

'I've alerted DS Poole and Dr Mortlock, sir. Both are on their way as I speak.'

'Good. Track down DI Ebdon and ask her to assemble a team, Don.'

'Already done, sir, and I've taken the liberty of sending a traffic car to pick you up. Are you at home?'

'No.' I gave him Gail's address.

'I'll give them a call on the air, sir.' Keegan paused. 'And a Merry Christmas, sir.'

'Get stuffed, Keegan.'

'Trouble?' asked George Sutton, once I'd terminated the call.

'You could say that, George,' I said. 'I've just had a call-out to a murder at Heathrow.' I sighed, stood up and made my way to the kitchen to break the news that I would be missing out on Christmas dinner.

'I expect you can get a sandwich at the airport, darling,' was Gail's somewhat dry response. She had grown accustomed to my disappearing at the most inopportune moments.

'This zone of the car park's closed, sir.' The speaker was a uniformed jobsworth who, all puffed up with piss and importance, was strutting back and forth across the entrance. There was a policeman standing nearby, but he didn't seem to be doing anything in particular.

'You may not have noticed,' I said, waving my warrant card under his nose, 'but this car has the word POLICE plastered all over it, and there are blue lights on its roof.' By now I was in a thoroughly pissed-off mood, and this guy was doing nothing to alleviate it. Just to emphasize the point, my driver gave the attendant an ear-splitting blast on the siren.

'Ah! Of course, sir. Very good, sir.' The official crossed to the control box, managing to combine haste with obsequiousness, and raised the barrier. 'Your chaps are already in there, sir,' he added helpfully.

An unnecessarily large area of the car park had been cordoned off with the familiar blue and white tapes. I got out of the traffic car and walked towards my latest investigation.

I was intercepted by a uniformed inspector who carefully recorded my name on his clipboard.

'Merry Christmas, guv,' said Dave Poole, striding towards me with a huge grin on his face.

Detective Sergeant Poole is my right hand; what I don't think of, he does. The grandson of a Bethnal Green doctor who arrived from the Caribbean in the nineteen-fifties, Dave graduated in English from London University, and it shows. When it suits him. Shunning the professional calling of his grandfather, and indeed of his chartered accountant father, Dave decided to join the Metropolitan Police. He often claimed, to the embarrassment of those who worry about diversity, that this made him the black sheep of the family.

'What's the SP, Dave?' I asked, even though Don Keegan had given me the broad picture.

'That guy over there, guv,' said Dave, pointing to a white-faced individual, 'is some sort of security dogsbody. At ten o'clock this morning, he was doing a routine patrol and came across the victim in a Jaguar XJ.' He pointed to the canvas screens now surrounding the crime scene. 'Doctor Mortlock's in there somewhere, working his magic.'

I opened the flap and found Henry Mortlock in the act of packing his ghoulish instruments into a small black bag.

'Merry Christmas, Henry,' I said.

'What's bloody merry about it?' muttered Mortlock. 'And before you ask, as far as I can tell without carving her up, she was killed by a number of knife wounds to the chest and abdomen. Quite deep, I should think. I'll be able to give you further and better particulars after the post-mortem.'

'When are you proposing to do the PM, Henry?'

Mortlock gave me a sour look. 'This afternoon, I suppose,' he said grudgingly. 'What a way to spend Christmas.' And belying that pithy comment, he went on his way, humming an extract from Good King Wenceslas.

I cast a cursory glance over the car that still contained the body of our murder victim. The dead woman had been a good-looking blonde, probably in her early thirties, and the quality of her outfit implied wealth.

Linda Mitchell, who enjoyed the title of senior forensic practitioner, was already standing by. Beyond the tapes was a van emblazoned with the words EVIDENCE RECOVERY UNIT. This, presumably, was another snazzy slogan to emanate from the funny names and total confusion squad at Scotland Yard. This unit is staffed by boy superintendents whose aim in life is to reach the very top of the constabulary tree without actually doing any police duty. But they're an absolute whizz at changing things that don't need to be changed and offering advice to officers who have no need of it.

'OK to make a start, Mr Brock?' asked Linda.

'Yes, carry on. Dr Mortlock's finished in there.'

'D'you want a word with Mr Shaw, guv?' asked Dave, as Linda disappeared behind the screens.

'Shaw?' I was becoming confused already.

'He's the car park guy who found the body.'

'Ah, right. Got it.' I crossed to where the pale-faced one was perched on a steel barrier, constantly sipping water from a plastic bottle. He looked as though he was about to be sick.

'I'm DCI Brock,' I said. 'And you're Mr Shaw are you?'

'That's me, guv'nor, Peter Shaw.'

'What time did you come on duty this morning?'

'Seven o'clock.'

'And at what time did you do your first patrol of this zone of the car park?'

Shaw looked decidedly shifty. 'Well, it must've been about, um . . .'

'Mr Shaw,' I said, 'I don't give a toss when you were *supposed* to have started patrolling, and I don't care what company regulations you might've broken by not being where you should've been *when* you should've been. I'm not going to run off and tell your boss, so just answer the question.'

'A couple of minutes before ten, guv'nor. You see, the lads in the control room, being as how it's Christmas, had put on a bit of—'

'Enough,' said Dave. 'Just answer the chief inspector's questions, otherwise he could get very nasty. And I should know,' he added. He was lying, of course. I hoped.

'Just before ten, sir,' said Shaw again.

'And tell me exactly what you found, Mr Shaw,' I said.

'I spotted this car, and saw that there was someone in it. That's against the regulations, you see. People are not allowed to—' Shaw noticed my frown, and returned to the facts. 'I tapped on the window, but the passenger didn't move. So, I opened the door and this woman fell out, all covered in blood. It gave me a nasty turn, guv'nor, I can tell you.'

'Must've been very upsetting for you,' murmured Dave.

'What did you do then?' I asked.

'I got in touch with the control room, and they sent for the police.'

'Are you able to tell me when this car came into this section of the car park?' I asked.

'Already done, guv,' said Dave. 'The car entered at exactly three minutes to seven yesterday evening.'

'That means that the body had probably been here since then,' I said.

'Looks like it, guv.'

'But surely there must've been other patrols through the night.' I found it difficult to believe that the body had lain undiscovered for that long.

'It was Christmas Eve, guv,' said Dave, assuming that to be a sufficient explanation for neglect of duty on the part of the car park authority. 'But Miss Ebdon is checking that now. She went straight to their office; she'll be up shortly.'

Kate Ebdon is one of my detective inspectors. A flame-haired Australian, she came to us on promotion from the Flying Squad where, it is rumoured, she gave pleasure to a number of its officers. Male ones, of course. She usually dresses in tight-fitting jeans and a man's white shirt, something that upsets our beloved commander. When Kate first arrived in HSCC, he suggested that I speak to her about her mode of dress, not wishing to do so himself. I pointed out that such an approach might be interpreted as sexism or even racism, Kate being Australian. As the commander is keen on diversity, that was the last I heard about it.

One of Kate's great assets is that she is a tenacious interrogator. I was already beginning to feel sorry for those officials who had failed to notice, until this morning, the presence of a dead body in an expensive car that, ostensibly, was under their protection.

'Do we know the identity of the dead woman, Dave?' I asked.

'Yes, guv. She had credit cards, a driver's licence and a passport on her. She's Kerry Hammond and according to her driver's licence she lives at Elite Drive, Barnes. The next of kin is shown in her passport as Nicholas Hammond, same address, presumably her husband. Oh, and she had a mobile phone with her.'

'Any cash?

'Yeah, about two hundred pounds sterling and five hundred US dollars.'

'It doesn't look as though robbery was the motive, then,' I said, stating the obvious. 'Does the car belong to her?'

'Possibly,' said Dave. 'It's registered to a company called Kerry Trucking Limited with offices at Scarman Street, Chiswick.'

'I wonder if that's a coincidence, it being Kerry Trucking and that the victim's first name is Kerry.'

'No doubt we shall find out in due course, sir.' From Dave's tone, I gathered that he didn't think it mattered; he always called me 'sir' when he thought I'd made a fatuous remark. And he always called me 'sir' in the presence of members of the public.

'Better put a stop on this Nicholas Hammond with the Border Agency, Dave, in case he's abroad and returns in the next day or two.'

'Already done, guv,' said Dave. 'Although there's nothing to suggest that he's gone anywhere.'

'I've checked the deceased's fingerprints, Mr Brock,' said Linda, emerging from the tent. 'No record.'

'That was quick,' I said.

'One of the miracles of modern science, Mr Brock.' Linda held up a small machine that looked to me like a mobile phone. 'But it'll take longer to examine the vehicle to see if anyone else has left their dabs.' And with that, she disappeared behind the screens once more.

Dave and I turned as Kate Ebdon approached the tapes, but the uniformed inspector with the clipboard stopped her.

'This zone's closed, miss,' said the inspector. 'Do you have a car here?'

'Yes,' said Kate, 'that one.' She pointed to the traffic car that was still parked outside the tapes. 'DI Ebdon, HSCC.'

'Oh, sorry, love,' said the inspector, not realizing that he was making a grievous mistake.

'I'm not accustomed to being called "love" by some uniformed idiot who's just standing around making a bloody nuisance of himself, *mate*,' she snapped back, and ducked under the tape. *Aussies one – Brits nil.*

'Good afternoon, Kate,' I said.

'Merry Christmas, guv.' Kate flicked open her pocketbook. 'They're a load of bloody drongos down in that control room,' she said.

'Go on.' By now I was beginning to get the hang of the Australian language, and gathered that the members of staff to whom she referred were idiots.

'The short answer is that no one did a patrol after about three o'clock yesterday afternoon. They were doubtless getting a few tinnies under their belts on account of it being Christmas. I told them I'd be taking it up with higher authority, just for the hell of it. That should've poured cold water on their festivities. I left Sheila Armitage to take statements, for what use they'll be.'

'Thanks, Kate, and perhaps you'd get someone to take a statement from Shaw over there, he of the pasty countenance.'

'Incidentally, guv, there's a bloke from our Press Bureau just turned up. He's in a lather about how much to release to the press.'

This was always a problem. I didn't want anything going out

until we'd at least made some preliminary enquiries. We frequently needed the help of the media, but it had to be carefully controlled to avoid telling the murderer something that might help him to evade capture.

'Tell him I don't want anything released at this stage, Kate. And while you're about it, have a word with the car park staff and emphasize that they're to say nothing to the press.'

'Don't worry, guv, I'll persuade them that it wouldn't be in their best interest to speak to anyone.'

Once again, I felt a certain sympathy for the occupants of the control room; Kate in a persuasive mood can be terrifyingly intimidating.

'We've completed our preliminary search of the car, Mr Brock,' said Linda Mitchell, as she emerged once again from the tent. 'I've arranged for a low-loader to take it to Lambeth, and then we can start on a scientific examination, including any stray fingerprints and anything else we can find.'

'What about the contents of the vehicle, Linda?' I asked.

'There was a handbag, a cabin carry-on bag, a faux fur coat, matching hat, and a pair of gloves. And a suitcase in the boot. She was wearing an expensive necklace, earrings, and wedding and engagement rings. I've bagged those. In the glove box I found a packet of sweets and an unpaid parking ticket.'

'All right to move the body, guv?' asked Detective Sergeant 'Shiner' Wright. Wright was the laboratory liaison officer whose task was to accompany the body in order to preserve continuity of evidence.

'Yes, go ahead, Shiner.' I looked around for a spare officer. 'John,' I said, setting eyes on DC Appleby, 'go with Linda to the lab, and list everything she unpacks.' I spotted a number of closed-circuit television cameras around the parking area. 'Seize the tapes from those, Dave, and then we can get back to Curtis Green, via Henry Mortlock's carvery, of course.'

Curtis Green is where we have our offices. Once a part of New Scotland Yard, it's in a turning off Whitehall, and very few people – including the police – know where it is. Right now, I was wishing I'd never set eyes on the place. All I could think of was Gail and her parents tucking into a sumptuous Christmas dinner.

TWO

We went straight from the airport to Horseferry Road, only to find that Henry Mortlock had already completed his post-mortem examination of Kerry Hammond.

'Nothing much to add to what I told you at the scene, Harry,' said Mortlock, as he peeled off his latex gloves and tossed them into the medical waste bin. 'Death resulted from five stab wounds, one of which penetrated the heart. The entry wounds were made by a broad-bladed weapon, at least four centimetres in width, I should think, and she'd been dead for between ten and sixteen hours. Best I can do.'

'Thanks, Henry. Enjoy the rest of your Christmas.'

'Fat chance of that,' muttered Mortlock. 'The damned house is overflowing with relatives.'

It was almost seven o'clock by the time we arrived at Curtis Green. The only redeeming feature of being there on Christmas Day was that there was no chance of our beloved commander showing up and faffing about with bits of paper. The commander loves paper. But today, I tried to visualize him wearing a paper hat and enjoying Christmas dinner with his harridan of a wife, a photograph of whom adorns his desk. Presumably it's been placed there as an awful warning to anyone contemplating matrimony.

'There is little we can do today,' I said, gathering my small team around me in the incident room. 'However, a number of questions need to be answered. Firstly, why was Mrs Hammond at Heathrow Airport? She didn't have an airline ticket with her. Secondly, did she arrive at the airport with someone else? If that was the case, we need to know who it was, and whether he, or she, took a flight somewhere.' I glanced at Detective Sergeant Flynn. As an officer who had previously served on the Fraud Squad, he knew his way around paper. 'Charlie, make a few enquiries at the airport, and see what you can find out.'

'Right, guv.'

'I've listed the property taken from the car, sir,' said DC Appleby.
'Anything interesting, John?'

'Nothing unusual, sir. The suitcase contained a selection of
women's expensive clothing, and what looked like a couple of gifts,
probably for her husband by the look of them. There was a pair of
gold cufflinks and a leather briefcase. I reckon that together they're
worth about two and a half grand.'

'Rich lady,' I said.

'I reckon so, sir. She had a bottle of Estée Lauder perfume in
her handbag that Linda said retails for about two hundred quid. And
her jewellery box contained some very pricey stuff: a gold and
diamond necklace, earrings and a ruby bracelet. She was wearing
a diamond engagement ring that was probably worth ten grand, and
a platinum wedding ring.'

'Rich husband as well. Thanks for that, John,' I said. 'In the
meantime, Sergeant Poole and I will go out to Barnes and break
the news to Mrs Hammond's family, if she's got any.'

'And if they haven't gone away for Christmas,' commented Dave.

'A possibility, of course, but if there's anyone there they might
be able to answer some of the questions I've posed already. Bring
the house keys that Linda found in Mrs Hammond's handbag, Dave.'

Elite Drive proved to be a secure estate in Barnes. The uniformed
custody guard examined our warrant cards carefully before opening
the electrically-operated ornamental gates and allowing us to drive
through.

Number seventeen, a large, square, double-fronted, detached
modern house, stood some way back from the road. A path across
a lawn, beautifully tended even for the depths of midwinter, led up
to the front door. There was garaging for two cars to one side of
the house, and the property itself, needless to say, was in good
repair. I took a private bet with myself that there would be a swimming pool in the basement or in a specially built chalet behind. At
a guess I reckoned the market value to be somewhere around a
couple of million, give or take a few hundred thousand.

I pressed the bell push and heard chimes sounding somewhere
inside the house. But there was no reply.

'Open up, Dave.'

'Are you sure, guv? We don't have a warrant.' Dave was always

at pains to prevent me from doing anything rash or unlawful, probably because a complaint would, inevitably, involve him too.

'It's justified because I have reason to believe that the person
who murdered Mrs Hammond might be on the premises, Dave,' I
said blithely, citing one reason that might justify our entry. I, too,
was thinking ahead to any complaint that might turn up. I'd been
on the wrong end of a complaint on more than one occasion in the
past, and it wasn't a pleasant experience. Any suggestion that the
police whitewash complaints is a fiction, believe me. 'Sure as hell,
I'm not going to look for a magistrate to sign a warrant on Christmas
Day.'

Somewhat reluctantly, I thought, Dave found the appropriate key,
and we were in. Sadly, there was no fleeing felon on the premises,
but I didn't really expect there to be.

The spacious sitting room was comfortably and expensively
furnished and richly carpeted, and contained the usual possessions
of the well off: a plasma-screen television, a music centre, an iPod
player, expensive ornaments, and one or two original paintings.
There was also a silver-framed photograph of a wedding couple
taken outside Caxton Hall register office. I recognized the woman
as Kerry Hammond, and therefore assumed the man to be her
husband. But, in an era of constantly changing spouses, one could
never be certain if it was her current husband. Marriage these days
tends to be like a Paul Jones dance: when the music stops you
change partners.

'I've found an address book, guv,' said Dave.

'Might be helpful,' I said. 'Bring it with you, along with that
wedding photo.'

'And I've checked the answering machine,' added Dave. 'There
are no messages on it.'

'We'll have a quick look round upstairs, and then have a chat
with the people next door, Dave,' I said.

The king-sized bed in the large main bedroom was made up, and
there were no clothes scattered about on the thick pile carpet. A
quick examination of the sweep of built-in wardrobes revealed
apparel for both sexes: expensive bespoke suits and casual wear,
and haute couture dresses. In a compartment at the bottom there
were at least twenty-five pairs of women's shoes.

On the wall opposite the windows was yet another original

painting. On closer examination, I noticed that the frame stood away from the wall, perhaps by a sixteenth of an inch. I pressed the right-hand side, releasing a magnetic catch, and the picture opened on a hinge. Inside, there was a small safe set into the wall. However, despite what crime writers would have you believe, there was no way of getting into it without knowing the combination. It is a fallacy to imagine that it's possible to hear the click of the tumblers as the ridged knob is turned. A stethoscope doesn't help either; I've tried.

But there were no signs anywhere of a hurried departure; everything pointed to the house having been meticulously tidied before the occupants went on holiday. It looked as though Mrs Hammond employed a cleaner. I doubted that a woman with an engagement ring worth ten grand would do her own household chores.

The man who answered the door of the nearest house was about forty. He looked to be a stuffy sort of fellow with his toothbrush moustache and rimless glasses. There was an incongruous paper hat on his head and he held a glass of wine in his hand.

'Sorry to bother you on Christmas Day, sir,' I said. 'We're police officers. I'm Detective Chief Inspector Brock of New Scotland Yard, and this is Detective Sergeant Poole.'

'Good heavens, this sounds serious.' The man swept off his paper hat. 'You'd better come in. We were just finishing our Christmas dinner.'

'I apologize for the intrusion, sir, but it is important. And you are?'

'Oh, sorry, I'm Peter Maitland.'

We followed Maitland into his huge dining room. Eleven people were seated around a long table, all wearing silly paper hats. The diners looked up enquiringly at our entry, their expressions indicating irritation that we'd just interrupted that stage of the meal where the host was about to commit arson on the Christmas pudding.

'These gentlemen are from the police at Scotland Yard,' announced Maitland to his guests, a statement that produced an immediate buzz of conversation.

'If it's a strippergram shouldn't they be in uniform?' queried one silly young woman, an alcoholic slur taking the edge off her consonants.

'Perhaps we could have a word with you and your wife in private, sir,' I suggested.

'Of course,' said Maitland. 'This is my wife, Janet,' he added, as a plain woman in a full-length red gown stood up at the far end of the table, and made her way towards us.

'I hope this won't take long,' said Janet Maitland curtly, clearly annoyed at having her dinner interrupted, and led the way into the sitting room on the front of the house.

'Do sit down, gentlemen,' said Maitland. 'Can I offer you a drink?'

'No, thank you.' Once we were all seated, I got straight to the point of our visit. 'We're making enquiries into the death of Mrs Kerry Hammond, your neighbour.' It was an announcement guaranteed to rivet the Maitlands' attention, and it did.

'Good God!' exclaimed Maitland, his jaw dropping.

'Oh, surely not,' said Mrs Maitland, her face paling significantly. Realizing that this was not an occasion for paper hats, she promptly removed the one she was wearing.

'What happened?' asked Maitland. 'Was it a car accident?'

'I'm sorry to have to tell you that she was found murdered in her car at Heathrow Airport earlier today.'

Mrs Maitland leaned back in her chair. 'Oh, how awful,' she muttered. 'But she was supposed to be going to New York to spend Christmas there with her husband. She was very excited about it.'

'D'you know if they left here together, Mr Maitland?' asked Dave.

'No, I don't know, I'm afraid. I was playing golf yesterday afternoon.'

'No, they didn't,' said Janet Maitland. 'Kerry said that she was going to meet Nick at the airport.'

'I take it that Nicholas Hammond is Kerry's husband,' I asked, wishing to confirm the entry in the dead woman's passport.

'Yes, that's correct. Just before she left, Kerry dropped in to leave her spare set of house keys with me. It's something she always does whenever she and her husband are away, just in case anything happens. We're quite good friends, Kerry and me.'

'What time would that have been?' I asked.

'It was between five and six, I suppose. Yes, I remember now because Kerry glanced at her watch and said that it was twenty past five and she'd have to run. She said she didn't want to be late checking in. Apparently the airport can get very busy on Christmas Eve, and so can the roads leading to it.'

'Have you any idea why Kerry and her husband should've travelled to the airport separately?'

'She told me that Nick had a last minute meeting in London. He runs his own estate agency business in Mayfair, and apparently he was near to closing a deal on some expensive property.'

'On Christmas Eve?' I wondered about that. It seemed strange for an estate agent to be clinching a deal on the day before Christmas, especially as he was apparently due to fly to New York with his wife.

'Well, that's what Kerry said,' confirmed Janet Maitland.

'And does Mrs Hammond pursue a career?' asked Dave.

'Indeed she does. She's involved with a haulage business in Chiswick, and from what I've heard, it's a pretty big concern. I believe they do quite a lot of carrying to and from Europe and beyond,' said Maitland. 'Kerry Trucking, I think it's called.'

That tallied with the registration details of the car in which Kerry Hammond had been found.

'D'you mean she owns the company?'

'She does now. Her husband started it. Her first husband, that is. His name was . . .' Maitland paused, and turned to his wife. 'What was his name, darling?'

'Richard Lucas,' said Janet. 'He was killed in a car accident about seven years ago,' she continued. 'It was a terrible tragedy, him being so young. He was on his way home from Sheffield in December and got involved in one of those awful pile-ups in the fog on the M1. The company became Kerry's when he died, and she's continued to run it ever since. Very successfully, I believe.'

'They certainly weren't short of money, if that's anything to go by,' said Maitland, and received a nod of agreement from his wife.

'Were there any children?' asked Dave, who was an inveterate collector of inconsequential bits of information.

'No, I don't think so,' said Janet. 'In fact, I'm certain.'

'But then she remarried,' I said, taking the wedding photograph from Dave and showing it to Mrs Maitland. 'Is this her second husband or her first?'

Janet Maitland put on a pair of spectacles, but needed only to glance briefly at the photograph. 'No, that's Nick, her second husband. I think they were married about five years ago. It was a couple of years after Dick died, I seem to recall. But she's only a young woman, early thirties, I suppose, so you can't really blame her for finding someone else.'

'Did they get on, Kerry and her husband?' asked Dave, just beating me to the question. 'Were there any rows, fights or disagreements, for instance?'

Janet Maitland looked shocked at that. 'No, they were a perfect couple,' she said, in a rather tart manner, as though it were impertinent for Dave to have posed such a query.

'It's a question we have to ask,' I said. 'You'd be surprised how often a woman is murdered by her husband. Or a husband by his wife,' I added as an afterthought.

'Really?' Mrs Maitland did not seem at all mollified by that particular statistic of the crime of murder. 'Well, I very much doubt that in this case you'll find that Nick has murdered Kerry. He's not the type.'

Don't you just love armchair detectives?

'Did Kerry enjoy a busy social life?' I asked. It was a question designed to prompt any revelations about extramarital affairs; not that I expected Janet Maitland to tell me even if there had been. She seemed very defensive of her friend Kerry Hammond's reputation.

'She was always on the go.' As I'd anticipated, Mrs Maitland declined to read between the lines of my question. 'And she and Nick enjoyed themselves socially. Well, they had the money, so why not?' she added. 'At one time, she was involved in charity work, too. Of course, I don't mean that she worked in a charity shop in the high street; it was more a case of charity balls in big West End hotels, and dinners at five hundred pounds a plate, that sort of thing.'

'D'you know which charity it was?' asked Dave.

'No, I don't, other than to say it had something to do with starving children in Africa.'

'The Hammonds had a pretty full life, then,' I said. 'I imagine they had a lot of friends.'

'Oh yes,' put in Peter Maitland. 'Dinner parties and drinks parties, but nothing rowdy, of course. No loud music. They've got a swimming pool in the basement, too. Well, all of us round here have,

but we don't use ours much. But the Hammonds used to hold parties
in theirs. We went to one or two. They were very generous hosts.'

'Thank you for your help,' I said, 'and my apologies for interrupting your festivities. If and when Mr Hammond returns,' I
continued, addressing myself to both the Maitlands, 'perhaps you'd
ask him to contact me as a matter of urgency.' I handed Peter
Maitland one of my cards, but sincerely hoped that the arrangements
to intercept Nicholas Hammond at Heathrow on his return, assuming
he'd actually gone, would obviate the necessity of Maitland breaking
the news to him.

There was a good reason for that. It's of invaluable assistance to
a detective to watch the reaction of a man when he's told of the
murder of his wife, particularly when he's suspected of that murder.
And in the absence of any firm evidence, and based on the history
of homicide, right now Nicholas Hammond had to be a front runner.
Wife-killers are devious people. It's surprising how often a bereaved
man is keen to appear on television, appealing for information about
his partner's murder, only for police eventually to discover that he's
the guilty party.

Having obtained all the information that we could, we left the
Maitlands to enjoy their Christmas pudding, although I suspected
that our visit had put a damper on the celebrations.

Back at Curtis Green, DS Flynn was waiting with news.

'Both Nicholas and Kerry Hammond were booked on the flight
to New York's JFK Airport that left Heathrow at twenty-hundred
hours on Christmas Eve, sir. But only Nicholas Hammond turned
up. He asked the passenger service agent to page his wife, but there
was no response. The man I spoke to said that Hammond seemed
extremely fraught that his wife hadn't arrived.'

'I wonder if he was covering his tracks,' I suggested. 'He could've
been making a fuss so that his concern about his missing wife would
be remembered. It wouldn't be the first time it'd happened.'

'Wouldn't surprise me, guv,' said Flynn, who shared most CID
officers' suspicions of the husbands of murdered wives. 'However,
when she failed to show, Hammond left his wife's ticket at the
airline desk, and asked the agent to tell her he'd gone on ahead.
He said to tell her he'd meet her in New York, and that she knew the
hotel they would be staying at.'

'Par for the course.' I was beginning to move Nicholas Hammond to the top of my suspect list; leaving the airport without knowing what had happened to his wife did not gel in my book. 'Did you find out which hotel they were staying at, Charlie?'

'No, guv. The man I spoke to didn't know and he said that Hammond hadn't mentioned it.'

'If the flight left at eight o'clock, what time would it arrive in New York?'

'About nine o'clock that evening local time, guv. New York is five hours behind GMT.'

'Just in time for a late-night dinner *à deux* at Cipriani's on Forty-Second Street.' On one occasion in the distant past, I'd sampled that famous restaurant's cuisine, and having seen the prices I was extremely grateful that the NYPD had picked up the tab.

'We could ask the New York police to try and track him down, guv,' suggested Dave. 'Shouldn't be too difficult as we know he was due to arrive at JFK at about nine o'clock New York time.'

'What, and alert him to our interest? If we did that, he might never come back, Dave, and then we'd be into extradition. Assuming, of course that he had murdered his wife. Not that we've got any evidence. Yet!'

'We won't have long to wait, sir,' said Flynn. 'Hammond's ticket was a return. He's due back the day after tomorrow, the twenty-seventh, and, as you suggested, Dave has already lodged his details with the Border Agency to intercept him on his return and notify police.'

'Excellent,' I said. 'Dave and I will be there to greet him. What time's he due in?'

'According to his return ticket, sir, he should be touching down at Heathrow at three in the afternoon, our time.'

It was now past midnight and very little had been achieved. Admittedly, we knew the identity of the dead woman, and had obtained a few sparse background details from the Maitlands. The next two important steps would be to interview Nicholas Hammond on his return from New York, and to visit the offices of Kerry Trucking. DS Flynn had said that Hammond would not be back until the twenty-seventh, but there was a chance that Kerry Trucking would be operating on Boxing Day, particularly if it had the international commitments that Peter Maitland had suggested it had.

I sent the team home, but told them that I expected to see them

the following day. There were a few groans, but a general acceptance that murder enquiries rarely fitted in with detectives' social
arrangements. It was not the first time my Christmas had been
ruined, and I don't suppose that it will be the last.

I arranged for a duty car from the Yard to take me home to my flat
in Surbiton. I'd decided that it would be most unwise to return to
Gail's house, not that I would have shared her bed in any event;
Gail is a little shy of sleeping with me when her parents are staying
with her. Apart from anything else, George and Sally Sutton were
travelling back to Nottingham later on Boxing Day, and that would
avoid my having to answer George's question about whether I
intended to marry his daughter. It also meant that I would miss out
on further gripping yarns about the land speed record and Formula
One motor racing. But I could live with that.

I was in the office by nine o'clock. Dave was already there, as were
Kate Ebdon and the rest of the team.

'Kerry Trucking is operating today, guv,' said Dave. 'It seems
they don't recognize Boxing Day. Bit like us.'

'In that case, we'll get out there.' I glanced at Kate. 'Anything
for me?' I asked.

'I've been checking on Kerry Hammond's mobile, guv. There
were several unanswered calls from Nick Hammond on Christmas
Eve at about the time he discovered she wasn't at the airport. And
over the past few days there have also been calls from a mobile
that goes out to a Gary Dixon. There were quite a few calls from
him over the preceding weeks, the last one being at about three
thirty on Christmas Eve. There were also a few from Kerry to a
Miguel Rodriguez. So far I don't know who Dixon or Rodriguez
are, but I'm working on it.'

'Well done, Kate, and thanks.'

'There's one other thing, guv,' said Dave. 'The CCTV tapes from
the airport car park.'

'Yes?' I asked hopefully.

'They were duff, guv. Half of them weren't working, and those
that were operative weren't focused on the area we're interested in.'

'Terrific!' I said. But it was no more than I'd expected.

THREE

Kerry Trucking occupied a huge area in Scarman Street, Chiswick. There were several Volvo articulated lorries in the yard, a couple of which were backed up to the loading bay. A group of forklift trucks stood in a rank at the other end of the compound where a bulk container was being hoisted on to a flatbed truck. Beyond it there were about twenty similar containers stacked in groups. And all this on Boxing Day. You didn't have to be in the haulage business to see that Kerry Trucking was a huge operation.

A security guard approached as we arrived.

'Can I help you, sir?'

I identified Dave and myself. 'Who's in charge here?' I asked.

'That'll be Mr Bligh, sir. Mr Bernard Bligh. He's one of the directors.'

'Is he here today?'

'Oh, yes, sir.' The security guard smiled. 'He seems to spend most of his time here.'

'Perhaps you'd tell me how I can get to his office.'

'No need, sir. That's him standing on the loading platform.' The guard pointed to a stocky figure whose gaze was sweeping back and forth across the yard. 'Either he or Mr Thorpe always like to keep an eye on things.'

'Who is Mr Thorpe?' I asked.

'He's the company secretary, sir, but he's also a director.'

Dave and I crossed to the loading platform and mounted the short flight of steps at the side.

'Mr Bernard Bligh?'

'That's me. Who are you?'

'Detective Chief Inspector Brock of New Scotland Yard and this is Detective Sergeant Poole.'

'What's this about, then? Illegal immigrants or bootlegged liquor?' Bligh sounded resigned to it being one or the other.

'Neither, Mr Bligh. It's about Mrs Hammond.'

'What's she been up to?'

'It might be better if we went into your office, sir,' I suggested, having noticed a loader doing a bit of earwigging.

'Yes, right, follow me.' Bligh led the way up a flight of wooden stairs and into an office that overlooked the loading bay. 'Always like to keep an eye on the drivers,' he volunteered. 'Never know what the buggers are up to otherwise. Now, what's this about Kerry?' He gestured towards a sofa upholstered in threadbare corduroy, and took a seat behind his paper-laden desk.

'She was found murdered in her Jaguar in a car park at Heathrow Airport yesterday,' I said, seeing no reason to avoid the stark truth.

'Good God!' For a moment or two, Bligh stared at me. 'Murdered? But what the hell happened?'

I gave Bligh the brief details of the finding of Kerry Hammond's body, and that she had been due to fly to New York with her husband on Christmas Eve.

'Do you know of anyone who might've held a grudge against Mrs Hammond?' I asked.

Bligh laughed. 'The haulage business is a pretty cut-throat game, Chief Inspector, but I doubt that any of our competitors would resort to murder.'

'Did she have any problems that you know of?'

'Doesn't everyone? But no, she'd none that I can think of. She was very much a hands-on sort of boss. She took over the company when Dick was killed.'

'That'd be Mr Lucas, I take it?' queried Dave.

'Yeah. He was killed in a car accident on the M1 about seven years ago. They were devoted to each other. Dick even named the company after her. He worked it up from nothing. Well, we both did, but he was the brains behind it.'

'But I understand that she got married again,' I said.

'Yeah, to Nick Hammond. They got spliced about five years back.'

'Does he have anything to do with the business?' asked Dave.

'Never comes near the place,' said Bligh. 'He runs some sort of poncey estate agent's outfit in the West End. I don't think he's doing too well, mind you. As a matter of fact, I think that Kerry had to bail him out a couple of times.' He paused and stared at me. 'Are you sure it was her? I thought she was off to the Big Apple for Christmas. That's what she told me, anyway.'

'I understand that those were her plans,' I said, 'but she only got as far as the airport.'

'D'you think Nick killed her?' asked Bligh bluntly.

'D'you have a reason for asking that?'

'Not really. I just wondered. They'd had the odd falling out, but no more than most married couples, I suppose.'

I had a gut feeling that Bligh wasn't telling us the whole truth. 'We've no idea who murdered her, Mr Bligh,' I said. 'It's early days yet, but our enquiries are continuing.'

Bligh laughed. 'That's what all the detectives on TV say.'

'Probably,' I said. I have an ingrained dislike of the way in which the CID is portrayed in fiction with, for the most part, airy-fairy pseudo-intellectual chief inspectors and dim sergeants.

'Does the name Gary Dixon mean anything to you, Mr Bligh?' asked Dave, referring to his pocketbook. 'Or Miguel Rodriguez? Kerry had spoken to both of them on her mobile over the last day or so.'

'Yeah. Dixon was one of our drivers up to about three months ago.'

'Why did he leave?'

'I sacked him. He got captured by the customs guys at Dover, bringing in a load of bootlegged booze from Calais.'

That was interesting. Dixon's calls to Kerry's mobile had continued long after he'd been dismissed. I wondered why, but I was not about to ask Bligh because I thought I could guess.

'And Rodriguez?' I asked.

'No idea. Never heard of him.'

'Is the company in a good way of business, Mr Bligh?' I asked.

'Couldn't be better,' said Bligh, 'despite the recession, although we've had to make one or two cutbacks. It's made Kerry a very rich woman. Well, good luck to her, I say. She worked bloody hard to learn the ins and outs of the trade after Dick was killed. And she did, despite knowing nothing about the haulage business to start with. But she knows a hell of lot about it now. She even got a licence to drive a forty-four tonner just so she'd know what the guys were up against.'

On the afternoon of the day after Boxing Day, Dave and I made our way to Heathrow Airport in good time to meet the aircraft that should be bringing Nick Hammond back to England from New York. Don Keegan, the relief incident room manager, had done something he called 'trawling the Internet' and discovered that the flight in which we were interested was estimated to land twenty minutes earlier than its scheduled time of three o'clock. Even so, I made a point of getting there at two o'clock. In my experience, aeroplanes are unpredictable beasts and could arrive much earlier or much later than they were supposed to.

As it happened, Hammond's aircraft did in fact touch down at twenty minutes to three, having benefited from a tailwind across the Atlantic. I'd made contact with the Port Watch police at the airport, and one of the unit's sergeants accompanied Dave and me to the arrivals area. Even though Dave had already done so, the sergeant then alerted the Border Agency officers to our interest so that they could identify Hammond for me, but it turned out to be unnecessary.

At five past three, the passengers started to trickle through the control. I immediately recognized the tall figure of Nick Hammond from the wedding photograph we had taken from his house at Barnes. Waiting until he had cleared the control, Dave and I approached him.

'Mr Nicholas Hammond?' I asked.

'Yes, I am he.' Hammond looked nervous. But so do most people arriving at an airport when they're stopped by a couple of officials.

'We're police officers, Mr Hammond. We'd like a word with you.'

'Is it about my wife?'

'Why should you think that?' asked Dave.

Hammond dropped his carry-on bag. 'Well, she didn't turn up here on Christmas Eve, and she didn't arrive in New York either. Has something happened to her?'

The Port Watch sergeant touched my arm. 'Would you like to use our office, sir?'

'Yes please, Skip.'

The sergeant led the way through a deserted customs hall and into a small office that had one-way windows large enough to see all that was happening in the arrivals area.

'I'll leave you to it, sir,' said the sergeant. 'If there's anything you need, I'm only in the next office. Just give me a shout.'

'What's this all about?' demanded Hammond, when the three of us were alone.

'Mr Hammond, I'm Detective Chief Inspector Brock of New Scotland Yard,' I began, 'and this is DS Poole. I'm sorry to have to tell you that your wife is dead.'

'Oh God, no! She can't be.' Hammond's face drained of colour, and he immediately started to perspire as he sank back into a chair before shooting off a number of staccato questions and statements. 'What happened? Was it an accident? She always tended to drive that damned car too fast. I've often told her to slow down. I knew something like this would happen.'

Interesting reaction, I thought. *Why should he assume that a senior detective from the Yard would be involved in telling relatives about a fatal traffic accident? Perhaps he watches too much television.*

'No, Mr Hammond, she was murdered, here at the airport.'

Hammond's mouth dropped open. 'Murdered? Who murdered her? Was it a robbery?'

'We're still attempting to establish who murdered her and why, but I'm satisfied that robbery wasn't the motive. Your wife was in possession of a substantial sum of money, her credit cards, and some quite expensive jewellery, all of which we found with her.'

'I can't believe it. Why? Why should anyone want to kill Kerry?'

'I was hoping that you might be able to help me there, Mr Hammond,' I said. 'As I understand it, you were meant to meet your wife here on Christmas Eve and that you and she had planned to go to New York together.'

'Yes, that's quite right, but I had a last minute business meeting in London, and to make matters worse the bloody deal fell through. I'd telephoned her early that afternoon asking her to meet me here, but she didn't show up.'

'But you went to New York, nevertheless,' said Dave incredulously. He obviously found such behaviour difficult to understand.

'Yes. I rang her again from here, several times, but I got no answer from her mobile. I left her ticket with the check-in people and asked them to tell her to get the flight if she made it in time, or to get the next available one if there was a spare seat. But I heard nothing. Aircraft at this time of year are usually fully booked, though, and I presumed that she couldn't get a flight. I tried ringing her mobile again from New York, but there was still no answer.'

'Did it not occur to you that perhaps you should've waited, Mr Hammond?' I suggested. 'That something might have happened to her.'

Hammond gave me a baleful look. 'If only I had,' he said, 'I might've prevented this awful tragedy.'

'I doubt that you would've done,' I said. 'Mrs Hammond's body was found in her car in one of the airport's car parks. She'd been stabbed, and we think she was murdered shortly after arriving here on Christmas Eve. She didn't even get the chance to make it to the terminal.'

'But who would've done such a thing?' Hammond shook his head in bewilderment as he repeated his question.

'Did the two of you often travel to places separately?' asked Dave. 'Or was this a one-off?'

'We're both heavily involved in businesses of our own,' said Hammond. 'I'm an estate agent with offices in the West End, and Kerry's the owner of a very successful haulage business.'

'Does the name Gary Dixon mean anything to you?' I asked, hoping that by a change of questioning I'd catch Hammond on the hop.

But he answered without hesitation; in fact, almost too quickly, and that made me suspicious. 'No, should it? Why d'you ask?'

'No particular reason,' I said. 'It's just a name that came up in the course of our enquiries.' I had no intention of telling Hammond of the frequent telephone calls that Dixon had made to Kerry Hammond's mobile, even after he'd been sacked by Bernard Bligh. It was quite possible that Kerry and Dixon were having an affair that Hammond knew nothing about, and I had no wish to add to his distress. 'Or Miguel Rodriguez? Does that name mean anything to you?'

'Oh yes, I know him,' said Hammond. 'He owns the Spanish Fly nightclub in Mayfair. Kerry and I often went there, when we had the time. We both have pretty heavy schedules.'

I stood up. 'I don't think there's anything else to ask you at the moment, Mr Hammond, but we shall need to see you again.'

'Of course.'

'There is one other thing. If you have no objection, I'll need to

see your wife's bank statements at some time.' What I didn't say
was that if he did object, I'd get a warrant.

'What on earth for?'

'It's a routine part of a murder enquiry, Mr Hammond,' I said.
'At the moment we are looking for a motive, and it might have
something to do with money. I imagine that your wife was a rich
woman.'

'Yes, she was,' said Hammond pensively, 'and she had a separate
account; separate from mine, I mean, but I'll get the details out for
you. Where would you like me to send them?'

'Don't worry about that,' said Dave. 'We'll collect them next
time we see you, which will probably be in the next day or two.
Are you likely to be at home? You live in Barnes, I believe.'

'Yes, I'll either be there or at my office,' said Hammond. He
produced a business card, and scribbled his home phone number
on the back.

'One other thing, Mr Hammond,' I said, as I pocketed the card,
'do you happen to know if Kerry's parents are still alive and, if so,
where they live? They'll have to be informed, you see.'

'Yes, of course.' Hammond gave us an address in Henley-on-
Thames. 'They're a Mr and Mrs King, Charles and Diana. Charles
is something to do with insurance. He's done quite well out of it,
I should think, if their lifestyle's anything to go by.'

'How are you getting back to Barnes?' I asked. 'D'you have a
car here?'

'No, I came by train. It saves all the hassle of parking, and
ploughing my way through the traffic. It's just as well; I don't feel
much like driving now. Is that it, for now?'

'Yes, it is, thank you.'

Hammond picked up his overnight bag and left the office, his
shoulders sagging and his head down.

'What d'you think, guv?' asked Dave, once the door had closed
behind Kerry's husband.

'I don't know, Dave. He could be a bloody good actor, but he
seemed genuinely taken aback by the news.'

'I wonder if their marriage was all that the Maitlands reckoned
it was,' said Dave. 'What's more, I wonder who gets control of
Kerry Trucking now that Mrs Hammond is dead. That might give
us a motive.'

'Good point, Dave,' I said. 'It's something we shall h.
out in due course. Bligh suggested that they had the occasr
but there's nothing unusual about that,' I added, speaking fror
experience.

'I still think he's sus, just pushing off to the States like that, ɛ
though his wife didn't turn up. I reckon he topped his missus a.
went to the Big Apple to have a dirty Christmas with some bird. I.
it'd been Madeleine, I'd've been worried sick and I certainly
wouldn't have got on a plane to New York without knowing what
had happened to her.'

I could understand Dave's viewpoint. His wife Madeleine was a
principal dancer with the Royal Ballet. She was five foot two and
gorgeous.

'Nice theory, Dave, but it'll take some proving.'

'NYPD might help, guv,' said Dave, unwilling to relinquish the
tenuous proposition he'd made earlier about asking the New York
police for assistance.

'And what sort of answer d'you think you'd get, Dave? How
about, "Sure thing, bud. Here in New York's Finest we've got so
many detectives doing nothing that we tail every visiting foreigner
to see if he's screwing someone else's wife."'

'Only a thought, guv,' said Dave moodily. 'What do we do next?'

'We're only about a half hour's drive from Henley, Dave. We'll
go and speak to Kerry's parents. Once we've done that, we'll find
Gary Dixon, and we'll have a word with Miguel Rodriguez, owner
of the Spanish Fly.'

FOUR

'The house occupied by the Kings, Kerry's parents, certainly bore out what Nicholas Hammond had said about their lifestyle. It was a large, red-brick detached house set back from the road in what was clearly a select part of Henley. As we stopped at the end of the Kings' lengthy drive, our headlights shone on a blue Bentley Infiniti parked in front of a double garage. The car's registration mark indicated that it was this year's model.

'You won't get much change out of forty grand for that beauty,' said Dave, as he parked our bottom-of-the-range CID runabout next to it.

A young woman, probably in her twenties, answered the door. She was tall and slender with short blonde, carefully-styled hair, and all her curves were in the right places. Her blue eyes gazed at us enquiringly.

'May I help you, please?'

'Good afternoon,' I said. 'I'd like to speak to Mr and Mrs King.'

'May I ask who you are?' The request was delivered in almost perfect English, but with a slight accent that sounded vaguely Scandinavian. I imagined her to be an au pair, or whatever they call home helps these days.

'We're police officers, miss,' I said.

'Please come in.' The girl opened the door wide, and we stepped into a white-tiled hall. There was a large circular table in the centre, and a broad staircase that wound its way up one wall leading to a gallery that ran the full width of the far end. There were several doors off this gallery that I imagined led to bedrooms.

'This guy must be worth a mint, guv,' whispered Dave, gazing round at the sheer opulence of the Kings' residence.

The girl disappeared into a room on the right, but returned almost immediately. 'Please come this way,' she said, leading us into the room she'd just left. 'The police officers, Mr King,' she announced.

'Thank you, Ingrid.'

'Detective Chief Inspector Brock from Scotland Yard, sir,' I said, by way of introduction, 'and this is Detective Sergeant Poole.'

'I'm Charles King.' The speaker was a tall man, probably in his early sixties. Casually dressed, he was wearing tan-coloured trousers and a polo-necked cashmere sweater. 'This is my wife, Diana.' He took a hand out his pocket to indicate a middle-aged grey-haired woman, very much of the twinset and pearls variety, who was reclining in an armchair. 'Please sit down.' He remained standing in front of the York-stone fireplace in which a log fire was burning. There was a Christmas tree in the corner, its fairy lights making a bright addition to the soft illumination of the two or three table lamps that were dotted around the room. 'Is there some sort of trouble, Chief Inspector?'

'I'm afraid I have some bad news, Mr King,' I said, as I started on the difficult task that policemen dislike the most. 'It's about your daughter Kerry.'

'Oh good Lord! What's she been up to now?' A half smile played around King's lips.

There was no easy way. 'I'm sorry to have to tell you that she was found murdered in a car park at Heathrow Airport on Christmas Day.'

'Murdered?' The smile on King's face was instantly replaced by a stunned look of disbelief.

'I'm afraid so.' I glanced at Mrs King. She was sitting perfectly still, a slight frown on her face, but displaying no immediate reaction to the tragic news that I'd just delivered. It appeared very much as though she was unable to take it in.

'God, this is awful.' Charles King crossed the room to a table and poured himself a large brandy with a trembling hand. He turned and glanced at me, the decanter still in his hand. 'I'm sorry, would you like something?'

'No thank you, sir,' I said.

'You say that Kerry was murdered.' King crossed the room a little unsteadily and sat down in the armchair next to his wife's. 'What are the circumstances, Chief Inspector?' he asked, resting his brandy glass on the arm.

'She was found in her car, Mr King, and she'd been stabbed. Beyond that, there is very little I can tell you at this stage.'

'Has Nick been told?' King took a sip of brandy.

'We've just come from the airport, sir,' said Dave. 'We met Mr Hammond off a New York flight and broke the news to him.' He went on to explain how Nicholas Hammond had left for the United States on Christmas Eve, but that his wife hadn't shown up.

'D'you mean he went on his own?' King sounded incredulous. 'We knew they were going to New York for Christmas, but we naturally assumed that they'd be going together.'

I explained about Hammond's excuse that he'd had a deal to settle.

'Damned funny business,' muttered King. 'Are you saying that he actually went to America without knowing what had happened to Kerry?'

'It would appear so, Mr King,' I said.

'I never liked that man,' said Diana King, speaking for the first time since our arrival. She looked sideways at her husband. 'I think I could do with a drink, Charles.'

King crossed to the table and prepared a gin and tonic for his wife.

'What didn't you like about him, Mrs King?' I looked at her; despite a valiant attempt to hide her grief, the tears had started to come. She took a handkerchief from her sleeve and dabbed irritably at her eyes, annoyed that she was unable to control her emotions.

'I think he was seeing other women. And he never looked you in the eye when you were speaking to him. He was nothing like her first husband, Dick Lucas. We liked him very much. He was killed in a car crash, you know.' Diana King took the glass from her husband and sipped at it.

'So I understand. We spoke to the Hammonds' neighbours, Mr and Mrs Maitland, on Christmas Day, and they told us about the accident.'

'If Kerry was found on Christmas Day why has it taken so long for you to tell us, Chief Inspector?' asked King, sitting down again. It wasn't so much a criticism as a genuine enquiry.

'We didn't know where you lived until we spoke to Mr Hammond earlier today,' I said. 'Your address wasn't among her possessions, and the Maitlands didn't know it.'

'Yes, I see. I quite understand.'

'As a matter of interest, had your daughter always lived at Elite Drive?'

'Yes. She and Dick moved in there when they were first married.'
King finished his brandy and returned to the table for a refill. 'Do
you have any idea who might have killed our daughter?' he asked,
as he sat down again.

'Not at this stage, Mr King, no. This might sound like a pointless
question, but are you aware of anyone who might've wanted to kill
her?'

'No,' said Diana King, answering the question. 'She was a bubbly,
outgoing sort of girl. Did very well at university.' Once again, she
dabbed at her eyes.

'Which one?' asked Dave.

'Cambridge. She got her degree in economics and then went on
to do a postgraduate course in business management. She took over
the company when Dick died. It's a haulage company in West
London somewhere . . .' Diana King paused. 'Where is it, Charles?'

'Chiswick,' said King.

'What sort of woman was your daughter?' I asked, hoping to
learn a little more of her background and lifestyle. In fact, anything
that might help us to find her killer.

Charles King seemed to weigh the question carefully before
answering. 'Pretty much what you'd expect a girl in her early thirties to be, I suppose,' he said eventually. 'Her first marriage was a
very happy one, and it was an absolute tragedy when Dick died. I
don't think she ever really recovered from it. She seemed to change
after that happened, got harder somehow. Whether it was that or
the fact that she'd taken over the company and become a hard-headed
businesswoman, I couldn't really tell.'

'I suppose the business took up most of her time,' I suggested.

'Oh no, not at all. She immersed herself in good works for a
while; charities and that sort of thing. But there was a period when
she became a good-time girl, always at parties and generally living
the high life. To be honest, we were quite worried about her. But
a couple of years after Dick's death, she married Nicholas and
seemed to settle down again. But she was never quite the same as
she was before Dick died.'

'When we arrived, you asked what Kerry had been up to now,
Mr King. What prompted that question?'

King leaned across and took a cigarette from a box on a nearby
occasional table. 'I'm sorry, do either of you smoke?'

'No thanks,' I said, although both of us did.

'I thought you'd come to tell us she'd been arrested in a drugs raid, or something of the sort,' King began. 'As I said just now, just after Dick was killed she became a bit wild, drinking to excess and generally behaving as though she couldn't've cared less what happened to her. For a time we feared she might've been on drugs, and she was certainly close to becoming an alcoholic. But then she met Nick. Despite what my wife said just now, I think that Nick was a sobering influence on her in more ways than one. But it always concerned us that she might've reverted to the bizarre behaviour of what we called her "in-between years".'

'Did she have any particular friends, Mr King?' asked Dave.

'There was one girl she was especially close to,' said Diana King. 'Susan Gough and Kerry were great friends. They'd met at university, but I do know that Susan got married shortly after coming down.'

'Do you know her married name?' I asked.

'I'm not sure.' King glanced at his wife. 'Diana?'

'Yes, it's Penrose.'

'D'you have any idea where the Penroses live?' Dave took out his pocketbook.

'I'm afraid not,' said Mrs King, 'but I do know that Susan's husband owns a couple of car showrooms, if that's any help.'

'There is one other question I have to ask, Mr King.' I said.

'I think you were going to ask if she was seeing any other men, Chief Inspector. I don't know, but, to be candid, I wouldn't be surprised.'

'I certainly wouldn't have blamed her,' said Diana King, displaying a frankness that was rare in the mother of a married woman.

'We'll keep you informed, Mr King,' I said, as Dave and I stood up.

'Thank you, that would be most kind,' said King. 'I'll show you out.'

We'd almost reached the sitting room door when Diana King finally broke down and began to sob uncontrollably. King shot me a sideways glance and shrugged. He seemed embarrassed by his wife's distress.

Back at the factory, as we CID officers call our office, Linda Mitchell's preliminary report had arrived. I read through it quickly, and then gathered the team round me in the incident room.

'It seems,' I began, putting the report aside, 'that a number of fingerprints were found in Kerry Hammond's Jag. Apart from Kerry's own, the only identifiable set goes out to a Gary Dixon who's got a bit of form. He's probably the same Gary Dixon who telephoned her a few times.'

'Has he got any previous for violence, guv?' asked Dave.

'Not for violence, no. The most recent conviction was for his run-in with customs at Dover when he got done for smuggling a lorry-load of hooch that he'd brought in from France. That, of course, bears out what Bernard Bligh told us. It seems that customs carried out a full-scale investigation and found that Dixon had been supplying a number of pubs with duty-free spirits over a fairly long period. So he'd obviously been at it for some time before he got caught. Customs had a field day and prosecuted about six or seven publicans and, of course, Dixon himself. But prior to that bit of nonsense, he had a few convictions for dishonesty, namely theft from previous employers, and one for aggravated burglary. He got nine months for that a couple of years ago.'

'Did he get sent down for the smuggling, guv?' Dave obviously thought that Dixon should be in prison.

'No, he was fined five thousand pounds, and it was paid.'

'Where on earth did a lorry driver get five grand from?' asked Dave, a look of disbelief on his face.

'That's something we'll need to find out,' I said. 'Maybe Kerry paid it.'

'But how the hell did he get a job as a driver with Kerry Trucking when he'd got that sort of form, guv?' asked Tom Challis, the ex-Stolen Car Squad sergeant, who took an interest in anything on wheels.

'They probably didn't take up references,' I said, 'but we'll ask Bernard Bligh when next we see him.'

'When d'you propose to do that?' asked Dave.

'Tomorrow, I think, Dave, but this evening we'll pay a visit to the Spanish Fly, and see what *Señor* Rodriguez has to say for himself.' I glanced around until I spotted DC Chance. 'You're a Spanish speaker, aren't you, Nicola?'

'Yes, sir.'

'Good, then you'd better come with us in case his English is a bit shaky.'

The Spanish Fly nightclub occupied large premises in Mayfair. Over the door there was a depiction of a blister beetle.

'I wonder why he called it the Spanish Fly, Dave.'

'Probably because of the misconception that Spanish fly is supposed to be an aphrodisiac, guv,' suggested Dave. 'Might be good for business.'

We approached the door and Dave pressed the bell.

It was opened by a shaven-headed individual, who appeared to be too large to fit into his badly cut dinner jacket.

'Are you members?' he enquired politely, glancing suspiciously at the three of us, and fingering his earring.

'I don't think we'd want to be,' said Dave, producing his warrant card.

'Ah! Is there a problem I can help you with, sir?' The doorman looked at me. He clearly didn't fancy engaging in a prolonged conversation with Dave.

'I doubt it,' I said. 'We've come to see Mr Rodriguez.'

'Just step inside, lady and gents, and I'll see if he's available.' The shaven-headed one turned to a house telephone and made a call. Within minutes of his replacing the receiver a young girl appeared. Attired in a furry bikini, she had long legs encased in the inevitable fishnet tights, and wore abnormally high-heeled shoes. 'This is Carmel,' said the bouncer, 'and she'll take you to Mr Rodriguez' office.'

We followed Carmel through the gloomy area of the nightclub. It was crowded to capacity with small candlelit tables, each of which was occupied, and upon which champagne seemed to outweigh any other form of beverage. Some were being served by girls wearing similar outfits to that worn by Carmel. On a dance floor not much bigger than a pocket handkerchief, a number of couples were shuffling around to the accompaniment of a three-piece combo dressed in Spanish costumes. At the far end was a bar, its clients, male and female, perched on high stools.

Carmel eventually showed us into an office where we were greeted by a man of indefinable age. He wore a silky sort of dinner jacket, and had jet-black hair plastered closely to his skull. Sideburns adorned his face and terminated in a point almost at his mouth. There was no doubt that he was Spanish, at least in appearance.

'Mr Rodriguez?' I asked.

'That is I, *señor*. I understand that you are from the police. I can assure you, *señor*, that I run a respectable club here. We have many distinguished patrons, including some lords and ladies. There is even a member of royalty who comes here occasionally, but I have to pretend I do not know who that person is. Also, I have many inspections from your Vice Squad, and they are completely satisfied.' Unsurprisingly, the entire monologue was spoken with a pronounced Spanish accent.

'Bully for you,' said Dave. 'How well d'you know Kerry Hammond?'

'Please take a seat, *señors* and *señorita*,' said Rodriguez with a flourish of his hand. 'May I offer you a drink?' His other hand hovered over a bottle of whisky on his desk.

I got the impression that Rodriguez was playing for time. 'No thank you,' I said, 'but perhaps you'd answer my sergeant's question.'

'Ah, *Señora* Hammond. A beautiful lady,' exclaimed Rodriguez. 'She comes here many times, and with her husband, also, occasionally. Yes, I know her. Of course I do.'

'When did you last have contact with Mrs Hammond, Mr Rodriguez?' I used the word 'contact' deliberately; Rodriguez had made several phone calls to Kerry Hammond's mobile over the preceding few days, far more than was warranted by someone whose relationship was ostensibly one of club owner and patroness.

'I think she and her husband was here perhaps a week ago.'

'That wasn't the question,' said Dave. 'My chief inspector asked when you last had *contact* with Mrs Hammond.'

'Ah, you mean on the telephone perhaps, *señor*?'

'Yes, I mean on the telephone perhaps,' said Dave slowly, as though dealing with an idiot.

Rodriguez glanced nervously at Nicola, obviously wondering why she was there, but he didn't have to wait much longer to find out.

Nicola smiled at Rodriguez, and then rattled off a couple of long sentences in Spanish. I have no idea whether it was perfect Spanish, but it was certainly fluent.

Rodriguez was taken aback; in fact, the term 'gobsmacked' sprang to mind. 'Oh, bloody hell!' he exclaimed in tones that obviously originated closer to Brixton than to Barcelona. 'I don't speak any Spanish, love. It's all a bit of an act I put on for the benefit of the punters.'

'Let's start again, then,' said Dave. 'And we'll begin with your name. Your real name.'

'It's Michael Roberts,' said the club owner miserably.

'I'll put my question to you again, Mr Roberts,' I said. 'When did you last have contact with Mrs Hammond?'

'We talked on the phone a few times over the days leading up to Christmas,' said Roberts, all pretence at a Spanish accent now gone.

'Why? I imagine it had nothing to do with her desire to book a table, or your need to drum up trade.'

'We'd been seeing each other, on and off,' said Roberts. 'Private like.'

'You mean you were shafting her,' said Dave brutally.

Roberts nodded his head slowly. 'Yeah,' he said, glancing at Nicola again. 'Sorry, miss.'

'Don't worry about me, Mr Roberts,' said Nicola. 'I'm a police officer, and I've heard it all before, and seen it all before.'

'But why all these questions?' asked Roberts.

'Because Mrs Hammond is dead,' I said. 'She was murdered.'

'Oh Gawd blimey!' exclaimed Roberts. 'When did this come off?'

I ignored his question, and countered with one of my own. 'Where were you on Christmas Eve, Mr Roberts?'

'Is that when it happened?'

'Just answer the question,' said Nicola. 'Or would you like it in Spanish?' she added sarcastically.

'I was here, up to midnight.' Roberts glanced at Nicola again; he obviously didn't know what to make of her.

'And can anyone confirm that?' I asked.

'Yes, my bar manager, Fernando.'

'And what's *his* real name?' asked Dave.

'Fred Goddard,' said Roberts, with a sigh.

'And where can we find him?'

'He's got an office behind the bar. I'll show you the way.'

Roberts led us out of his office, and through the main area of the club. He was about to open the door of a room behind the bar when Dave put a hand on Roberts's arm. 'We'll take it from here.'

'Thank you for your assistance,' I said, and waited until Roberts was on his way back to his office.

Dave pushed open the door of the bar manager's office. 'Are you Fred Goddard, *amigo*, otherwise known as Fernando?'

'Yes, but who the hell are you?'

'Police,' said Dave, 'and my boss, Detective Chief Inspector Brock of New Scotland Yard, has a question to ask you.'

'What d'you want to know?' Goddard stood up, and gazed apprehensively at the three of us.

The telephone rang, but Dave placed his hand on the instrument. 'Leave it,' he said.

I allowed Dave to carry on; he was skilled at extracting information.

'*Señor* Rodriguez, otherwise known as Mike Roberts, reckoned he was definitely *not* here at any time on Christmas Eve. Is that right?' Although we could have found it ourselves, Dave had cleverly permitted Roberts to escort us to the bar manager's office, thus preventing him from telephoning Fred, alias Fernando, and fixing himself an alibi. The phone call that Dave had just prevented Goddard from answering was probably from Roberts. Then, he'd cunningly reversed what Roberts had said about having been in the club all Christmas Eve. 'And you'd better make it the truth, Fred, because this is a murder investigation, and anyone lying to the police would be in serious shtook. Like copping a few years in the nick.'

'Yeah, it's right what he said, guv'nor. He definitely wasn't here,' agreed Goddard readily.

'Good,' said Dave. 'That's all. For the time being.' Dave always liked to leave a threat hanging in the air, particularly when dealing with those he thought suspicious. And there were precious few people he didn't regard as suspicious.

We left Goddard to get on with his bar managing, and wondered what would happen when Roberts asked him about his interview with us. I guessed it would not be a happy exchange.

'I'll put money on our Fernando there having a bit of form,' said Dave, as we made our way to the main door and back into the street. But Dave assumed that everyone had 'a bit of form' until the contrary was proved.

'I don't think that Roberts has an unblemished record, either, Dave,' I said, and turned to Nicola. 'What was it you asked him in Spanish, Nicola?'

'I didn't ask him anything, guv. I recited a couple of verses of a Spanish poem I'd learned when I was studying the language.'

'What d'you make of Roberts claiming to have been at the club when Fernando says he wasn't there, guv?' asked Dave, when we'd finished laughing at Nicola's subterfuge.

'Clever question of yours, Dave,' I said, always believing in giving credit where it was warranted. 'We'll wait a day or two and then interview Roberts again. He'll probably say that he was with a woman.'

'But if that was the case, why didn't he say so?' asked Dave.

'Probably because he was screwing the arse off someone else's wife and is worried that you'll want to check his story,' said Nicola, demonstrating once again that she was not the demure young lady that she appeared to be.

'Well, I shall,' I said. 'In due course.'

FIVE

On Saturday morning, Dave and I went, once again, to the premises of Kerry Trucking at Chiswick.

We found Bernard Bligh in his office overlooking the loading bay.

'Good morning, Mr Bligh.' I looked enquiringly at the other man in his office.

'This is Carl Thorpe, fellow director and the company secretary,' said Bligh.

'I'm Detective Chief Inspector Brock, Mr Thorpe. I'm investigating Mrs Hammond's murder.'

'Yes, Bernard told me.' Thorpe stepped across the office and shook hands. 'Are you getting anywhere with finding out who killed her, Chief Inspector?' he asked.

'We're following a few leads, Mr Thorpe,' I said, 'but these are early days.'

'I suppose so,' said Thorpe.

'Perhaps one of you can answer a question for me, though.'

'Fire away,' said Bligh.

'We're interested in tracing the present whereabouts of Gary Dixon, the driver you sacked.'

'I've no idea where he is,' said Bligh, and turned to Thorpe. 'You keep the staff records, Carl. Have you still got an address for him?'

'It should be in the office somewhere.' Thorpe glanced in my direction. 'Bear with me a minute, Chief Inspector, and I'll go next door and get my girl to have a look.'

'D'you know who takes control of the business now that Mrs Hammond's dead?' I asked, while we were waiting for Thorpe to rummage through his records.

'No, I don't,' said Bligh. 'As matter of fact, Carl and I were discussing what was likely to happen when you arrived. I've got a thirty-five per cent holding in the company and Carl holds ten per cent, but Kerry held the majority shareholding of fifty-five per cent. So it all depends on what's in her will. If she's left her shares to that waster of a husband, and he's allowed to get his hands on the business, he'll likely make as big a mess of it as he has of his own. And then we'll all go down the tubes.'

'Last time we were here, you told me that Nick Hammond is an estate agent.'

'Of sorts,' said Bligh dismissively. 'He's got flashy offices in the West End somewhere, but personally, I'd never consider letting him sell a house of mine. He's a bit dodgy, if you ask me. I reckon he'll go belly up before long, and if he gets the chance to siphon off cash from this company to support his own, he'll be throwing good money after bad. And we'll be left high and dry.'

It was an interesting comment that Bligh had made about Nicholas Hammond's business acumen, or lack of it, particularly as it came from an established and successful businessman. I decided that I'd have someone take a careful look at Hammond's estate agency.

'Did he and Mrs Hammond get on?' asked Dave.

'As I said the last time you were here, I think they had one or two ups and downs, but they seemed to have resolved whatever differences they had. And like I told you previously, I believe she had to shore up his finances once or twice.' Bligh lowered his voice. 'What's more, the way she put herself about at times led me to think that Kerry wasn't averse to having the occasional fling, and I don't suppose that contributed anything to marital harmony.'

That was not only interesting, but had been vaguely hinted at by Kerry's parents. And if it were true it opened up the possibility of having to seek an incalculable number of lovers.

'Have you got any names, Mr Bligh?' asked Dave.

'Names? What names?'

'The names of anyone with whom she might've been having an affair.'

'Oh, I see. No, it was just a sort of feeling I got,' said Bligh, but he gave the impression that he wasn't being completely frank about Kerry's private life.

'I've only got the address we had for Dixon when he was working here,' said Thorpe, coming back into Bligh's office with an open file in his hand. 'According to his HGV licence, he was living at twenty-five Hardacre Street, Ealing.'

'Did you take up references for Dixon when he started work here, Mr Bligh?' asked Dave.

'I suppose we must've done.' Bligh glanced at Thorpe. 'Carl?'

'I imagine so,' said Thorpe, 'but if I remember correctly it was Kerry who engaged him. She just told me to put him on the books, so I suppose she must've run some checks.'

'Why d'you ask?' queried Bligh.

'Because he had previous convictions,' I said, breaching numerous regulations that forbade me from imparting Dixon's criminal history to a third party. 'Apart from the one for which you sacked him.'

'Bloody hell!' exclaimed Bligh. 'If I'd known that, he'd never have got through the gate. I wonder what was so special about Dixon that Kerry took him on.'

'So do I,' I said, but in view of what Bligh had just told me about Kerry having the occasional fling, I thought I could guess.

'It looks as though he slipped through the cracks as far as references are concerned,' said Bligh. 'But I'm not surprised at what you say, Mr Brock.'

'Any reason in particular?'

'I never trusted Dixon, and I was always worried that we'd get a phone call from a customer saying that there was a shortfall in the load they'd received. Or, worse still, he'd been caught bringing in a load of illegal immigrants. I was concerned, too, that his load might be hijacked one day and that he would claim to be the innocent party, a scam that's as old as the hills. But in a way, I was proved right to be suspicious when the customs people nicked him for bootlegging. What really annoyed me was that they told me he'd been at it for some time. I always prided myself on spotting a dodgy driver, but I obviously didn't suss him.'

'When exactly did you sack him?' asked Dave.

'Eleventh of September last,' said Thorpe promptly, who still had Dixon's file in his hand. 'It was after the customs people turned up here making enquiries about him. They told us he'd been arrested at Dover and was being charged with the illegal importation of a large quantity of spirits. We were damned lucky that the vehicle wasn't impounded, or even confiscated. But I think that only happens if the vehicle has been specially adapted for smuggling,' he added as an afterthought.

That comment about a specially adapted vehicle made me think, and I determined that I would look into it.

'I wasn't having any drivers who got up to that sort of malarkey,' said Bligh firmly. 'So he was out on his ear the same day.'

'What was Mrs Hammond's reaction to you giving Dixon his cards?' asked Dave.

'As I recall, she just shrugged. I got the impression that she was a bit put out by it, but she didn't say anything. She couldn't really argue with me for giving a driver the elbow when he'd been nicked by customs.'

'Did Nick Hammond ever come here?' I was interested in the Hammonds' relationship, and whether he'd shown any desire to become involved in Kerry's haulage company.

'Occasionally,' said Bligh. 'But only ever at the end of the day, and that was usually to collect Kerry when they were going out somewhere. I don't think she liked him poking his nose into the business. She probably thought that his inefficiency was contagious.'

We left it at that. We'd added a little more to what we knew of the Hammonds, but not much.

'I think this afternoon might be a good time to have another word with Nick Hammond, Dave,' I said, as we drove back to Curtis Green.

'Is he likely to be at home, guv? Most estate agents I know of are open on Saturdays. Sundays even.'

I rang Hammond's home phone number from my mobile, confirmed that he was at Barnes and made an appointment to see him that afternoon.

When we returned to Curtis Green, I spent an hour or two scanning the pitifully few, and largely useless, statements that we'd acquired since the discovery of Kerry Hammond's body. I then set Kate Ebdon to checking on the address that Thorpe had given us for Gary Dixon.

'D'you want him nicked if I find him, guv?' Kate asked.

'Yes, he's worth a pull if he's there,' I said. 'If not, find out what you can about him. Have a word with his wife, assuming he's got one.'

'He has, guv. Well, I imagine so. I did a voters' list check and it shows a Sonia Dixon living there.'

Dave and I grabbed a quick bite to eat, and made our way to Barnes.

Exuding what I was certain was a false air of bonhomie, Nick Hammond gave all the appearance of a man who had quickly recovered from his wife's death. Wearing a sweater over a blue shirt, chocolate brown chinos and expensive loafers, he invited us into the sitting room.

'I'm having a bit of a job finding Kerry's bank statements,' he said, as we sat down.

'That's a pity,' said Dave. 'It means that we'll have to get a Crown Court judge's warrant to serve on her bank.' He took out his pocketbook and flicked it open, ready to record details. 'Perhaps you'd give me the address of the branch where she banked.' He looked up expectantly.

The ploy worked. 'Oh, hang on, though,' said Hammond, flicking his fingers at feigned recollection. 'If you can give me a minute or two, I've just thought where she might've kept them.' He jumped up and hastened from the room, and I heard him going upstairs, presumably to the safe I'd discovered in the bedroom.

I wondered why Hammond should've made such a blatant attempt to prevent us from seeing his late wife's bank statements, and I was now even more interested to see them in the hope that they might reveal some secret that would aid our investigation.

Taking advantage of Hammond's absence, Dave took the wedding photograph from his briefcase and placed it on the side table whence he had taken it three days previously.

'These are the last two years' statements,' said Hammond, flourishing a sheaf of bank documents as he returned. 'Kerry always got online statements, but then printed a copy of them to keep here. I think she kept a duplicate set at the office as well. Very good with paperwork, was Kerry.'

'Seems a bit pointless, getting online statements and then making a hard copy,' commented Dave, who knew about these things. He glanced quickly at the statements and then put them in his briefcase.

'I suppose so,' said Hammond, 'but Kerry was very much a belt and braces girl.'

'Does the name Gary Dixon mean anything to you, Mr Hammond?' I asked. I'd posed the same question to him at the airport when we'd told him of Kerry's death, but I was interested to hear what he had to say this time. I was disappointed.

'You asked me that at the airport,' said Hammond, 'and no, the name means nothing to me. Why, is it important?'

'I've no idea, Mr Hammond,' I said, 'but a murder enquiry is a bit like a jigsaw puzzle: you collect all sorts of odd pieces and try to fit them together.'

'I see.' Hammond appeared unimpressed by this novel approach to solving serious crime. 'When am I likely to get Kerry's car back, Chief Inspector?'

'There are still a number of scientific tests to be carried out on the vehicle, Mr Hammond.' Although I'd noticed a new Mini Cooper on the drive when we'd arrived, it seemed that Hammond was more concerned about getting his hands on the Jaguar. Certainly more concerned than he seemed to be about his wife's murder. But I was on the point of disillusioning him. 'However, the Jaguar will be returned to its owners, Kerry Trucking Limited, once we've finished examining it.'

'But it's Kerry's car, surely?'

'It's registered to the company,' said Dave, 'and it's the company that'll get it back.'

'But Kerry owned the company.'

'Not all of it,' said Dave. 'It's something you'll have to take up with her fellow directors.'

'Which leads me to my next point, Mr Hammond,' I said. 'Do you have a copy of Mrs Hammond's will?'

Hammond hesitated long enough for me to know that his answer, when it came, would be untrue. 'Er, no, I'm afraid not,' he said eventually. 'In fact, I'm not sure she'd made one,' he added, belying his previous statement that Kerry was a belt and braces girl. 'Is it important?'

'Not really,' I said offhandedly, in an attempt to imply that it was of no real interest to me. But I was sure that a businesswoman with the assets that Kerry Hammond possessed would not have died intestate. Doubtless Bernard Bligh would know about it, and it was a possibility that Kerry Trucking's company solicitors would have taken care of drawing up a will for Kerry.

But Hammond answered that question for me. 'I do know that she used the company's solicitors for private stuff, like the purchase of this house.'

'Is the house jointly owned by you and your wife?' asked Dave.

'No, it's in Kerry's name,' said Hammond tersely. I got the

impression that such an arrangement did not please him greatly. 'She lived here with her previous husband.'

'Do you know where I can find these lawyers?' I asked.

'I'm afraid not. I seem to recall Kerry saying that all the paperwork, including the deeds for this house, were kept by a solicitor, but I've no idea which one. I dare say that someone at her offices in Chiswick will be able to help you.' And then Hammond reverted to our previous conversation. 'I imagine that the bulk of her estate will come to me,' he volunteered, 'although we'd never discussed it. Certainly mine would have gone to Kerry. Quite frankly I didn't expect a woman of her age to die when she did. Well, you don't, do you?'

'I understand that Bligh and Thorpe, being directors, have a holding in the company,' I said.

Hammond gave a short, humourless laugh. 'Oh, poor Mr Bligh wasn't very happy that Kerry gained control of the company when Dick Lucas died. Dick was her first husband.'

'So I understand, but why was Bligh upset?'

'Kerry once told me that Bligh and Dick Lucas were instrumental in setting up the company. In fact, they were virtually equal partners, but when Lucas died and left the company to Kerry, Bligh was bloody furious, so she told me, and the thirty-five per cent holding he was given didn't please him. He thought he should've been given control.'

'And if he doesn't get the company now, he'll be even less pleased, I suppose.'

'I imagine so.'

'Did you and your wife get on?' asked Dave suddenly.

'What sort of question's that?' demanded Hammond. He glanced across the room at the replaced wedding photograph and did a double take, his expression indicating that he was puzzled by its reappearance. But human nature being what it is, he'd probably blame his cleaning lady.

'A quite simple one, Mr Hammond. Did you and your wife have rows?'

'The occasional tiff,' admitted Hammond, returning his gaze to Dave once again. 'We had disagreements from time to time, like most married couples, I suppose, but nothing serious.'

That might've been true, but he probably didn't know about the 'occasional flings' that Bligh had suggested she'd had. Speaking from personal experience, I knew that the husband is usually the last person to find out about a wife's infidelity. And, to be fair, probably the other way round too.

'I understand that she had to help you out financially once or twice,' I said.

'Who told you that?' snapped Hammond. He seemed irritated at the change in questioning.

'Well, did she?'

'When I first set up business, yes. Things were a bit shaky to start with, what with house prices rocketing at the time and the market stalling, but I'm flourishing now.'

That remained to be seen, even though Bligh didn't seem to think so. But Bligh's view might've been prompted by animosity. If Hammond *was* in financial difficulties, and Kerry had left everything to him, he had just provided us with a good motive for murdering her. But that rather depended on what was in her will and whether Hammond knew what was in it.

That said, I was still surprised that a man who claimed to have had only the occasional slight tiff with his wife should have gone to New York without knowing what had happened to her. *Unless he knew what had happened to her.*

It was five o'clock by the time that Dave and I returned to Curtis Green. Nothing had happened during my absence, but I hadn't expected it to. I briefed Charlie Flynn, my ex-Fraud Squad sergeant, to find out just how successful Nick Hammond's estate agency was, or wasn't. But I told him that there was no point in starting before Monday.

That done, I decided that there wasn't much more that could be undertaken between now and Monday. One or two members of the team were working on various assignments that I'd given them, but I gave the others the weekend off, what little remained of it.

It was half past six when I arrived home at my flat in Surbiton, a place I saw but briefly when I was in the middle of a murder investigation. Those rare moments of my off-duty time that I enjoyed were usually spent at Gail's house, and I kept a change of clothing there.

As usual, my flat was clean and tidy, and it was apparent that Mrs Gurney had been at work. Gladys Gurney is the uncomplaining middle-aged lady who 'does for me' two or three times a week, and she takes care of all the things that I don't have the time to do myself. She tidies everything, polishes everything, gathers up my abandoned clothing and puts my laundry in the washing machine, and irons my shirts. Gladys is an absolute gem, and I'd be completely lost without her. On this occasion, she had left one of her charming little notes on the kitchen worktop along with a small parcel that had been carefully wrapped in tissue paper:

> *Dear Mr Brock,*
>   *I found one or two of Miss Sutton's bits and pieces lying about in the bedroom. I give them a wash for her and perhaps you'd let her have them back.*
>   *Yours faithfully*
>   *Gladys Gurney (Mrs)*

Carefully removing the tissue paper, I discovered one of Gail's lacy bras and a thong. It's a mystery to me how she manages to forget her underwear when she goes home.

For one brief, impish moment, I was tempted to post them from central London with a note saying, 'Thanks for a wonderful weekend,' and signing it 'Fred', just to see her reaction, but I changed my mind and decided to deliver them personally. I cause Gail enough grief without going out of my way to antagonize her. I rang her to say that I was on my way.

'Is the coast clear?' I asked, when Gail opened the door. I handed her a bunch of flowers, but kept hold of the chilled bottle of champagne I'd had the foresight to bring with me.

'Of course it is,' said Gail. 'You know Mum and Dad went back on Boxing Day. Are you going to open that?' she asked, pointing at the champagne, 'or is it just to look at?'

We moved into the sitting room, and Gail produced a couple of champagne flutes. I poured the wine and we settled down.

'Dad wanted to know if you'd proposed to me yet.' Gail gave me one of her mischievous smiles.

'*What?*' I'd hoped that George wouldn't raise the question with Gail.

'You heard, lover. He wanted to know if you were going to make an honest woman of me.'

'And what did you say?'

'I told him that you hadn't said a word about marriage, and that I was beginning to feel like a wronged woman.'

I was completely taken aback at this turn in the conversation. 'But we *have* discussed it.' I was floundering now. 'You always said that once was enough and that you were quite happy with our arrangement.'

'Gotcha!' Gail threw back her head and laughed at my embarrassment. 'Well, I am, and that's what I told him.'

'Oh! That's all right, then. And what did he say to that?' I'd almost forgotten her propensity for teasing.

'Nothing much.' Gail held out her glass for a refill. 'Apart from saying that he thought it was a bit unconventional.'

'Really? I never took George for someone who was concerned about the proprieties.'

'Don't worry,' said Gail laughing again. 'Mum reminded him that they'd lived together for a few months before they were married. She told him that I was a big girl now, and that he was not to interfere. Dinner?'

'Please.' I stood up and followed my girlfriend downstairs to the dining room.

As befitted Gail's superb culinary skills, she produced an excellent meal. The roast beef was done to perfection, and the roast potatoes and steamed cauliflower, with a delicious sauce, were out of this world. The meal was accompanied by an expensive bottle of Malbec that Gail said was a gift from her father.

'I do wish that murder wouldn't keep me away from your cooking,' I said, standing up to get the Armagnac. 'I'm sick of grabbing a pie and a pint at the local pub.'

'You should try going on the stage if you really want to know what it's like to rough it,' said Gail, as usual displaying no great sympathy for a policeman's lot.

I poured the brandy and placed a glass in front of her.

'Bring it with you,' said Gail, rising from the table and leading the way upstairs. All the way upstairs.

SIX

I arrived at the office at nine o'clock on Monday morning. As was his invariable practice, the commander arrived on the stroke of ten. It was a habit that reminded me of the annual Trooping the Colour ceremony for which Her Majesty the Queen always arrived on Horse Guards Parade as the clock struck eleven. And the commander always arrived at Curtis Green as Big Ben struck ten.

'Mr Brock, a moment of your time.' The commander didn't even break step as he passed the open door of my office. Nor would he ever address me as Harry like real CID commanders did, presumably for fear that I might call him by his first name. I'm not sure he could cope with that.

But the commander is not a real detective, even though he fancies himself as one. After a lifetime in the Uniform Branch, he was visited upon us by some genius in Human Resources at Scotland Yard who probably imagined that it would widen our illustrious leader's experience – and doubtless add a new dimension to the way we poor workers set about our mundane task of investigating murders. I'm not sure, however, that his knowledge of curbing unruly football crowds and instituting diabolical traffic schemes would help us very much. Mind you, he was very good, and very prolific, when it came to writing memoranda.

I followed the great man into his office.

'Did you have a pleasant Christmas, sir?' I enquired, not that I cared, but such social niceties tended to put him off his stroke, albeit temporarily.

'Oh, er, yes, thank you, Mr Brock. Very quiet, of course. Very quiet.' The commander settled himself behind his desk, and spent a moment or two surveying his overflowing in-tray with the sort of relish with which a hungry man contemplates a hearty meal. 'Be so good as to bring me up to date on this suspicious death you're investigating at the airport, Mr Brock.'

He would never call a suspicious death a murder in case it turned out to be manslaughter or even suicide. A bit of a pedant, is our commander.

I summarized what we knew so far. 'But I'm not too happy about Nicholas Hammond, the dead woman's husband, sir,' I continued, intent upon feeding in a few red herrings, and explained how he'd gone to New York without knowing what had happened to her. 'Seems a strange sort of thing to do,' I added.

'Yes, very strange, very strange indeed, Mr Brock. Are you considering arresting him?'

'Not at this stage, sir. In the meantime, I'm having enquiries made about his business. It's in Mayfair.'

'In Mayfair, eh?' The commander was always impressed by prestigious addresses.

'But there are others in the frame,' I said.

'In the frame?' The commander contrived to look both irritated and mystified at the same time. He knew perfectly well what I meant, but he always affected ignorance whenever any of us used the jargon he abhorred.

'Yes, sir, Bernard Bligh for one. He's one of the directors of Kerry Trucking who was apparently annoyed that control of the company didn't pass to him on Richard Lucas's death. Lucas was Kerry Hammond's first husband.'

'Her *first* husband? You mean she was married before? This all seems rather complicated, Mr Brock.'

It seemed fairly plain to me that if she was now on her second husband, she'd been married before. 'And then there's a former driver called Gary Dixon who was prosecuted by customs for smuggling.' I said, managing to confuse the commander even further, which, of course, was my intention.

'He sounds like your principal suspect, then,' said the chief confidently. In his simplistic view, anyone previously convicted of a crime must have committed the one currently under investigation.

'I don't think it's as straightforward as that, sir,' I said. 'But time will tell.'

'Yes, but don't waste *too* much time, Mr Brock. I expect to have a result soon.' Using his customary technique of implying dismissal, the commander put on his half moon spectacles, intended to lend him gravitas, and drew the first file from the top of his in tray. But then he paused and looked at me. 'I should be inclined to detain this Nicholas Hammond and interrogate him thoroughly. From what you say, he sounds like a suspect.'

'Thank you, sir. That's a very good suggestion if I may say so. I'll bear it in mind.' But I had long ago come to the conclusion that the commander's advice was best ignored.

'Be so good as to keep me informed of your progress, Mr Brock.'

'Of course, sir.'

Detective Inspector Ebdon had been busy over the weekend, and was waiting for me in the incident room.

'Gary Dixon, guv.'

'Have you found him, Kate?'

'Not yet. I called at Dixon's Hardacre Street address, and had a chat with his wife Sonia. She hasn't seen him since just before Christmas, and she's no idea where he is now.'

'Guilty knowledge, guv,' said Dave, but he always said that. He set down a tray bearing several cups of coffee that he'd made on the unauthorized machine we kept tucked away in a cupboard out of sight of the Commissioner's 'electricity police'. Every so often, a jobsworth would arrive in search of illegal coffee-making equipment. But he never had any luck; Dave was far too cunning for him.

'Maybe,' said Kate. 'But I had a heart-to-heart with Sonia. Apparently Gary is a bit of a womanizer, and she thinks he might've gone off somewhere with a bird. I asked her to tell him we wanted to see him, if and when he comes back, and if that results in him doing a runner, she'll give us a bell. But somehow, I don't think we'll hear anything.'

It was no more than I'd expected. 'Better put him on the PNC, Kate.'

'Already done, sir.' Colin Wilberforce, now back from his Christmas break, glanced up from his desk.

'I don't suppose that'll help much.' said Kate. She had no greater faith in the Police National Computer as a method of tracking down criminals than I had. In my experience, wanted villains were often nicked in the most unlikely circumstances. Frequently by a traffic policeman doing a routine stop and asking embarrassing questions

such as: 'What's your name, and where d'you live?' Followed up
by the crippler: 'Got any ID?'

We'd been lucky enough to find Susan Penrose's telephone number
plumbed into Kerry Hammond's mobile. Dave had done a subscriber
check with the cellphone service provider and found that she lived
at Barling Towers, Royal Dock Road, in that expensive area of east
London which had once been a thriving dockland.

The barefooted girl who answered the door was wearing a full-
length yellow kaftan. She had brown, cropped hair and her only
make-up was a minimal amount of lipstick and delicately applied
mascara. For a moment or two, she gazed pensively at us.

'Can I help you?'

'Mrs Penrose?'

'Yes, I'm Susan Penrose. Who are you?'

A man appeared behind the woman. 'What is it, Sue?'

'We're police officers,' I said, producing my warrant card. 'I'm
Detective Chief Inspector Brock of Scotland Yard, and this is
Detective Sergeant Poole.'

'Oh, God, not another break-in, surely,' said the man. 'You'd
better come in.'

The sitting room was vast, and a picture window, taking up most
of one side, afforded the occupants a panoramic view of the River
Thames. Adjacent to the window was a door that gave access to a
balcony running the full width of the room.

'I take it you're Mr Penrose,' I said, as the four of us sat down.

'Yes, that's me, old boy, I'm Dudley Penrose. So, one of
my places has been broken into, has it? What's been taken this
time?'

Penrose was a smooth individual, probably pushing forty, and
judging by the casual clothes he was wearing would have died rather
than be seen in something from a high street chain. He was the sort
of know-it-all who holds forth in the local chic gastropub about
everything and anything. He would always know the chief man in
any organization, and he'd been wherever you'd been, but more
often. And even more often to places to which you'd never been.

'If you're talking about your car showrooms, Mr Penrose,' I said,
'the answer's no. We're here to ask Mrs Penrose a few questions
about Kerry Hammond.'

'Oh, what's the dear girl been up to now?' asked Penrose, still not taking the hint that I was talking to his wife.

'She's been murdered,' I said flatly.

'Oh no!' Susan Penrose was visibly shocked. 'When?'

'Her body was discovered in her car on Christmas Day at Heathrow Airport,' I said.

'Was it the indigo blue Jaguar XJ?' asked Penrose, taking a sudden interest in what I was saying.

'It was, as a matter of fact. Why d'you ask?'

'Only professional interest,' said Penrose. 'I supplied it to her or, technically speaking, to her company, Kerry Trucking.'

'This is no time to talk about your damned business, Dud,' snapped Penrose's wife, tears running unchecked down her face. 'Didn't you hear what the chief inspector said? Kerry's been murdered. It's my best friend we're talking about here, damn you.'

'Sorry,' mumbled Penrose. 'Can I get you guys a drink?'

'No thanks,' I said.

'Well, it was good of you to let us know.' Penrose stood up. 'I'll show you out.'

'We didn't come here to deliver a death message,' said Dave sharply. 'If that had been necessary, which it wasn't, we'd've sent a uniformed constable.' He'd obviously taken a serious dislike to Dudley Penrose, but he probably disliked car dealers as a species.

'Just sit down and shut up, Dud.' Having delivered that rebuke to her husband, Susan Penrose turned to me. 'You obviously want to know anything about Kerry that might help you find out who killed her.' She took a tissue from a handy box and dabbed gently at her eyes, being careful to avoid smudging her mascara.

'We know about her first husband's death in a car accident,' I began, 'and we know about her second marriage. We have actually interviewed Mr Hammond, and Kerry's parents, Mr and Mrs King.'

'In that case, I doubt if there's any more I can tell you,' said Susan.

'Mr King said that after the death of Kerry's first husband, and before she remarried, two years later I understand, she became something of a good-time girl. I suspect that that might've been a euphemism for something more serious.'

'She certainly went off the rails a bit,' said Susan. 'She was drinking far too much and associating with a lot of odd people that

she met in nightclubs. She wasn't too choosy about who she slept
with, either.'

'Was there anyone in particular?' asked Dave.

'Not that I know of. She spent a lot of time at a club called the
Spanish Fly. In fact, I've an idea that she had a fling with the guy
who owns it, a rather oily Spaniard called Miguel something.'

'Yes, we know about him,' I said, without revealing that he was
British and otherwise known as Michael Roberts.

'Then she met Nick Hammond and a couple of months later she
was married to him.' Susan Penrose looked pensive for a moment
or two. 'God knows why,' she said. 'He didn't seem her type at all,
but after that she shrugged off her frenetic lifestyle and appeared
to settle down to playing with her lorries.'

'D'you know where she met Nick?' I asked.

'Believe it or not, at a tennis club dance. She was mad keen on
tennis for a while. It was one of the fads that she went through.
Her "get fit" phase, I called it. I met Nick once, but he was a
humdrum sort of a guy, a bit of a wimp. I think he was an estate
agent. At the time, I asked her if she knew what she was doing in
marrying him, but she was quite adamant. Frankly, I didn't think it
would last, even though it lasted for about five years. Between you
and me, though, I don't think that Kerry was averse to having the
occasional fling.' Susan paused, a sad expression on her face. 'Not
that she will any more,' she added, giving her red-rimmed eyes a
final dab.

On Tuesday morning, DS Flynn came into my office.

'You wanted to know about Nicholas Hammond's business in
Mayfair, guv.'

'Yes, Charlie?'

'I was lucky enough to find an obliging lady who keeps a shop
opposite Hammond's place.'

'How obliging?' I asked.

'I wasn't that lucky; she was a grandmother,' said Flynn, with a
laugh. 'I spun her some fanny about drug dealers, and she let me
keep obo from an upstairs room. She even made me tea and sand-
wiches, and lent me a pair of binoculars.'

'And what did you learn about Hammond and his business from
this comfortable little observation post, Charlie?'

'I took up the obo at about eight o'clock, and a guy I presumed to be Hammond turned up on foot about twenty minutes later. It was a plush sort of place, carpeted throughout. There were four or five expensive desks with computers on each of them. Hammond has got a couple of assistants, a man and a woman. But he doesn't seem to do much in the way of business; not that that means much nowadays.'

'I suppose that in this modern age a lot of house sales are conducted on the Internet, or on the phone,' I suggested.

'Could be,' said Flynn. 'But at about midday a couple of well-dressed but shifty-looking Arab types turned up who didn't give the impression that they were interested in buying any property. They had a quick glance up and down the street before going in, and the minute they walked through the door, Hammond ushered them into a back room. They were there for about twenty minutes, and then they pushed off.'

'I wonder what that was about,' I said.

'I was in two minds whether or not to follow them, guv, but I thought it was better to stay where I was. Anyway, apart from our two Arab friends, only a handful of seemingly bona fide clients walked through the door until he shut up shop at six o'clock. By the way, I had a casual glance at the property he'd got in the window. All expensive stuff, but not one of them was marked "sold". I reckon he's running a front for something. Surveillance might tell us more.'

'It could be a sham, Charlie, although God knows for what, but it'd take a lot of manpower to put on round-the-clock observation. Whatever Hammond's up to, I don't think it'd have much to do with Kerry's murder. We'll have to wait and see,' I said. 'But in the meantime, I think I'll have him into the nick and give him a good talking to.'

But that idea was thwarted almost immediately by a telephone call.

'It's the commander here, Mr Brock. Be so good as to step into my office.'

The commander's office was two doors down the corridor, but he had to ring me. Alan Cleaver, the detective chief superintendent, would have strolled into my office, cadged a cup of illegal coffee and sat down for a chat.

'You wanted me, sir?'

'Close the door, Mr Brock.' The commander drew a sheet of paper towards him, and glanced at it; he makes a note of everything. 'I've just received a telephone call from the DAC in charge of Counter-Terrorist Command. He wishes to see you immediately, and you're to go alone.'

'Very good, sir,' I said, wondering what the hell that was all about. I couldn't think of any complaint against me that might've come from that quarter, although you never can tell.

'And when you've seen him, you're to come straight back here and report to me.'

I decided to walk. I could do with the fresh air and it would give me time to think. And at this time of year, there were few foreign tourists to stop me and ask inane questions. Even though I wasn't wearing a policeman's costume, I looked English.

I walked along Parliament Street, cut across Parliament Square, into Victoria Street and finally to New Scotland Yard.

Over forty years ago, the Metropolitan Police had been ousted from its headquarters on Victoria Embankment by parliamentarians who wanted the building for themselves. Consequently, the Yard was now housed in a glass and concrete pile in Broadway that possessed all the architectural appeal of a third world tenement block.

I'd not previously met the deputy assistant commissioner for counter-terrorism, but he turned out to be an affable fellow, and obviously a real detective.

'DCI Brock from HSCC, sir. I understand you wanted to see me.'

'Good morning, Mr Brock,' said the DAC, waving me into a chair. 'It's Harry, isn't it?'

'Yes, sir.'

'This is David Simpson, Harry,' said the DAC, indicating a man seated in an armchair. 'He's from the Security Service. And before we proceed, nothing you hear in this room must go any further. Is that clearly understood?'

'Yes, sir.' I shook hands with the man from MI5, but guessed that his name wasn't really Simpson. Such shadowy characters never give their real names when dealing with ordinary mortals like me.

'I understand that you have an interest in Nicholas Hammond, Mr Brock,' said Simpson.

'He's a suspect in a murder enquiry,' I said bluntly, even though I wasn't sure that he was. 'I'm investigating the death of his wife who was discovered in her—'

'Yes, I know all about the case,' said Simpson, holding up a hand, and glancing at the DAC. 'I have to tell you that Mr Hammond is one of our officers.'

'Bloody hell!' I said.

The DAC laughed. 'I thought that'd surprise you, Harry.'

'Do you consider Nicholas Hammond to be a viable suspect, Mr Brock?' asked Simpson.

'One of several,' I said, unwilling to offer Simpson any quarter.

'I see.' Simpson lapsed into silence for a moment or two. 'I'm going to ask a favour of you, Mr Brock. Is it at all possible that you could avoid interviewing him at his Mayfair premises, or taking him to a police station? You see, it would quite possibly compromise a rather special operation in which he's currently involved.'

'Well, don't leave it there, David,' said the DAC. 'You're putting Mr Brock in a very difficult position and it's only fair you tell him what he's up against.'

It obviously went against all the principles of the Security Service for Simpson to say any more than he had to, but he eventually capitulated.

'Of late, Nick Hammond has been cultivating a number of inform-ants, mainly expatriate Iranians, and he's also been in touch with our liaison in the United States.'

'By which, I presume you mean the CIA, Mr Simpson,' I said.

'Er, yes, exactly.' Simpson seemed mildly irritated that I'd seen through his euphemism. 'He's engaged in very important work.'

I told Simpson about the two shifty Arabian characters that Charlie Flynn had seen entering Hammond's Mayfair estate agency.

'Good God!' exclaimed Simpson, clearly appalled, 'd'you mean you've been keeping observation on the place.'

'It's standard practice,' commented the DAC, hiding a smile, 'and in all fairness, Mr Brock knew nothing of Hammond's background until now.'

'Yes, I see,' said the unhappy Simpson. 'But I'd deem it a great favour if you discontinued the observation.'

'I've done so already,' I said. 'But my officers got the impression that Hammond's business is a bit of a front.' It was a comment that seemed to discomfit Simpson even further.

'D'you think Hammond's up for this topping, Harry?' asked the DAC, clearly enjoying the difficulty in which Simpson found himself.

'I don't honestly know at this stage, sir. He didn't seem too cut up about the death of his wife, *and* he went off to New York on Christmas Eve without waiting to find out what had happened to her. In fact, to the best of our knowledge she was already lying dead in one of the airport car parks.'

'He had to go to New York, Mr Brock,' put in Simpson. 'There was no way he could not have gone. I'm sure you understand.'

'Over Christmas?' I said. 'Another meeting with the American spooks at Langley, Virginia, I suppose.' I now assumed that Hammond's excuse of 'closing a deal' had nothing to do with buying and selling houses.

'Quite so,' muttered Simpson, who seemed unhappy that I was aware of the location of the CIA, despite it being widely publicized. But I got the impression that he was the sort of guy who'd lock a newspaper in his safe if MI5 was mentioned in its pages. And I noticed that he'd readily agreed that Hammond had met with the CIA, even though Langley, in Virginia, was at least three hundred miles from New York. But I didn't suppose that Simpson's circumspection affected my enquiry.

'I think we've just made your job harder than it was already, Harry,' said the DAC, 'but if you come up against any insurmountable problems, let me know, and I'll see what can be done. And if you get to the point where you intend charging Hammond with his wife's murder, I'd be grateful if you'd let me know before you nick him. Not that his current employment will make any difference. He wouldn't be the first MI5 officer to grip the dock rail at the Old Bailey.' It was a throwaway line that caused Simpson to frown.

'Of course, sir,' I said. 'Incidentally, I've learned that on at least a couple of occasions his wife injected some capital into this estate agency that Hammond's running.'

'That's easily explained, Mr Brock,' said Simpson smoothly. 'It was all part of the cover, in case anyone looked into the background of his business. It would make it seem more genuine, you see.'

'I suppose so,' I said, but as a simple policeman, I failed to see the logic of that. Surely to God, if any financial shoring up was required, the secret fund would be able to provide it *and* keep it secret. But who am I to understand such arcane matters?

'And one other thing, Harry,' said the DAC. 'I must remind you once again that nothing you've heard in this office is to be passed on to any other person at all. And that includes your commander. Understood?'

'Absolutely, sir.' The DAC's embargo on telling the commander was about the only thing to emerge from the interview that gave me any pleasure. I stood up to leave.

'And a Happy New Year, Harry,' said the DAC, and laughed.

SEVEN

When I got back to Curtis Green, the commander was hovering in his doorway. It was a most unusual sight and one that underlined his curiosity about my visit to the Yard.

'Come in, Mr Brock, and close the door. Now, what was this interview with the DAC Counter Terrorism all about, eh?'

'I'm afraid I'm under strict orders from the DAC personally not to divulge anything about it to anyone, sir.'

The commander afforded me a strained smile. 'Yes, but that doesn't include me, surely?'

'As a matter of fact, the DAC made a particular point of saying that you were not be told, sir.' Although I derived some satisfaction from that, I was fairly certain that I'd be the one on the receiving end of the commander's wrath. If not today, then certainly later on.

'But that's absolutely preposterous, Mr Brock.' The commander's face reddened quite noticeably. 'I'm sure you must have got that wrong. The DAC couldn't possibly have said such a thing. Does he think I'm not to be trusted?' Suddenly he realized that he was implying criticism of a senior officer to a junior one. 'I'm sure you must have misunderstood the direction, Mr Brock,' he said, hurriedly backtracking. 'I shall speak to the DAC immediately.' And with that, he waved an imperious hand of dismissal. He was, to use one of Kate Ebdon's favourite phrases, not a happy bunny.

Understandably, I never learned the details of the commander's conversation with the DAC, but it was apparent that from that day forth he seemed to lose interest in the murder of Kerry Hammond.

I returned to my office, shouting for Dave on the way.

'Yes, guv?'

'Shut the door and sit down, Dave.'

'Sounds serious,' said Dave, sprawling in my only armchair. 'Not a complaint, is it?'

'We've got a problem,' I said, ignoring Dave's question. Despite the DAC's prohibition, I'd decided that I could not keep this

information from Dave, and I told him what had taken place at the
Yard.

'Bloody hell!' exclaimed Dave. 'That's going to make life a bit
difficult.'

'If Hammond's our man it means that we'll have to be very
circumspect in our dealings with him. No obos, no interviews in a
nick. Which leaves us with talking to him on his own turf, and that
always puts us at a disadvantage.'

'Perhaps we ought to pursue the other suspects first, guv.'

'Agreed. But right now, the most pressing job is to get a sight
of Kerry Hammond's last will and testament. That might steer us
in the right direction. And we need to speak to Gary Dixon sooner
rather than later.'

'We've got to find him first, guv.'

'We'll leave that to Miss Ebdon for the time being,' I said, 'but
first there is the question of Mrs Hammond's will.'

I telephoned Bernard Bligh at Kerry Trucking and asked him for
the name of the company solicitor. After querying why I wanted to
know, and getting no answer, Bligh furnished the name of the lawyer
and told me that she had offices in Lincoln's Inn Fields.

I was expecting to be greeted by a horse-faced harridan, but Kerry
Trucking's solicitor was a striking young blonde, a first in my
experience of the legal profession.

The solicitor's secretary, who looked old enough to be the lawyer's
mother, served coffee.

'And now tell me how may I help you, gentlemen,' said the
lawyer, once the secretary had left the office.

'Did you draw up a last will and testament for Mrs Kerry
Hammond, the managing director of Kerry Trucking?' I asked.

'Yes, I did, but what's your interest?'

'I'm investigating her murder.'

'Yes, of course. A tragic event. Mrs Hammond had a lot to live
for.' The solicitor spoke to her secretary on the office intercom and
asked for Kerry's will. Minutes later, the document was placed on
the lawyer's desk.

'What exactly did you want to know, Chief Inspector?' Having
spent a few minutes reading the document, the solicitor looked up.

'The names of the main beneficiaries,' I said.

'There's only one: Nicholas Hammond, Kerry Hammond's husband. Everything goes to him: the business, the house in Barnes, the one in France, and a considerable sum of money.' The lawyer paused and glanced at the document again. 'The last estimate put the entire estate somewhere in the region of twenty million pounds, give or take a few million,' she added with a smile.

'Interesting,' I said, in the absence of anything more constructive to say.

'Does that provide you with a motive, Mr Brock?'

'It might,' I said cautiously. 'As a matter of interest, where is this house in France?'

The solicitor glanced at the will again. 'It's in St-Tropez, in the rue Gambetta. A very upmarket property, I should imagine. D'you know St-Tropez, at all?'

'No, I can't say that I do.'

'I do,' said Dave. 'Madeleine and I spent a holiday there a few years ago.'

The solicitor regarded Dave with renewed interest, but said nothing. Perhaps she thought that he was bent; that's what most lawyers think about policemen who appear to be living above their means.

'Is Mr Hammond aware of the contents of his wife's will?' I asked.

'Almost certainly, Mr Brock. She asked specifically that a copy should be sent to him when it was drawn up.'

That too was interesting; Hammond told us he knew nothing about it. It must've been the old MI5 secrecy kicking in.

'Would Bernard Bligh have been made aware of the contents of the will?'

'I certainly haven't told him, but maybe Kerry Hammond did.'

'Would you have any objection to my telling him?'

'Not at all, but remember that it has yet to go to probate. Is there anything else you'd like to know?'

'Not at present, no,' I said, 'but I may have to come back to you.'

'Fine. You can always email me, of course, if it'll save you a visit.'

'Thank you.' I forbore from saying that I wasn't into emailing.

'Well, Dave,' I said, once we were back at Curtis Green, 'that rather points a finger at Nicholas Hammond.'

'So he knew about the will, despite having denied all knowledge of it.'

'So it would seem, but perhaps secrecy comes naturally to him.'

'I reckon Kerry's topping's got to be down to him, guv.'

'It's beginning to look that way, although how the hell we're going to prove it without having him into the nick, I don't know.'

'Well, I know what I'd do,' said Dave. 'I'd nick him and let the secret squirrel you saw across at the Yard pick the bones out of that. Anyway,' he added, 'I thought that MI5 weren't supposed to operate outside the UK, but you said that he'd been to the States to talk to the CIA.'

'There are a lot of things they're not supposed to do, Dave, but it doesn't stop them.'

'There are a lot of things we're not supposed to do, either,' said Dave, 'but we do them. Like nicking people on suspicion whether they're spies or not.'

'If only it was that easy, Dave,' I said.

'There is another aspect, guv,' said Dave thoughtfully. 'Given the possibility that Bligh is ignorant of the will's contents, he might've been under the impression that he was going to get the company when Kerry died. And that would make for a motive.'

'Yeah maybe, Dave, but we've got to find some solid evidence.'

I was surprised that we had managed to achieve so much, given that it was New Year's Eve. Britain grinds to a standstill between the twenty-fourth of December and the second of January, or even longer if our revered government has thrown in an extra bank holiday or two. Consequently, it's a miracle that anything at all gets done.

I decided that I couldn't do a lot more on New Year's Day, so I didn't try. Instead, I spent a lazy day with Gail, drinking too much and eating too much.

On the Thursday morning, however, I resolved to speak to Bernard Bligh again, mainly to see his reaction to the news that his new boss was to be Nicholas Hammond.

'There can't be anything else you want to know, surely?' Bligh's reaction to our visit was a little more wary than hitherto, and I wondered whether it was because he'd had something to do with Kerry's death.

'Not at the moment, no.' Dave and I accepted Bligh's invitation to sit down in his pokey little office. 'I was wondering whether you'd heard about Mrs Hammond's will.'

Bligh's eyes narrowed. 'What about it?'

'It seems that Nicholas Hammond gets everything, and that of course includes the control of this company.'

For a few moments, Bligh stared at me, stunned by the disastrous news I'd just given him. 'I don't bloody believe it,' he said eventually. 'Kerry wouldn't do something like that to me. Are you absolutely sure, Chief Inspector?'

'I spoke to the company solicitor the day before yesterday, and she assures me that Nicholas Hammond is the sole beneficiary of his wife's will.'

Bligh shook his head in disbelief. 'But Kerry told me that if anything happened to her, and that included serious illness, she would hand the company over to me. She always looked to the future, even though she was in the best of health.' He pulled open a drawer in his desk and took out a bottle of whisky. He poured a substantial measure of Scotch into a glass and drank it down neat. 'Oh, would you like a drink?' he asked, as an obvious afterthought.

'No thanks.' It's a fallacy that policemen don't drink on duty, and I'm not usually averse to accepting one, but I make it a practice never to drink with suspects. And right now, Bligh was beginning to look that way.

'I helped Dick Lucas build up this business from scratch, you know, Mr Brock.' Bligh poured more whisky into his glass and stared at it moodily. 'In fact, we worked at it together, driving our first two trucks ourselves, and working our damned fingers to the bone. Every day and every hour that God gave. And this is all the thanks I get for it. It was bad enough when Dick died and left the company to Kerry, but at least she made a good fist of running it. But Nick Hammond'll spend all the profits and run it into the ground. That guy is a tosser, pure and simple.'

There was something at the back of my mind that told me that he and Thorpe could, should they so desire, take legal proceedings to have Nicholas Hammond removed as managing director. Especially if his stewardship proved to be detrimental to the running of the company. But I kept my silence; I know very little of civil law. No doubt the company solicitor would advise them, for a hefty fee.

'Where were you on Christmas Eve?' asked Dave.

The suddenness of the question caught Bligh unawares. 'Er, Christmas Eve. I was, um . . . yes, of course, I was at home with the wife.'

'Wrapping the kids' Christmas presents no doubt,' suggested Dave.

'We don't have any children,' responded Bligh sharply. 'Anne and I have tried, but it was no good. We're thinking of trying the IVF programme now, or even adoption.'

'Were you at home all day?' Dave was not greatly interested in Mrs Bligh's childbearing problems.

'Until the evening, yes. We had the usual Christmas party at The Bull, the pub round the corner from here. We hold it there every Christmas Eve, in a big private room upstairs. It's a way of saying thank you to all the boys and girls who work for us, but I think it'll probably be the last one.'

'Why is that?' asked Dave.

'It's the recession, of course,' said Bligh, as though the answer was obvious. 'The state of the economy means that we have to watch every penny.'

'Presumably there were people at this party who saw you there,' said Dave.

'My wife was with me, along with Carl Thorpe and his missus,' said Bligh, 'and there were about eighty others,' he added, somewhat sarcastically. 'They'll vouch for me if necessary, but I hope you're not thinking that I had anything to do with Kerry's murder.'

'Where d'you live, Mr Bligh?' Dave asked the question casually, as if he were collecting inconsequential information.

'Hatton. Carmen Avenue. I've always thought that Carmen Avenue is a suitable sort of name for a road that a haulier lives in, don't you think?' Bligh gave a nervous laugh.

Dave made a note in his pocketbook, but said nothing. He didn't have to; we both knew that Hatton was practically within walking distance of Heathrow Airport.

'I've no doubt that both the company solicitor and Mr Hammond will be in touch with you shortly to finalize details, Mr Bligh,' I said. With that we left Bernard Bligh to mull over a future under the thumb of Nicholas Hammond. As we got into the car, Dave gave voice to what I was thinking.

'I reckon we might have another murder on our hands before long, guv, once Hammond starts interfering.'

'One's enough,' I said. 'But while we're in the area, we'll pop into The Bull and check Bligh's alibi.'

The bottle-blonde barmaid was definitely in her forties, but probably claimed to be forever thirty-something, and had the appearance of a resting soap actress: curvaceous and brassy.

'What can I get you, love?'

'The licensee, if he's around,' I said. 'But in the meantime, I'll have a pint of best bitter, and my friend here will have an orange squash.'

'On the wagon, then, is he?' asked the barmaid.

'No, he's driving.'

The barmaid, whose name tag proclaimed her to be Yvonne, laughed. 'I shouldn't worry, love. You never see a copper round here.'

'Well, today's your lucky day,' said Dave. 'You've found two now.'

'Oh! That's nice.' Yvonne served our drinks. 'I'll see if the guv'nor's about.'

Moments later, a dapper individual appeared behind the bar. He was short, slightly built, and his black hair was heavily greased so that it lay flat on his head, giving him the appearance of a gigolo rather than a pub landlord, an impression enhanced by his pencil-thin moustache. He certainly had the look of a sickeningly enthusiastic ballroom dancer.

'I'm the licensee, gentlemen. Yvonne tells me you're from the police. There isn't any trouble, I hope.'

'We haven't found any yet, Mr . . .?' Dave opened his pocketbook and waggled his pen.

'Mr Butler.'

'First name?'

'Reginald. Reginald Butler.'

'I understand that Kerry Trucking holds its Christmas party here, Mr Butler.'

'Yes, that's right, every Christmas Eve, but they're never any trouble.'

'I don't much care if they are, Mr Butler,' I said, taking a sip of my beer. 'D'you know any of the people from there?'

'Oh, yes. They're a nice bunch. Their Mr Bligh is the one who makes all the arrangements. They invite all the staff every year: office people, drivers, everyone. And that Mrs Hammond always comes. She's the boss, you know. Mind you, she wasn't here this Christmas just gone.'

'She wouldn't have been. She was murdered on Christmas Eve.'

'Oh, good grief, surely not?' Butler fingered his moustache. 'I didn't see anything about that in the papers.'

'That's because it hasn't been released to the press,' said Dave, 'and we'd be obliged if you'd keep it to yourself for the time being. Otherwise you'll find that your pub is suddenly full of journalists, and they're notorious for not buying a drink.'

'What a terrible shock,' said Butler, clearly stunned by the news. 'Who would've wanted to murder Kerry?'

'That's what we're trying to establish,' I said. 'Mr Bligh has told us that he was here on Christmas Eve, with his wife and Mr and Mrs Thorpe. D'you know if that's the case?'

Butler glanced at his barmaid. 'Yvonne, you were looking after the Kerry party on Christmas Eve. Perhaps you can answer these officers' questions.' He glanced down the bar, and then back at me. 'D'you mind if I serve those customers?' he asked, indicating a couple of thirsty-looking men.

'No, you carry on, Mr Butler.' I'd already come to the conclusion that Yvonne was likely to know more about the party than her boss.

'It's always a big do,' said Yvonne. 'Must've been about a hundred of them all told. The staff bring their partners, and I think there's one or two of their clients who get invited. But Kerry Hammond wasn't here this year, or her husband, but now that I hear she's been murdered, I know why.'

'They'd planned a holiday in New York,' I said, 'but only Mr Hammond got there.'

'What a bleedin' tragedy, her getting killed,' said Yvonne, shaking her head. 'Life and soul of the party, that girl was.'

'Really?' said Dave. 'In what way?'

'Well . . .' Yvonne leaned forward, resting her folded arms on the bar and revealing an inch or two more of cleavage. 'The Christmas before this one just gone, she turned up in the skimpiest

Father Christmas outfit you've ever seen. Nothing to it, there wasn't. Short skirt, bare midriff and a low-cut bra, all in red furry stuff, and she was wearing black tights and heels the height of Blackpool Tower. Left nothing to the imagination, I can tell you, love. Not something I'd wear. Mind you, I might've done twenty years ago.' She sighed and her face assumed a wistful expression. 'And she wasn't above putting herself about.'

'Meaning what?' I asked.

'Flirting with all the men, and at one stage she disappeared for about half an hour with her secretary. That was the year before last, of course.'

'What, with a woman?' Dave took a sudden prurient interest.

'No, silly, a bloke. Only a young chap, he was. About twenty, I should think.'

'Any idea of his name, Yvonne?' I asked. The barmaid's information tallied with both Bernard Bligh's and Susan Penrose's suspicions about Kerry's promiscuous behaviour.

Yvonne thought about that for a moment. 'Bryce, I think. Yes, I'm pretty sure it was Bryce.'

'What was his first name?' asked Dave.

'That was his first name, but I don't know what his surname was.'

'Was there anyone else she seemed particularly close to?'

'Yeah, there was a shaven-haired hunk called Gary; one of the drivers he was. Common sort of bloke with an earring and tats, but him and Kerry seemed very friendly, if you get my drift. P'raps Kerry liked a bit of rough.'

'What sort of tattoos?' asked Dave, pocketbook at the ready.

'Nasty serpent thing up his left arm, and a skull and crossbones on the other,' said Yvonne. 'It put me right off, I can tell you. I don't like men with tats.'

'I'd put money on that being Dixon, sir,' said Dave.

'Sounds like him.' I redirected my attention to Yvonne. 'Was Kerry's husband here on that occasion?'

'Who, Nick? Yeah, he was here; bit of a wimp by the look of him. I didn't take to him at all.'

'Didn't he mind what Kerry was getting up to?' asked Dave.

'It didn't seem to bother him, love. He just sat in the corner and got slowly pissed. I think a couple of the drivers poured him into a taxi at about half past nine, but Kerry stayed on till midnight.'

'And about this guy with the tattoos: did he have a wife or a girlfriend with him?'

'Not that I know of,' said Yvonne. 'He only seemed interested in Kerry.' She glanced up and down the bar, and then moved her head even closer to us. 'I did hear that she was having an affair with someone, mind you,' she added in a conspiratorial whisper. 'You'd be surprised what you pick up when you're behind the bar.'

'Have you any idea of his name?' asked Dave.

'No, love, but from the way she was flaunting herself, I think there might've been more than one. Quite blatant, she was. It takes another woman to know the signs, and I think she was looking to get laid.'

'To get back to Mr Bligh,' I said. 'What time did he arrive?'

'About eight o'clock. That's when it began. They start it that late to let the drivers go home and get changed, Mr Bligh said. Them as weren't away on a driving job, of course.'

'Was Mr Bligh here all the time?'

'Well, he was here, love, but I can't swear that he was here all the time. I was behind the bar and too busy serving drinks to keep an eye on everyone. Why? D'you think he done it?'

'We don't know who did it,' said Dave.

'Thanks, Yvonne,' I said, deciding that we'd extracted as much as we could from the informative barmaid.

'Well, I hope you catch the bugger who did for Kerry. Despite what I said, she was a nice girl.'

'We shall, Yvonne,' I said confidently, but secretly I wasn't so sure. There was a long way to go yet.

EIGHT

'It's only about twelve miles from here to Heathrow, guv,' said Dave, as we drove away from the pub. 'Bligh could've gone out there, done the deed, and then gone on to the party.'

'It's possible, Dave. But from what Henry Mortlock said, it's possible that she died at any time between six o'clock and midnight on Christmas Eve. And you've established that Kerry's car checked into the car park at three minutes to seven.'

'We could ask his wife if he disappeared *before* going to the party,' suggested Dave. 'Or at any time during it.'

I laughed. 'And what d'you think she'd say?'

'She'd agree, guv,' Dave said with a sigh. 'So are we going back to the haulage yard to interview this Bryce bloke?'

'No, Dave. I'll get Miss Ebdon to send one of the team out there to get a list of all the employees together with their home addresses. Then we'll interview Bryce at home. If we talk to him at the office, I've no doubt that Bligh will get to hear why we talked to him. And in his present mood, he'd probably sack the bloke. After all, Bryce has got no one to be a secretary to now, has he?'

'No, sir.' Dave was calling me 'sir' again, probably because he didn't like the construction of my last sentence.

We returned to Curtis Green and checked with Kate Ebdon to see if there was any more news of Gary Dixon. But there was none, and if Dixon was the tattooed partygoer who Kerry fancied, he remained on our wanted list. Having given Colin Wilberforce the details of Dixon's tattoos for inclusion on the PNC, I decided that Dave and I would pay Mrs Dixon a visit.

We grabbed a quick bite to eat, and made our way to Ealing.

Hardacre Street, where the Dixons lived, was a narrow road of terraced houses that had cars parked bumper to bumper on both sides. Green wheelie bins blocked the pavement, from which I presumed that it was dustbin day, although it could've been that the residents were too idle to take in their bins. Or had nowhere to put them if they did take them in.

I guessed that the woman who answered the door was in her mid-twenties, but she had a careworn appearance that made her look older. She was wearing jeans and a crop top that revealed the tattoo of a bird power-diving towards her navel. It seemed that tattoos were popular in the Dixon family. The baby girl she held in one arm stared at us with big blue eyes and chewed on a dummy.

'Yes, what is it?' the woman asked listlessly.

'We're police officers. Are you Mrs Dixon?'

'That's me.' Sonia Dixon's response was delivered in a resigned tone of voice, as though she was accustomed to frequent visits from the police. 'I s'pose you've come about Gary again. There was a lady copper here a few days ago asking about him.'

'That's correct, Mrs Dixon. Inspector Ebdon is one of my officers.'

'I told her I never knew where he'd gone, but you'd better come in, I s'pose.' She turned from the door, leaving Dave to close it, and showed us into the front room. It was surprisingly tidy, the windows shining and the curtains clean, and it was apparent that Sonia Dixon was one of those women who did her best to keep everything in order. Despite having a womanizing husband who came and went as he pleased.

A three-year-old boy was sitting on the floor, totally absorbed in a programme on the television.

'Go and play in your room, Gerard.' Sonia Dixon turned off the television oblivious to the boy's howls of protest. 'Go!' The boy grabbed hold of a Harry Potter toy model of Grawp the Giant, and wandered off mumbling to himself.

'We're anxious to speak to your husband, Mrs Dixon,' I began. 'He could be a vital witness in a murder enquiry.' Not that I thought Dixon would fall for that excuse, even if Sonia relayed it to him. 'Have you any idea where he might be?'

'I wish I knew. One thing's certain: he'll have collected his benefit from the social, but if he has, I ain't seen nothing of it.'

'Is he claiming unemployment benefit, then?' asked Dave. 'Or Jobseekers Allowance, I think they call it now,' he added, in a tone that indicated his dislike of euphemisms.

'Course he is,' said Sonia. 'He ain't been in work since he got the sack from Kerry's.'

'About three months ago, your husband was fined five thousand pounds for illegally importing alcohol,' I said. 'D'you know how he paid that fine, given that he's on unemployment benefit?'

'*Five thousand pounds?*' exclaimed Sonia, her mouth opening in an expression of utter amazement. 'You must've got that wrong, mister. Where would Gary have got that much money from? We're practically on our beam-ends. And I never knew nothing about him bootlegging. That is what you mean, innit?'

'Yes, that is what I meant. And you knew nothing about it?'

'Not a word. He never said nothing to me.' The baby girl started to grizzle, and Sonia rocked her back and forth until she quietened. 'Is that why he got the sack?'

'Probably.' There was no point in discussing Dixon's smuggling activities any further, and I switched to another line of enquiry. 'Did you ever meet Mrs Hammond, Mrs Dixon?'

'Was that one of his fancy women?'

'Did he have any fancy women, then?'

'A few, but it's what men do, innit?' Sonia sounded resigned to the infidelity of husbands in general and her own in particular. 'But he always come back, 'cept this time.'

'Mrs Hammond was his boss at Kerry Trucking.'

'Oh, I didn't know that. No, I never met her.'

'Did your husband ever take you to the firm's Christmas party at The Bull in Scarman Street, Chiswick?'

'What, with two kids to look after, and not a cat in hell's chance of getting a babysitter? Leastways, not round here. No, Gary went, but I never.'

'You said just now that Gary received unemployment benefit, Mrs Dixon,' said Dave. 'How did he get it? Paid into his bank, was it, or did he collect it in cash?'

'His bank?' scoffed Sonia. 'We ain't got no bank account. Gary wouldn't have no truck with banks. Anyway, we'd have nothing to put in it even if we did have one.'

'Well, how *does* he get his money?' asked Dave, a note of exasperation creeping into his voice.

'He's got one of them cards what he takes to the post office and they give him cash over the counter. Not that I see much of it.'

'Does he go to any particular post office?'

'I haven't got a clue. Gary don't tell me nothing.'

That closed that line of enquiry. It meant that we'd be unable to set a trap for Dixon at a specific post office; with a post office card, he would be able to collect his benefit anywhere in the country.

'When he returns, Mrs Dixon, perhaps you'd ask him to contact me,' I said, repeating the request that Kate Ebdon had made of the woman. I handed her one of my official cards with no hope whatever that Dixon would turn up at Curtis Green one fine morning.

But as we turned to leave, Sonia Dixon spoke again.

'There was a man what come here a few days ago, looking for Gary. Was he one of your lot?'

'No, he wasn't. Did he give a name, this man?'

'Nah! He just said he had a bit of business to discuss.'

'What did he look like?'

'He was a tall bloke, well dressed an' all. Good looking, he was.'

'Was there anything particular about him, such as the way he spoke, for example?'

'Nah, he was just ordinary.'

'Did he say what this business was, that he had to discuss with your husband?'

'Nah, he never said.'

And we left it at that. From the brief description of the mysterious caller that Sonia Dixon had given, it crossed my mind that it could've been Nicholas Hammond. Or a hundred other men.

'I think it's time we had another word with Nicholas Hammond, Dave,' I said, once we were back at the office. 'I want to hear what he has to say about his amorous wife.'

'Is that wise, guv? Aren't we supposed to tread a bit warily with him, as he belongs to the funny farm lot?'

'It is the duty of police to keep the victim's widower informed of the progress of our enquiries, Dave,' I replied loftily.

'What progress, sir?'

It was getting on for eight o'clock when we arrived at Hammond's house. The door was answered by a slender woman of about thirty with long, dark hair. She looked as surprised to see us as I was to see her.

Nicholas Hammond appeared behind the woman. 'Oh, Mr Brock, I wasn't expecting you. Er, you'd better come in,' he said, with a reluctance that indicated his embarrassment at our arrival.

We were conducted into the living room, and Hammond effected introductions.

'This is Natasha Ellis, a friend of mine. She, er, just popped in to see if I was coping all right.'

'Of course.' *A likely story,* I thought.

'These gentlemen are the police officers investigating Kerry's murder, Tash,' said Hammond.

'Oh, I see.' Natasha stood up. 'In that case, I'll leave you to it, Nick. I'll look in again tomorrow evening, just to make sure that you're all right.'

'I'll see you out.' The expression on Hammond's face, as he escorted Natasha to the front door, suggested that our arrival had spoiled a romantic dinner, or even more. Much more.

'It didn't take him long to install a replacement for Kerry,' whispered Dave.

'What's so important that you had to call at this time in the evening?' asked Hammond, returning to the room. He sounded a little piqued at our interruption. 'You could've made an appointment.'

'I'm afraid that in a fast-moving investigation we can't always do that, Mr Hammond,' I said smoothly. The truth of the matter was that, far from being fast moving, our enquiry was practically stationary. 'So I'll get straight to the point. On the last two occasions we spoke to you, you told me that you'd never heard of Gary Dixon.'

'That's correct. I've never heard of him.'

'We have received information . . .' Dave opened his pocketbook and paused, as if searching for the right place in his notes. There was always something ominous about the way he did that. 'Ah, yes, here we are. We've received information that the year before last you and Mrs Hammond attended the Kerry Trucking Christmas party at The Bull in Chiswick. It is said that your wife was wearing a revealing Father Christmas outfit.'

'So? Kerry liked to show herself off. She was a great one for fancy dress parties.'

'We have also been told that one of the company's drivers, whom we believe to have been Gary Dixon, was there too, and that he was paying a great deal of attention to your wife. In fact, we understand that she was flirting with him.'

'Who the hell told you that?' demanded Hammond angrily.

'We never reveal our sources, Mr Hammond,' I said. 'Bit like your other job.'

'What d'you mean by that?'

'I have been advised officially of your real occupation,' I said.

'You have?' Hammond was clearly taken aback that I'd been told that he was a Security Service officer. He switched his gaze to Dave. 'And I suppose you know, as well, Sergeant Poole.'

'Know what? You're an estate agent, aren't you, sir?' Dave's face assumed a masterfully feigned expression of perplexity. 'However, do you still maintain that you don't know this man Dixon?'

'She was having an affair with him.' Hammond let out a sigh, and his shoulders slumped as he made the admission.

'Did she have many affairs?' I asked.

'I don't really know; I imagine it was quite a few. But why are you so interested in this man Dixon or, for that matter, anyone else Kerry might've slept with?'

'Very simply because one of them might've murdered her, Mr Hammond.' *And*, I thought, *that might've been a good reason for you to have murdered her.*

'Oh, I see.' Hammond responded to that truism lamely.

'So, I have to ask you if you know of any other men that your late wife might've been seeing on a regular basis.'

'No, I don't, but our marriage wasn't always plain sailing, as you might say. With me being away a lot, I never knew what she was up to.'

So now we had confirmation of what had been hinted at by Bernard Bligh, Susan Penrose and Yvonne, the barmaid at The Bull. Kerry Hammond seemed to be in the habit of playing the field. And that opened up a whole list of new suspects who might've had reason to kill her. If only we could find them.

On Friday morning things started to come together.

'Sheila Armitage obtained a list of all the employees of Kerry Trucking, guv,' said Kate Ebdon, 'and I've got one of the lads going through the address book that Dave seized from the Hammonds' house. I'm surprised Hammond didn't notice it had gone,' she added.

'Perhaps he hasn't looked for it. Anyway, he probably thought that Kerry had taken it to the office with her, or to the airport.'

'Do you intend to interview all these people?' asked Kate, flour-ishing the staff list.

'How many are there?'

'All up, about eighty or so, including the drivers, of course.'

'Not unless I have to,' I said, appalled at the prospect of conducting that many interviews.

'It wouldn't be all of them. I was able to confirm that twenty of the drivers were out of the country at the time of Kerry's murder.'

'What, over Christmas?'

'It seems that the haulage business doesn't stop for the festive season.'

'Bit like us,' muttered Dave, with a measure of bitterness.

'And presumably you've got an address for this Bryce bloke, Kate. He was Kerry's secretary.'

'His name's Bryce Marlow, he's twenty-four, unmarried, and he lives in Cumber Road, Chiswick. It's within walking distance of the office.'

'What time does he normally finish work, Kate?'

'Six o'clock, according to Bligh. When he wasn't acting as PA to Kerry Hammond he was helping Thorpe with the general admin.'

'Did Bligh want to know why we were interested in Marlow?'

'I didn't let him know we were interested in him, guv.' Kate frowned, an indication that she thought I was impugning her profes-sionalism. 'I told him that we might have to interview all of the firm's staff, and I asked him about the work hours of a few of the others. Mind you, I wouldn't be surprised if Bligh didn't go in for a bit of leg-over himself from time to time.'

'Come on to you, did he, *ma'am*?' asked Dave.

Kate scoffed at the very idea. 'You must be bloody joking, *Sergeant*,' she said. 'But he did ask me if I fancied having a drink with him at some time.'

'What did you say to that, Kate?' I asked.

'I told him I was much too busy arresting sex offenders and stalkers to waste time on adulterers, guv.'

I almost felt sorry for Bernard Bligh. As I've said many times before, it doesn't pay to get on the wrong side of Kate Ebdon.

'Let me know if and when you get anything interesting from Kerry's address book, Kate,' I said.

NINE

We arrived at Bryce Marlow's Cumber Road address in Chiswick at half past six.

The woman who answered the door to Marlow's semi was too old, sixty or so perhaps, to be Marlow's wife or girl-friend, and I assumed that she was Bryce's mother. We knew that he was into fancying older women, but not that old.

'Yes?' She glanced suspiciously at us. I was accustomed to such wariness. It was not the first time that the arrival on someone's doorstep of a tall, reasonably well-dressed man and a heavyweight black guy has been regarded with apprehension.

'We're police officers, madam,' I said. 'We'd like to have a word with Mr Marlow, Mr Bryce Marlow, if he's here.'

'I'm his mother,' said the woman. 'Whatever's wrong?'

'Nothing at all, madam,' I said, attempting to calm her. 'We're making enquiries into the death of Mrs Kerry Hammond. I under-stand that your son was Mrs Hammond's secretary.'

'Oh, I see. Yes, he was. What a terrible thing to have happened. It was an awful shock to poor Bryce. You'd better come in, then, Mr, er . . .?'

'Brock, madam, Detective Chief Inspector Brock, and this is Detective Sergeant Poole. You are Mrs Marlow, I take it.' It was a valid question. Although she'd admitted to being Bryce Marlow's mother, she might've remarried.

'Yes, I'm Doreen Marlow,' she said, leading us into the sitting room. 'Would you like a cup of tea?'

'Thank you. That's very kind, but I don't want to put you to any trouble, Mrs Marlow.' I didn't really want tea, but I'm all for giving the impression that the constabulary are a friendly lot. I once forced myself to eat two slices of a spinster's home-made seed cake, which I detest, in order to be amiable, and thus securing the withdrawal of a complaint that had been made against three of my officers. They'd been careless enough to misread the address on the search warrant, and insisted on rummaging through the old lady's flat until she'd eventually convinced them that they should've been searching the flat upstairs.

'It's no trouble,' said Mrs Marlow. 'I was just about to make some anyway. I'll get Bryce for you. I think he's upstairs doing something on his computer.'

The man who entered the room looked younger than his twenty-four years, but that was probably accounted for by his long blond scruffy hair. He was wearing jeans with a hole in one of the knees, a greyish sweater, and he was barefooted. Personally, I couldn't understand what Kerry Hammond had seen in him, but then I'm not a woman.

'Mum said you wanted to see me,' said Marlow, flopping into an armchair. 'She said it was about Kerry.'

So, Bryce Marlow called his boss by her first name. When I left school, I took a job with a water company, and I was there for three long and tedious years before joining the police. If anyone had dared to address the chief executive by his first name, particularly his secretary, they'd've got the bum's rush very smartly. But, I suppose, things have moved on since then.

'I understand you were employed as Mrs Hammond's secretary, Mr Marlow,' I said.

'Yes, that's right.'

'But there was a lot more to it than that, wasn't there?' suggested Dave, getting quickly to the point of our interview.

'More to it?' Marlow shot a quick glance at the closed sitting-room door. 'I don't know what you mean.' He looked decidedly shifty, and failed to disguise the fact that Dave's question had unnerved him.

'Really?' Dave leaned forward in his chair, resting his elbows on his knees, and linking his hands. It was a menacing attitude. 'We've been told that you and Mrs Hammond were having an affair. A sexual relationship,' he added, so that there would be no doubt in the young man's mind.

'Who told you that?' Marlow had blushed scarlet and began fidgeting, his fingers playing a devil's tattoo on the arm of his chair.

'Never mind who, but we were told that you and she disappeared for half an hour at the firm's Christmas bash the year before last. What was that all about? Surely the pair of you didn't nip out for a quick smoke behind the bike sheds.'

'It was her idea.' Marlow blurted out the words and looked extremely uncomfortable.

'What was?'

'I don't see that it has anything to do with you.' Suddenly Marlow developed a little steel, and stared angrily at Dave.

The door opened and Mrs Marlow entered with a tray of tea. 'I'll let you pour it yourselves, if you don't mind,' she said, placing the tray on a small table. She glanced at each of us in turn, and it seemed that she had detected a tension in the room, but she said nothing more.

Once his mother had left, Bryce Marlow spoke again.

'I don't see that my private life is anything to do with the police.'

'Mr Marlow,' I said, 'as I'm investigating the murder of Mrs Hammond, I shall ask any questions I like and I expect truthful answers.'

'But surely you can't think I was involved in her death, can you?'

'I don't know who was responsible for her death, but I must say that your reticence to answer my sergeant's questions makes me wonder. Now then, did you have a sexual relationship with Mrs Hammond?'

There was a long pause before Marlow answered, during which time he stared at the ground. 'Yes,' he said eventually, shooting another glance at the door.

'At whose instigation?' Dave asked.

'It was Kerry's.'

'And how did that come about?' asked Dave. 'Did she just proposition you one day? Say something like, d'you fancy hopping into bed for a quick screw?'

'No, it wasn't like that.' Marlow probably viewed his affair with his boss as a romantic tryst, rather than the sordid coupling that Dave was implying. 'It was when she took me to Paris. She had to go there on business, she said.' Now that he had admitted to an affair with Kerry, he seemed to be more relaxed in answering our questions.

'When was this?'

'About eighteen months ago, I suppose. Yes, it was in July of the year before last, and she said she intended taking me with her. It was natural enough for me to accompany her, she said, as I was her secretary, and she wanted to show me the sights. I'd never been to Paris before, you see. She told me that it would be a bit of a reward for all the hard work I'd done for her.'

'And that's when the affair began, I suppose,' said Dave.

'Yes. Kerry certainly knew her way about when it came to travelling. We went by Eurostar, first class of course, and had champagne and a meal on the train. At the Gare du Nord, she got a taxi to take us to a super hotel in the rue de Rivoli, and we stayed there for the whole time. I think that she'd stayed there before because the staff seemed to know her.'

'And what exactly was this business that she had to do in Paris?'

'That's the funny thing about it; there didn't seem to be any, unless she did whatever she had to do on her laptop or on the Internet.' Marlow gave the impression of being baffled, but it wasn't convincing. 'But then, why bother to go to Paris? She could've done all that in England.'

'It looks as though she'd planned the whole thing just to get you into her bed,' said Dave, half to himself.

'I suppose so,' said Marlow quietly, as though loath to admit that he'd fallen into the clutches of a scheming woman several years older than he was. 'We had separate rooms in the hotel, with a communicating door, and after we'd arrived and unpacked, she invited me into her room and ordered a bottle of champagne from room service. We sat and chatted for a while, and then she took me out to dinner at a swish restaurant in the Champs Elysees.'

'Did Mrs Hammond speak French?' asked Dave.

'She spoke it fluently,' said Marlow, 'which was just as well because I don't understand a word of it.'

'And then you returned to the hotel . . . after your cosy little dinner, did you?'

'Yes, and I thought that was the end of the evening. But at about half past eleven, Kerry came through the communicating door into my room without knocking. I hadn't locked it from my side, you see. In fact, I didn't know you could. I'd never stayed anywhere like that before, but I found out later that there was a lock on each side of the door.'

I wondered if Bryce Marlow really was an innocent abroad, or whether he was pretending to be. 'Were you asleep when she came in?' I asked.

'No, I was reading. But I was absolutely amazed because she

wasn't wearing anything. I couldn't believe that my boss would do such a thing.'

'Did she speak?'

'No, she didn't say a word; she just got into bed with me.'

'How long were the pair of you in Paris, Mr Marlow?'

'Four days.'

'What did you do during that time?' I glanced at Dave and thought I detected a smirk on his face.

'We spent each day sightseeing around the city. She took me to see the Mona Lisa in the Louvre, and one evening we had dinner on the Seine on one of the *bâteaux mouches*; I think that's what they call them. And we did a fair amount of shopping. Kerry bought a lot of clothes for herself, and a couple of expensive shirts and two ties for me.'

'Did she pay all the bills for the hotel and the meals?'

'Yes, she paid for everything. Well, actually she said the company was paying, but that was the same thing really, wasn't it?'

'And presumably you and Mrs Hammond slept together from then on.'

'Yes, we did. And then each morning, she'd go back into her room and untidy her bed so that it looked as though she'd slept in it.'

'I wonder why she bothered. The French are quite accustomed to that sort of thing. In fact, it's almost a national sport,' said Dave, in an aside. 'And I suppose you each had a double bed.'

'Yes. Kerry said she'd particularly asked for each of us to have a double bed because they're more comfortable. She said that some French beds are shorter than English ones, but I didn't notice any difference.'

I was far from convinced by Marlow's account of what was supposed to have happened. He was twenty-four years of age, for God's sake, and I very much doubted that he was the inexperienced youth he was purporting to be. I thought it just as likely that the events he'd described had occurred the other way round: that Marlow had gone into Kerry Hammond's room on the off-chance of her being willing, and found to his delight that she was. I certainly didn't believe his story of not knowing that hotel communicating doors could be locked from both sides. On the other hand, her insistence on double beds seemed to indicate Kerry had done a bit of what we in the police call forward planning.

'Did this relationship continue after you returned to England?' I asked.

'Yes. It became quite a regular thing after that. I usually went to her house in Barnes when her husband was away. He was away quite often.'

'And this affair lasted until Mrs Hammond was murdered, did it?'

Marlow nodded sadly. 'Yes, it did.'

'D'you think that Mr Hammond knew that you had become his wife's lover?'

'God, I hope not.'

I think that Hammond probably did know, but none of that mattered a damn unless Marlow had murdered Kerry. 'Where were you on Christmas Eve, Mr Marlow? This Christmas Eve just gone.'

'I was at the company's party in Chiswick.'

'From when until when?'

Marlow gave the impression of considering the question carefully. 'I suppose I got there about a quarter past eight. I didn't stay long because I don't like leaving my mother alone, especially at Christmas, not since my father died a couple of years ago. But Mum was quite adamant that I should go.'

'What time did you get back home?' I asked.

'It must've been about ten. It's only a five minute walk from here, and I had my mobile with me in case Mum wanted me.'

'Where were you before going to the party?'

'Here, of course. I'd finished work at midday on Christmas Eve, and I came straight home and had tea with Mum.'

'And she can vouch for that, can she?'

'Certainly. D'you want me to call her?'

'That won't be necessary.' I was sure that Mrs Marlow would confirm her son's story, whether it was true or not. That was always the problem with alibis provided by relatives.

'What's going to happen to you now, Bryce?' asked Dave. 'As you were Mrs Hammond's secretary, there won't be a job for you any more, will there?'

'I'm hoping they'll find me something,' said Marlow. 'I'm thinking of trying for a heavy goods vehicle driver's licence. I rather fancy driving one of those Volvo artics across Europe.'

'Do you have a driving licence, then?' Dave asked.

'Oh yes, but only for a car.'

'And do you own a car?'

'Yes, it's that old VW outside.'

We thanked Mrs Marlow for the tea and left.

Dave took a note of the VW's registration mark before we drove out of Cumber Road. 'Do we keep Marlow on the list, guv?' he asked.

'He could've done it, Dave, despite claiming he was at home at the relevant time. We know he was at the party, but we only have his word for when he got there and when he left. Yvonne the barmaid won't be much help, either. Bryce admits to owning a car, and he would have had plenty of time to get to Heathrow and then go on to the party. Or return to it.'

It was now nearing eight o'clock, and I decided that it was time for another talk with Michael Roberts, alias Miguel Rodriguez, dodgy proprietor of the Spanish Fly nightclub. I wanted to know where he was on the night of the murder, because sure as hell he hadn't been where he'd said he was.

The bouncer recognized us immediately, but bouncers have an innate ability to remember policemen who call at the nightclub where they work.

'He's not here, guv'nor,' said the bouncer, in reply to our query for Rodriguez.

'Where is he, then?' demanded Dave.

'Haven't a clue,' said the bouncer, with a shrug of his steroid-developed shoulders.

'What's your name?'

'Elliot.' The bouncer seemed loath to admit it.

'First name or last name?' asked Dave.

'First,' said Elliot.

'And your last name?'

'Williams.'

'When did you last see Mr Rodriguez, Elliot?'

'A few days ago.'

'How many days are a few days?'

'Well, it's, like, a few days.'

'I should've been a dentist,' muttered Dave.

'What?' Williams looked completely baffled by Dave's throwaway remark.

'Because getting information out of you is like pulling teeth, old son.' Dave took a pace closer, invading the bouncer's personal space. 'Where is he, Elliott?'

Williams moved so that his back was against the wall. 'I don't know, guv'nor, really I don't.'

'Who's running this place in Mr Rodriguez' absence, then?' I asked.

'That'd be Fernando, the bar manager, sir. He's, like, the maître d', if you know what I mean.'

'Good, now we're getting somewhere,' said Dave. 'Is *he* here, then?'

'Oh yeah,' said Elliot. There was a pause. 'Well, I think so. I'll get Carmel to show you the way.'

'Don't bother,' said Dave. 'We know where he hides himself.'

We entered the main area of the club and were immediately approached by the man himself.

'Good evening, *señors*. A table for two?'

'No thanks, Fred,' said Dave. 'Just a word in your shell-like.'

'Oh blimey, it's you,' said Goddard, alias Fernando, as he recognized us. He looked decidedly put out by our arrival.

'Yes, it's us,' I said. 'Where's Mike Roberts, otherwise known to the punters as Miguel Rodriguez?'

'I haven't the foggiest. I haven't seen him since last Friday.'

That was interesting. Last Friday was the day we called at the Spanish Fly and discovered, courtesy of Goddard himself, that Roberts had been absent from the club on the night Kerry Hammond was murdered. Despite Roberts claiming that he *had* been there.

'Didn't he say where he was going?'

'No, not as such. He had a go at me for telling you he'd been adrift on Christmas Eve. He said that I'd got it wrong, and that I'd landed him in bother with the Old Bill.'

'How did he know what you'd said?'

'Well, he came down here after you'd gone, and asked me what I'd said. So I told him that he'd told you he wasn't here, and that I'd agreed with you. Then he just took off. He said something about having some business to attend to.'

'Have you got a phone number for him?' asked Dave. 'A mobile, for instance?'

'No, but he never lets on what he's up to. I dunno why I bother. Half the time I'm running this place by myself.'

'It must be a hard life,' commented Dave.

'When he shows up, tell him I want to see him. And tell him I don't want to come round here with a warrant.' I tucked one of my cards into Goddard's top pocket. 'Because there's no telling what I might find, is there, Fernando?'

We left a very despondent maître d' mulling over the consequences of a police raid on the Spanish Fly.

'I reckon *Señor* Fernando is thinking about a change of occupation, guv,' said Dave, as we regained the comparatively fresh environment of the Mayfair streets.

'I wonder why Roberts did a runner,' I said.

'It's got to be down to him,' said Dave.

'Not necessarily, Dave. I reckon that *Señor* Rodriguez has his fingers in some other pies. Put him on the PNC when we get back to the factory.'

All in all, it had been an unproductive day. First we had Bryce Marlow spinning us a yarn about being taken advantage of by his boss, a tale I didn't altogether believe, and then we found that Mike Roberts had done a runner. Just as Gary Dixon had done.

On Saturday morning, we returned yet again to Kerry Trucking's Chiswick haulage yard. An odour of diesel fuel hung in the cold, crisp air.

'Oh, so you're here again.' Bernard Bligh was standing on the loading platform with his hands in the pockets of a heavy parka jacket, and greeted us with a barely concealed expression of annoyance. 'What is it this time?' His eyes were everywhere, watching and checking. At a previous interview, he'd told us that he'd once been a heavy-goods driver himself, and I didn't doubt that he knew all the tricks and all the scams that a driver could pull. Like fiddling the tachograph; like filling up the fuel tank of his own car and using the company credit card to pay for it; like picking up and delivering private loads and pocketing the cash, and a dozen others. I was convinced that not very much would get past Bernard Bligh, and he was keeping a careful watch to make sure it didn't.

'Mrs Hammond's bank statements,' I said. 'Her husband told me that she kept copies here.' I didn't mention that we'd already obtained a set from Nicholas Hammond, and I was working on the possibility that she kept a different set in her office.

'Aren't you supposed to have a warrant for that sort of thing?' said Bligh, at last turning to face me.

'We can get one, if you insist,' said Dave, and glanced searchingly around the yard, now busy with vehicles being loaded and unloaded. On the far side a crane was lowering a huge bulk container on to an articulated flatbed lorry, accompanied by shouted instructions to the crane driver. 'Mind you, the warrant would have to be for a search of the entire premises, and that would mean closing down the business for a few hours.'

'You'd better come into Kerry's office,' said Bligh churlishly, admitting defeat. 'If they're anywhere, they'll be in her safe.'

Kerry Hammond's enormous office, the only one in the building to have Venetian blinds and curtains, was considerably better appointed than Bligh's own. Carpeted from wall to wall, it featured a huge desk placed strategically across one corner. On the desk were a state of the art computer and a telephone so complicated that I wouldn't have known how to answer it, let alone make a call. Behind the desk was a high-backed, leather executive chair. A conference table with six chairs, and two club armchairs completed the picture of the successful businesswoman's seat of power.

'This is some office,' I observed, looking around in admiration. It was far superior even to that enjoyed by our beloved commander.

'Cost a bloody packet,' muttered Bligh, as he began twirling the dial on a large security cabinet. 'But that was Kerry; no expense spared when it came to her own comfort.'

'Kerry gave you the combination to her safe, did she?' Dave asked.

'No, but she was foolish enough to use her date of birth for it,' said Bligh, as he opened the door. 'I like to keep my finger on the pulse, if you know what I mean.'

'I imagine that Nick Hammond will be moving in here soon, then.' Dave's suggestion was deliberately meant to provoke Bligh, and it worked.

'Don't bloody talk to me about that waster,' said Bligh, almost spitting the words. He continued to rummage about in the security cabinet, but eventually turned to me empty handed. 'I can't find any bank statements in here, Mr Brock. I don't know why Hammond should've thought she kept them here. Perhaps she kept them on her computer at home.'

That was possibly true, but we'd already obtained a hard copy of the last two years' statements from Hammond. There was clearly something a bit underhand going on.

'What'll happen to Bryce Marlow now?' I asked. 'He was Mrs Hammond's secretary, I believe.'

'Her toy boy more like,' said Bligh dismissively. 'He'll be out on his ear as soon as I can get around to it. Between you and me, I can't stand that poncey little twit.'

'He told us he was hoping to become one of your drivers,' I said. 'Once he'd got his HGV licence.'

'In his dreams,' scoffed Bligh. 'I wouldn't even let him ride one of the firm's box tricycles,' he added derisively. 'If we had any.'

'I understand that he accompanied Mrs Hammond to Paris on one occasion, Mr Bligh.'

'Yes, he did, and I know what that was all about. A business trip to Paris my arse! A few days' jolly at the firm's expense, and she and Marlow have been at it like alley cats ever since. And he wasn't the only one.'

'Oh?'

'Dixon was another.' Bligh sat down behind Kerry's desk, and invited us to seat ourselves in the club armchairs. 'She decided to go on what she called a fact-finding trip across France in Dixon's truck.'

'And did she find out any facts?' asked Dave.

'Only the facts of life,' said Bligh, with a grim smile. 'But I reckon she knew more than enough about those already.'

'Was there anyone else that she knew rather well?' I asked.

'I suppose you mean that she slept with?' Bligh laughed. 'No, but I wouldn't mind betting there were a few.'

That made three paramours that we knew about so far: the missing Rodriguez, alias Roberts, owner of the aptly-named Spanish Fly; Bryce Marlow; and the absent Gary Dixon, whose affair with Kerry had been confirmed by Nicholas Hammond. A picture of a voracious sexual adventuress had emerged, and if there were even more lovers, our investigation would become increasingly widespread. And a damned sight more complicated.

TEN

B ack at the office, I gave Charlie Flynn, the ex-Fraud Squad sergeant, the task of examining Kerry Hammond's bank statements.

'Those are her statements for the past two years, Charlie. They were the ones we got from her husband, but she didn't keep any in her safe at the office. See what you can make of them.'

'Anything in particular, guv?' asked Flynn.

'Any large unexplained movements of funds,' I said. 'In fact, anything that might lead us to Kerry's killer.' The task I'd set him was one with wide parameters, but he knew his job.

First thing on Monday morning, Charlie Flynn produced a breakdown of Kerry Hammond's financial affairs, at least, those that could be deduced from the past two years' statements. But it was enough to set us on another path.

'For a start, guv'nor, we're dealing with two separate accounts here. One set are for the household bills which Kerry paid for their Barnes property: gas, electricity, council tax, that sort of thing, so we can forget those. The second account, which is kept at a different bank from the first one, is much more revealing.'

'I'm beginning to think that Kerry Hammond was a devious woman, Charlie.'

'It looks that way, guv,' said Flynn. 'On the nineteenth of October she wrote a cheque for five thousand pounds payable to Lewes Crown Court.'

'So she covered Gary Dixon's fine for bootlegging,' I surmised.

'What's more, she paid a thousand pounds a month into his personal bank account.'

'Well, there's a surprise,' said Dave, 'especially as Dixon's wife said he didn't have a bank account.'

'But now it gets really interesting,' continued Flynn. 'There were transfers of substantial sums at intervals over the last two years; I won't bother you with actual amounts, guv, but I've prepared a breakdown of the figures so that you can look at them later. They comprised payments made to a French wine merchant called Marcel Lebrun, who appears to be based somewhere in the Marseille area. The last payment was in August of last year, five months ago. Then there were monies coming in over the last two years and occurring at intervals of about six weeks after each of the payments out. In all, those receipts totalled close to three-quarters of a million pounds and were payable to a set-up called Kerry Wine Importers. But there is no indication where that money came from.'

'Did the statements show any payments of income tax, Charlie?' asked Dave, who had a passionate interest in people who didn't pay tax. Probably because he had no option; his tax was deducted from his pay.

'Not that I could see, Dave,' said Flynn, 'but tax on legitimate wine importation is paid either at the excise duty point – normally when the wine is delivered for consumption – but occasional importers must pay the duty to Revenue and Customs before the wine is shifted.'

'What do we know about this wine importing firm, Charlie?' I asked.

'Nothing, guv. I interrogated the Companies House computer at Cardiff, and there's no trace of it. We don't even know if it's an occasional importer.'

'Or if it imports wine at all,' said Dave. 'Might be a front for something else. Perhaps Bernard Bligh can shed some light on it, guv,' he suggested.

'It's possible he knows nothing about it,' I said thoughtfully. 'It looks as though Kerry was running a wine business on the side, and probably using the firm's trucks to bring it in. And that could be why she kept all her statements at home. We know that Bligh had access to her safe.'

'But it doesn't make sense,' said Flynn. 'There are no payments for use of the transport, and that would be a tax-deductible expense. And there's no reason why she shouldn't have set up a company in her own name. It would have nothing to do with Bligh or Kerry Trucking.'

'I wonder if it was a load like that which got Dixon weighed off at Lewes Crown Court,' said Dave. 'The whole arrangement could've been illegal.'

'And Bligh might just have been a part of it, Dave,' I said, although I had to admit that we were straying into unfamiliar areas. 'I think we'll speak to him again. I'm pretty sure he knows more than he's told us. But this time I think we'll need a warrant, just in case he doesn't feel like cooperating.'

'Tomorrow morning, then?' queried Dave.

'Yes, and we'll take Tom Challis along as well,' I said. DS Challis's Stolen Vehicle Squad experience meant that he knew a thing or two about lorries.

'I think that Kerry Wines might have been set up for money laundering, guv,' suggested Flynn.

'I'd already come to that conclusion, Charlie,' I said.

It was possible that we might need to examine personal and financial records at Kerry Trucking. This, of course, complicated matters; the law dictated that I was obliged to apply for the warrant before a circuit judge. Having spent most of Tuesday morning preparing my 'information' and taking it to the Crown Court in Newington Causeway, it was almost one o'clock by the time I eventually obtained my search warrant.

'We'll grab a bite to eat,' I said, glancing at Dave and Tom Challis, 'and then we'll hit Kerry Trucking.'

We adjourned to a nearby Costas coffee shop. Dave bought three cups of latte and I gathered up a few snacks that would have to do for lunch. We found a table in the crowded seating area and settled down.

'It's going to take us a while to search a haulage yard, guv,' said Tom Challis.

'That depends, Tom. If Bligh is cooperative, we might find what we're looking for straight away.'

'What are we looking for, guv?'

'We haven't the vaguest idea, Charlie,' said Dave.

Bernard Bligh looked extremely apprehensive when the three of us confronted him on the loading bay.

'I have a warrant to search these premises, Mr Bligh,' I said, 'but it'll be quicker if we have your cooperation.'

'What the hell's this all about?' demanded Bligh aggressively.

'It's about a firm called Kerry Wine Importers,' I said, thinking that that would do for a start.

'Never heard of them. What do they do, then?'

'Import wine, presumably,' suggested Dave, with a hint of sarcasm.

'Well, I don't know anything about that. It must've been one of Kerry's sidelines.'

'Did she have many sidelines?' I asked.

'None that I know of.' Bligh looked furtive, and I doubted that he was telling the truth. On the other hand, it was a common enough reaction to the arrival of police armed with a search warrant, even on the part of those who were completely blameless. 'But there was no telling with Kerry.'

'Does the name Marcel Lebrun mean anything to you?' I asked.

'No. Sounds like a Frenchman.'

'I've no doubt he is,' I said, 'given that he appears to be a wine merchant based in the Marseille area.'

'Well, I'm sorry, but I can't help you,' said Bligh.

'In that case,' I said, 'we're going to have a look round. Tell me, Mr Bligh, do any of your trucks make a regular run to Marseille?'

'That one over there,' said Bligh, pointing to a Scania articulated box lorry parked on the opposite side of the yard. 'Why? What's so special about Marseille?'

'Because, Mr Bligh, Marseille is where Marcel Lebrun carries on business as a vintner.' I was uncertain whether Bligh was dense or just pretending to be. On balance, I thought he was pretending to be. 'Do any of your drivers usually do that run?'

'A new guy called Sharpe, Billy Sharpe. Well, he's comparatively new.'

'How new?'

'Sharpe's been with us for about three months now. Kerry took him on after I sacked Dixon.'

'And before that, did Dixon usually do the Marseille run, Mr Bligh?'

'Yes, he did. Look, what is all this?' Bligh was beginning to get tetchy at our persistent probing.

Ignoring Bligh's question, I turned to DS Challis. 'Give that vehicle the once-over, Tom, and see if there's anything in it that attracts your interest.'

'If there is, I want to know about it,' put in Bligh. 'If Sharpe's up to something, he'll be out on his ear.'

Challis took a pair of navy blue overalls from his holdall and slipped them on.

'What are you hoping to find?' asked Bligh nervously. 'All our trucks are legit. I told you that I'd sacked Dixon when he was done for bootlegging booze through Dover.'

'So you did,' I said, choosing not to tell him that Kerry Hammond was almost certain to have paid Dixon's fine.

Descending from the loading bay, Tom Challis crossed to the Scania that Bligh had pointed out. He crawled under the box trailer and spent a few minutes examining it. Then he opened the rear doors and climbed inside the cargo area.

Standing beside the two of us, Bligh fidgeted with his ballpoint pen, clicking it repeatedly. He was clearly worrying about something.

A couple of minutes later, Challis reappeared on the tailboard. 'Looks to be all right, guv,' he shouted, 'but perhaps you'd like to give it the once-over.'

I suspected that Challis had discovered something interesting that he didn't want Bligh to know about. Dave and I crossed the yard and clambered aboard the trailer.

'What've you found, Tom?'

'It's the oldest trick in the book, guv.' Challis led us to the front of the cargo area. 'I'll put money on this partition being false,' he said, rapping on the bulkhead with his knuckles.

'It doesn't sound hollow, Tom.'

'It's probably lined with some sort of soundproofing,' said Challis. 'Whoever installed this knew what he was doing.'

It was obviously a very professional job and I imagined that the work had been done by a skilled craftsman. The panel, covering the entire width and height of the trailer, was securely bolted in place. To the casual observer, it would appear to be an integral part of the unit.

'Can you be sure, Tom?' I asked.

'Not without taking a few measurements, guv, and then dismantling it, but I'd put money on it.' Challis took a compact laser meter from his overalls pocket, and measured the inside of the truck. He jumped down and swung the offside door round so that it was at right angles to the body of the truck, away from Bligh's view. 'Hold that door, Dave.' He walked to the front of the cargo area and measured the outside. 'As I thought, guv, the exterior is sixty centimetres longer than the interior.'

'What's that in English, Tom?' asked Dave.

'About two feet,' said Challis.

'It's obviously used for smuggling,' said Dave, 'but smuggling what?'

'I doubt if it's alcohol,' I said, 'not if Kerry was running a legitimate wine importing business.'

'If she was, why did Dixon get captured bringing in a load of booze?' asked Dave.

'Perhaps, he was doing a bit of moonlighting on the side,' said Challis. 'Don't forget that the customs guys followed it up, and prosecuted a few publicans for receiving smuggled alcohol.'

'Would you be able to take that panel down, Tom?' I asked.

'I don't have the right tools with me, guv,' said Challis. 'In fact, I don't have any.'

'Traffic,' said Dave.

'What about traffic?' Once again, I had a problem with Dave's verbal shorthand.

'We could send for the Traffic Division chaps and get them to open it up for us, *sir*.' Dave spoke carefully and precisely.

'Good idea. Do it. But it's now called a Traffic Operational Command Unit, Dave.' I always enjoyed those rare occasions when I was able to correct him.

Dave spent a few minutes on his mobile, and ten minutes later, a traffic unit arrived in the yard.

'PC Sam Buxton, guv. Luckily we were in the area when we got your call. I understand you've got a problem,' he said, as he sauntered across to join the three of us. 'And this is Jim White, my other half.'

I explained to the two traffic PCs what I wanted them to do, and why it was necessary for us to see what, if anything, was behind the panel in the Scania. 'D'you reckon you can manage it?' I asked Buxton.

'Piece of cake, guv. Fortunately, we've got the right tools with us, seeing as how we're accident investigators.' Buxton paused, and put a hand to his mouth in a charade of contrition. 'Oh, I shouldn't have said that,' he added. 'The powers that be now insist that accidents are called collisions. Although how one vehicle turning over because it took a bend too fast can be called a collision beats me.'

The boy superintendents of the funny names and total confusion squad had clearly been at work again.

'Well, get to it,' I said, laughing. 'And wear gloves in case there are any fingerprints that we can identify.'

'Of course, sir,' said Buxton, raising his eyebrows.

Buxton and White quickly went to work on the panel that had aroused Tom Challis's suspicions. As the last bolt was removed they gently lowered the false bulkhead to the ground. As Challis had suggested, the back was lined with a thick material than looked like polystyrene, doubtless to prevent it sounding hollow when tapped. In the space that had been shielded by the panel there were two metal boxes, each measuring about a foot high, a foot deep, and four feet long. They were bolted to the floor of the truck.

Tom Challis donned a pair of protective gloves and opened the boxes one by one. Each was empty. 'You don't have to be a firearms expert to identify the odour of gun oil, guv,' he said.

'Bloody hell!' exclaimed Dave. 'Kerry was a gunrunner.'

'And those boxes are large enough to have contained rifles as well as handguns,' volunteered Challis.

'All we've got to do now is find whoever she was supplying,' I said hopelessly, as the enormity of the task struck me. 'And any one of them could've topped her.'

'If she *was* the supplier,' said Dave. 'She might not have known anything about it. It's good fun, this coppering lark, isn't it?'

I turned to the two traffic officers. 'Can you put that all back, lads, so it looks as though it hasn't been removed?'

'No probs, guv.' Buxton and White began the work of replacing the panel.

'Can you read a tachograph, Sam?' I asked, as he put the last bolt in place.

Buxton looked mildly offended. 'Yes, sir,' he said, using the honorific in much the same way as Dave did when I'd posed a fatuous question.

'Perhaps you'd check the back tachograph records for this vehicle when we get back to the office, Sam. But if there's anything untoward don't show it in front of the guy up there.'

'Won't take a minute, guv,' said Buxton.

'Thanks for your help with the panel, lads,' I said. 'Let DS Poole know where he can find you so that he can take statements from you at a later date.'

'All in a day's work, guv,' said Buxton, and gave Dave the phone number and details of his and White's hours of duty.

We returned to the loading bay where Bligh had been standing and watching while we'd carried out our examination of the Scania.

'Find anything?' he asked, attempting an air of nonchalance.

'No, nothing,' I said.

'Not surprised,' said Bligh. 'As I said before, we run a legit operation here.' He glanced at Buxton, identified as a traffic officer by his white-topped cap. 'What's he doing here?'

'Routine check for roadworthiness,' I said, 'and he'd like to see the tachograph records and driver's log for the last two months.'

'What the hell for?' Bligh was becoming rattled.

'Routine,' I said, using an excuse beloved of television detectives, but rarely used by real ones.

We followed Bligh into his office. It took ten minutes for him to unearth the appropriate tachograph records, and hand them to Buxton.

'When is that vehicle next scheduled to go to Marseille, Mr Bligh?' I asked.

'I don't know offhand.'

'You must have details here.'

'Yes, I should have. D'you want me to look for them?'

'Yes, please. At the same time, perhaps you'd find out the last time it went to Marseille.'

'I'll have to check on that, too,' said Bligh, picking up a mountain of manifests, and thumbing through them. 'The last time it went to Marseille was Wednesday the second of December,' he said eventually, handing me the relevant document.

'And when is it next due to do that run?'

'Tomorrow.' Bligh glanced at a calendar on the wall. 'That's the eighth.'

I sensed a certain reluctance in his responses. 'What for?' I asked.

'To pick up a load, of course, something that Kerry booked before she died. I don't know what it is, though.'

'You must have details of it here somewhere, Mr Bligh.'

After a quick search through his paperwork, Bligh handed me another document. 'See for yourself.'

'Well, well,' I said. 'To collect a consignment from Marseille. But you don't you know what it is?'

'First I knew of it, and I don't know what the load is,' said Bligh again, but he was unconvincing.

'When is this vehicle due back here?'

'This coming Friday, the tenth.'

'I see the driver on the December trip was this Billy Sharpe you mentioned as Dixon's replacement,' I said. 'Is he here today?'

'Yes, he's about the yard somewhere.'

'Good. I want a word with him.'

Bligh opened a window and shouted to a passing loader to find Sharpe.

Five minutes later, a man of about thirty entered the office. He was of medium height, had a thin moustache and wore an earring in his left ear.

'You wanted me, guv'nor?' said the man.

'This is Billy Sharpe, Mr Brock,' said Bligh, and faced his driver. 'The police want a word with you, Billy.'

'I ain't done nothing wrong, guv'nor,' said Sharpe, as he turned towards me.

It was the typical reaction of a petty criminal, and I had little doubt that Sharpe would have a bit of form. I wondered if references for him had been taken up. Dave wasn't impressed either, but for a different reason; I noticed that he'd frowned at Sharpe's use of a double negative.

'What did you pick up, the last time you went to Marseille, Billy?' I asked.

'A consignment from a geezer called Lebrun, guv'nor.'

'Where exactly in Marseille?'

'A little place called St-Circe. It's just outside Marseille.'

'What did the load consist of?'

'No idea, guv'nor.'

'Who loaded it? Was it you?'

'No, the drivers never do the loading. The blokes at Lebrun's depot did it,' said Sharpe. 'The boss there told me to buzz off and get a meal, and that it'd all be done and dusted by the time I got back. All I do is a quick glance at the load to make sure it doesn't shift, because I'm the bloke who drives the bloody thing.'

'That's all right, then,' I said. 'Have a safe trip tomorrow.'

'Yeah, right. Cheers, guv.'

'I told you there was nothing wrong, Inspector,' said Bligh, once Sharpe had left the office. 'That lad's as straight as a die.'

'My guv'nor takes grave exception to being called "inspector",' observed Dave mildly. 'He's a *chief* inspector, and that earns him about eight grand a year more than an inspector.'

'Oh!' said Bligh, and lapsed into silence.

Buxton gave Bligh the tachograph record of the Scania and the driver's log. 'All in order, guv'nor,' he said.

'Of course it is,' snapped Bligh. 'Is that all?' he queried sarcastically. 'Or is there something else you want to poke your noses into?'

'No, that's all,' I said, and we left Bligh to get on with running his business.

'What about the tachograph, Sam?' I asked, as we walked back across the yard.

'On the December run, guv, the tacho showed a break of about an hour, thirty minutes before he finished the run. It wasn't a statutory break, and his log doesn't show the reason for the stop. In fact, the log doesn't show a stop at all.'

'I suppose there's no way of knowing where that stop was made.'

Buxton shook his head. 'Fraid not, guv.'

'Well, once again, thanks for your help.'

'What do we do now, guv?' asked Dave, as the traffic car drove out of the yard. 'Shift this lot to Lambeth so that Linda Mitchell can give it the once-over?'

'No, Dave, we run with it, and we monitor it.'

'D'you mean we follow it across France?' There was enthusiasm in Dave's voice at the prospect of a trip across the Channel.

'No, Dave, we don't. I'll arrange for the French police to follow it. They'll be as interested as we are if they can nick an arms dealer on their patch. And the customs lads at Dover will be keen to turn it over when it gets back.'

I was far from satisfied that Bligh was innocent in this Marseille operation, but I was pinning my hopes on the outcome of a combined operation that would have to include the French police and the United Kingdom Border Agency.

ELEVEN

I t was almost seven o'clock by the time we returned to Curtis Green, and it would be necessary for me to move at lightning speed if I was to arrange a combined operation with the UK Border Agency and the French police.

The rule book suggests working through either Interpol or that European Union organization called Europol. But I knew from experience that involving the former would take forever and a day, and the latter I dismissed as more of a sop to the concept of European cooperation than a reality.

I intended, therefore, to rely on what we call the 'old boy net' in the person of my good friend Henri Deshayes, an *inspecteur* in the *Police Judiciaire* in Paris.

Over the years, Henri and I had been involved in several cross-Channel enquiries, and Gail and I had dined with Henri and his delightful wife Gabrielle on several occasions in both London and Paris. But it was during our visits to Paris that Henri and I were at our most fraught. As a former dancer with the famous *Folies-Bergères*, Gabrielle had much in common with Gail, which was fine when they were discussing the theatre, but when they started talking about fashion, an obsession with them both, Henri and I knew that worse was to come. There is nothing more soul destroying for men than following two stylish women around the haute couture establishments of Paris, particularly when they have empty credit cards.

However, it wouldn't come to that on this occasion; there just wasn't the time for a trip to the French capital. Nor, for that matter, was there a valid reason.

'Gavin,' I said to Detective Sergeant Creasey, the night-duty incident room manager, 'see if you can reach *Inspecteur* Deshayes at the quai des Orfèvres in Paris, and tell them it's urgent.'

It took Creasey about twenty minutes before he was eventually connected to an English-speaking detective, only to be told that '*M'sieur* Deshayes left the office for 'ome, about fifteen minutes ago and, by the way, we don't 'ave *inspecteurs* any more. *M'sieur* Deshayes is now called a *capitaine*. It 'as all been changed.'

It appeared that the Paris police also had a funny names and total confusion squad. I flicked open my diary, found Henri's home telephone number and promptly rang it.

''*Ello*?' A female voice answered the phone.

'Gabrielle?'

'*Oui*.'

'Gabrielle, it's Harry Brock.'

''Ello, 'Arry, 'ow are you?' said Gabrielle in her delightfully sexy French accent. 'And 'ow is Gail?'

'We're both very well, thank you. And you?'

'Yes, we are also well.'

'Is your man there?' I asked.

'No, but my 'usband is,' said Gabrielle impishly. 'You want a word?'

That little chat having taken its usual course, there was a short delay and Henri came on the line.

'*Bonjour*, 'Arry.'

'*Bonjour* yourself, Henry.' I always called him Henry to compensate for him omitting the H from my name. It was unfair really; I knew that the French always had trouble with aspirates.

There followed the usual enquiries about our respective health and that of Gail, followed by the customary badinage that forms a part of any conversation between policemen, even of differing nationalities. I then explained briefly about the murder of Kerry Hammond and the connection with Lebrun, the wine merchant in St-Circe near Marseille, who had possibly played some part in Kerry's death. Finally, I told him about the vehicle in which we'd found the secret compartment, and our suspicion that it was used for gunrunning.

'So, Henry, can you put me in touch with one of your people in the Marseille area?' I said in conclusion.

'I'll speak to them myself, 'Arry. That way you won't 'ave difficulties with the language, *non*?'

'Thanks, Henry, that's great.'

'OK, now give me the exact details.'

I gave Henri the number of the truck, the name of the driver and told him that it was due to leave the United Kingdom tomorrow.

However, since telling Dave that we would run with it, and that

we'd ask the Border Agency at Dover to search the vehicle on its
return, I'd had second thoughts.

'I'd rather that the vehicle was not intercepted, Henry, because
I'd like to know where its load is going when it gets back here,' I
said. 'I suspect that there's an arms dealer somewhere in the UK,
probably London, and I'd like to lay hands on him. At the moment,
it looks very much as though Lebrun supplies the weapons, but
that's mere speculation.'

'*D'accord!*' said Henri. 'I will ensure that the *douaniers* do not
search it at Calais, but our people will want to raid this place after
your man has left with the goods.'

'Of course,' I said, 'but it would be helpful if any arrests were
kept from the press until we'd located our man.'

'That can be arranged, 'Arry. Leave it with me. I'll have our
people pick up the vehicle at Calais and see where it goes. What
time will it arrive there?'

'About midday, Henry.'

'*D'accord!*' said Henri again, 'but you will let me know what
happens at your end, *n'est pas*?'

'Of course, Henry, and perhaps you'll let me know what your
people find at Lebrun's place. But I understand that this St-Circe is
about seven hundred miles from Calais.' I'd looked it up on a map,
and I thought that the distance might present the French police with
some difficulties.

'*Pas de probléme*, 'Arry. We 'ave plenty of policemen and lots
of shiny new police cars.'

I next spoke to John Fielding, a senior customs investigator. John
and I had had several outings together over the years, and I'd kept
a note of his home telephone number.

I explained about the murder of Kerry Hammond, and went on
to tell John about our discovery, at Kerry Trucking's haulage yard,
of the vehicle with the secret compartment and our suspicion that
it was being used for gunrunning.

'I suppose there's always a risk that your guys at Dover might
search the vehicle on the off chance when it arrives, John, but I'd
rather—'

'Harry,' said John, cutting me off, 'there are over three thousand
goods vehicles arriving at Dover from abroad every day. It's as
much as our officers can do to search vehicles about which they

have some intelligence, so the chances of a random search picking up your guy are non-existent. But, like you, we'd want to know where this stuff is going. Give me details of the vehicle and I'll make absolutely sure our chaps give it a clear run.'

'Thanks, John.'

'But what are you doing about surveillance, Harry?'

'I'll have a team on standby at Dover ready to follow the truck when it comes in,' I said, secretly hoping that I could make the necessary arrangements in time. 'But I suppose you'll put on a team to follow it as well.'

'Not a chance, Harry. We don't have the manpower since the Chancellor of the Exchequer's swingeing cuts. We'll be happy to leave it to you, but perhaps you'd let us know where it finishes up. Then we can meet you there and have a look at what customs offences have been committed.'

I'd been involved in combined operations with customs before; it was complicated, and there was often a heated discussion about who should have first bite at the cherry. Or, to put it into laymen's terms, someone would have to decide which of us would take the culprits to court and on what charges.

All of that, however, was secondary to the next problem: that of assembling a surveillance team that could be in position by Friday. That's not as easy as you might think; a team has to be found, and permission obtained for it to work outside the Metropolitan Police District.

And that meant that I would have to speak to the commander, if he was still in his office; it was unlikely as he'd usually gone by six o'clock. But, to my surprise, he was still here, and was standing behind his desk attired in evening dress. On his left lapel were two miniature medals, one of which was for distinguished police service. It made me wonder what yardstick had been used in assessing our beloved commander for this award.

'I hope this won't take long, Mr Brock. My wife and I have been invited to a livery dinner in the City.'

'I hope you have a pleasant evening, sir,' I said, not that I could've cared one way or the other. I outlined my request. His response was predictable.

'D'you realize what this would cost, Mr Brock?' The commander's reaction was one of horror combined with trepidation at the prospect of sanctioning an expense that might subsequently be called into question. 'I'm not sure that the DAC would be prepared to approve it.'

The commander invariably invoked the deputy assistant commissioner's opinion even before he'd sought it, let alone heard it, but he was always reluctant to make any serious decisions without referring them to higher command. And as he regarded *all* decisions as serious, it meant that he never had to make *any* decisions.

'It is, of course, entirely a matter for you, sir,' I said, firmly whacking a volley into his court. 'But if we don't run the operation it might well result in our failure to bring Mrs Hammond's murderer to justice.'

'Yes, yes, of course.' The commander dithered. 'Leave it to me, Mr Brock. I'll let you know as soon as I have arrived at a decision.' And that meant when the DAC had arrived at a decision.

'Of course, sir, I'm sure you appreciate that time is of the essence,' I said, adding to his discomfort.

'I'm well aware of that, Mr Brock,' said the commander tetchily, but then he had another thought. 'Could we not perhaps ask the Kent police to arrange this observation?' he said, as if he'd just come up with a brilliant idea. 'In their police district, of course.'

'Not a reliable arrangement in the circumstances, sir.' I shook my head slowly to imply serious doubt. 'Such a plan would entail a handover at the border between Kent and the Metropolitan Police District, and that might blow the gaff.'

'Blow the gaff?' The commander wrinkled his nose; he had an abhorrence of CID argot.

'If the handover was clumsy or in any way obvious, sir, it might alert the suspects to the surveillance,' I said, swiftly translating. 'Counterproductive, as I'm sure you'd agree.'

The commander grunted, and I returned to my office and fretted.

Ten minutes later, my phone rang, and I was summoned to return to the presence.

'The DAC has agreed to the mounting of a surveillance operation out of town, Mr Brock.' Our leader did not look happy, and I got the impression that he disliked parting with the Commissioner's money as much as he hated spending his own. Even though the decision, and therefore the responsibility, was not his.

'Thank you, sir,' I said.

Now began the difficult part, but I had a way of dealing with
that. Rank hath its privileges, or RHIP as we say in the Job, and
I'd lumber someone else to do it. Returning to my office, I sent for
DI Ebdon.

'Kate, I want you to assemble a surveillance team to be at Dover
on Friday to follow Sharpe's vehicle to London.'

'What time, guv?' Kate was completely unfazed by the gargantuan
task I'd just set her.

'Better make it from six in the morning, Kate,' I said, 'but I
hope to hear from the French police in good time when it's due
to arrive at Calais. That means that the start time could vary
either way.'

'No worries, guv, I'll get on it.'

Kate Ebdon has a wonderful way of charming the impossible
out of senior officers in other departments who are reluctant to part
with manpower, and within an hour she reported back that it was
all set up.

'They're mainly motorcyclists, guv, with one or two nondescript
vehicles, all of them leapfrogging. It'll be the usual professional
operation.'

'I hope so, Kate.'

'And I've arranged for radio contact to be maintained in the
incident room here at Curtis Green.'

All we had to do now was to wait.

I had thought that there was little I could do until Friday, but it was
not to be. That, however, is police work for you.

I arrived at Curtis Green at about eight thirty on the Wednesday
morning, and was followed into my office by Detective Sergeant
Wilberforce waving an email printout in my direction.

'That looks ominous, Colin.'

'It's about Gary Dixon, sir.'

'What about him?' I asked, accepting a cup of coffee from Dave.

'He's in intensive care at Ealing Hospital, sir. He was found late
last night about two hundred yards from his home, and according
to the local police he'd been the victim of a severe beating. The
CID at Ealing did a routine check on the PNC, found we were
interested and informed us.'

'Has he said anything that might be of assistance, Colin?'

'According to this, sir,' said Wilberforce, flourishing the printout, 'he hasn't yet regained consciousness.'

'I hope he doesn't snuff it,' said Dave, 'at least, until we've had a chance to talk to him.'

'Is there any information as to his injuries, Colin?' I asked.

'I've spoken to the hospital, sir, and he's suspected of having a broken arm, several broken ribs, a possible hairline fracture of the skull, and severe general bruising. They've promised to let us know as soon as he's fit enough for us to have a chat with him.'

As it happened, we didn't have long to wait. At two o'clock, the hospital telephoned to say that Dixon had recovered consciousness, was out of intensive care and was now fit enough to be interviewed.

Gary Dixon was a sorry sight. He had a black eye, his left arm was in plaster, his head was swathed in bandages, and he was connected to all manner of weird tubes that were attached to even weirder machines.

'I'm Detective Chief Inspector Brock of Scotland Yard, Gary,' I said, 'and this is DS Poole.'

'I dunno nothing,' said Dixon.

'Well, that *is* a surprise,' muttered Dave.

'Who attacked you, Gary?' I asked.

'No idea. Two guys jumped me from behind. I never got a good look at 'em. Anyway, they was wearing ski masks.'

'Can you think of anyone who would've wanted to put you out of action, Gary?'

'Nope.' Dixon's response was too quick to be convincing.

'Well, I can think of a few,' I suggested. 'I understand that you were very friendly with Kerry Hammond, your former employer.'

'Never heard of her.'

I ignored that predictable reply. 'You phoned her mobile frequently, the last occasion being at about half past three on the afternoon of Christmas Eve. And we know you were having an affair with her,' I said, having fairly strong evidence that that had been the case.

'All right, so I did know her,' mumbled Dixon. 'There ain't no law against it.'

'No, but murdering her is punishable by life imprisonment,' put in Dave.

Dixon attempted to sit up, but let out a groan of pain. 'I never murdered her. I never even knew she'd snuffed it.'

'You were also involved in smuggling firearms,' I continued, convinced that he did know about Kerry's murder. 'But that all finished when you were turned over by customs at Dover last September bringing in a load of booze. That resulted in you being fined five grand, and we know that Kerry paid the fine for you. We also know that she paid a grand a month into your bank account after Bernard Bligh sacked you. What was that for? To make sure you kept your mouth shut?'

'I dunno where you got all that from,' said Dixon.

'Where were you between the twenty-third of December and when the police found you last night, Gary?' asked Dave.

'At home, weren't I?'

'No, you weren't,' I said. 'On Saturday, the twenty-eighth of December, your wife Sonia told one of my officers that she hadn't seen you since a few days before Christmas.'

'Oh yeah, I forgot. I was away on a job.' Dixon was struggling to field each of our increasingly difficult questions.

'On a job, eh?' said Dave. 'Who were you working for?'

'I'm sorry, but I'm feeling rather tired,' said Dixon, and promptly feigned sleep.

We met a nurse on our way out.

'How much longer d'you think that Mr Dixon will be kept in, Staff?' I asked.

'I've no idea, but why don't you ask the doctor. That's her over there.' The nurse pointed to a young good-looking black girl of about thirty, a stethoscope in the pocket of her white coat, who was in conversation with another doctor.

We introduced ourselves, and Dave asked the all-important question.

The young doctor laughed. 'Tomorrow, I should think. The X-rays showed that there was no hairline fracture of the skull, and what we thought was a broken arm turned out to be a dislocated elbow. The bruising will go down in due course, and the ribs will take care of themselves now that they're strapped up. In the meantime, we'll give him a bucketful of pain killers and send him home.'

'Mr Dixon is someone in whom we have an interest, Doctor,' I said. 'Would you have any medical objection to my placing a police

guard on him until he's ready to leave, at which point he'll be taken
into custody.'

'Not at all,' said the doctor. 'In fact, we'd be delighted. Might
stop him making a bloody nuisance of himself. He's always
complaining about something or another.'

I turned to Dave. 'Perhaps you'd make the necessary arrangements, Dave,' I said, but he was already on his mobile to Ealing
police station.

On Thursday afternoon, Gary Dixon limped into the interview room
at Charing Cross police station whence he'd been transferred from
the station at Ealing.

'I want to know why I've been nicked,' he said, as he sat down
slowly and carefully. He adjusted the sling supporting his left arm,
and glared at us.

'Just sit there quietly and we'll tell you,' said Dave. He turned
on the recording machine and announced who was present.

'We know that you were involved in smuggling firearms from
France, Gary.' I based that allegation purely on Tom Challis's claim
that he'd sensed gun oil in Sharpe's lorry. 'We found the secret
panel in the rig you drove before you got the sack from Kerry
Trucking.' I took a gamble on it having been installed while Dixon
was working for Kerry Trucking, if not before, and my belief that
the smuggling had been going on during Dixon's time with the
company.

'Secret panel? What the hell are you talking about?' demanded
Dixon. 'I don't know nothing about no secret panels. That's all
James Bond stuff. Who d'you think I am: Double-O-Seven?'

Dixon's reaction was so genuine that I was almost inclined to
believe him, and the confirmation I needed was, therefore, unlikely
to come from him.

'And even if I did know anything,' Dixon continued, 'I'd be
asking for more than a beating up if I grassed on whoever was at
it. Gunrunning's heavy stuff.'

'So you know about that, do you?' suggested Dave.

'Nah, but I've read about it. In the past, like,' Dixon added
hurriedly.

'Are you still not going to tell us who attacked you?' I asked.

'I told you in the hospital, I don't know. I never saw their faces.'

'D'you think that Kerry Hammond's organization was behind it?' I asked, still intent on getting an answer. 'Perhaps whoever took over the operation from her arranged for someone to give you a going over.'

'Why should they do that? All I know about Kerry is that I was screwing her,' said Dixon. 'She was all for it. Couldn't keep her hands off of me. She come with me on a trip to France, fact-finding she called it, but it was only an excuse to get me into bed in Gay Paree. But who was I to argue with the boss? When she said jump, I jumped.' Dixon gave a lascivious laugh.

'Why was Kerry paying a grand a month into your bank account?' asked Dave.

'I s'pose she felt sorry for me after Bligh give me the push. She never knew nothing about it until it was too late, and I never got no redundancy or nothing like that. But that Bligh's a nasty bastard.'

'When we spoke to you yesterday, you said that you were away from home over Christmas doing a job. What job was that?'

'All right, so I was with a bird what I met on one of my runs up to York. She give me a bell to say she'd be down in the Smoke over Christmas to visit her sister, and how did I fancy spending a few days with her in a hotel. At her expense, like. Well, I said I was all for it. And before you ask, her name was Tracey, and no, I dunno where she lives.'

Unfortunately, we'd been forced into giving Dixon time to dream up an alibi. Nevertheless, I had to try to break it.

'What was the name of the hotel?'

'Can't remember exactly, but it was up West somewhere.'

All of which amounted to a most unlikely story. I suspected that Dixon had been engaged in some pursuit of a felonious nature, and that the generous and willing woman from York was a figment of his imagination.

'Why did you telephone Kerry Hammond at about three thirty on Christmas Eve, Gary?' asked Dave.

'I wanted to know if she was up for it, didn't I? But she said as how she was about to leave for the airport because she was off to the Big Apple with her husband. I told her that she'd have a better time with me, but she said it was too late. She reckoned it was all booked, and I should've got in touch earlier.'

'But you just said that you were with an obliging girl from York over Christmas.'

'Yeah, but not all the time. Like I said, she had to pop out and visit her sister.'

I had rapidly come to the conclusion that Dixon knew little of the gun-smuggling operation, and that, even if he did, he wisely intended to keep his mouth shut. But he was still not out of the woods insofar as Kerry Hammond's murder was concerned.

'I'm going to admit you to police bail to return to this police station in one month, Gary,' I said. 'Should we not require you again, we'll let you know before then.'

'Bloody liberty, I call it,' said Dixon as he struggled to his feet and shuffled out of the room. He was clearly in a lot of pain.

TWELVE

Much to Gail's annoyance, I left her bed at a quarter to five on the Friday morning. I was annoyed too, because, like Marilyn Monroe, Gail wore nothing but Chanel No 5 in bed and, on occasions such as this, temptation comes very close to overcoming the demands of duty. I'd arranged for a car to pick me up and was in the office at just before six.

Kate Ebdon and Dave Poole were already there, along with Gavin Creasey, the night duty incident room manager.

'The team is at Dover, guv,' said Kate, 'all set up and raring to go. Captain Deshayes telephoned earlier to say that the suspect vehicle is booked on the oh-seven-hundred hours ferry from Calais.'

'That means it will be at Dover at about eight thirty.'

'Nearer seven thirty our time, guv,' said Kate smugly. 'The French are an hour ahead of GMT. Incidentally, Captain Deshayes said he'll ring you later to fill you in on what happened in France. But he did say that Sharpe picked up a load just outside Marseille at a place called St-Circe, as you said he would. He doesn't know what the load was because he didn't want his people to show out. However, he added that the police were now searching the warehouse where Sharpe stopped.'

'Excellent,' I said.

'So far as our surveillance is concerned,' Kate continued, 'our call sign here at Curtis Green is Trading Post, and the various guys doing the following are called Trader followed by a number. They're calling the suspect vehicle Jumbo.'

'I suppose that all makes sense,' I said, being none too well informed about technical matters of that nature.

For an hour and a half, we lounged around the incident room, drinking countless cups of coffee and reading the newspapers. And those of us who smoked were smoking, despite all the silly rules that forbade it.

At twenty minutes to eight the radio crackled unto life.

'Trading Post from Trader One. Jumbo now leaving port area. On to the A20. Over.'

Dave flicked a switch on the console. 'Received, out.'

Ten minutes later, another message came wafting through the ether.

'Trading Post from Trader Five. Jumbo now on to M20 in light traffic. Over.'

And so it went on until a quarter past eight when the first hiccup arose. Believe me, if anything is going to foul up a police operation, it's usually the police who do the fouling up. Today was no different.

'Trading Post from Trader Three, we have a problem. A Kent traffic unit has just pulled Jumbo into a lay-by for speeding between junctions ten and nine. It looks as though they're taking an unhealthy interest in what Jumbo's carrying. Over.'

Dave acknowledged the message, and turned to me. 'What do we do about that, guv? It could wreck the whole operation.'

'I'll deal with it,' said Kate, and grabbed a telephone. Within seconds, she was connected to the Kent Police control room via the direct link from the Yard.

'This is DI Ebdon, Metropolitan,' she began. 'We've got an operation running on the M20 and your traffic guys have just given our target a pull between junctions ten and nine.' She gave details of Jumbo before adding, 'Could you ask them to lay off, otherwise the whole show could be a blowout?'

'Well?' I asked, when Kate had finished.

'Done, guv. Kent have radioed their traffic car and told them to leave Jumbo alone.'

Three minutes later, we received another message from Trader Three. 'Panic over. The Kent guys have suddenly lost interest and cleared off. We're on the move again.'

I breathed a sigh of relief.

And so it continued, with occasional updates, until a quarter past ten. Then came the message we'd been waiting for.

'Trading Post from Trader Seven, Jumbo has arrived at a warehouse at twenty-seven Cantard Street, Walworth. It's a turning off the Walworth Road about half a mile south of the Elephant and Castle.'

Dave enquired what was happening, and was told that our suspect vehicle had driven into the warehouse, and that the doors had been closed. Significantly, they reported that Sharpe immediately left the warehouse and had made his way to a nearby coffee shop. Forty minutes later, the surveillance team reported that Sharpe had returned and that Jumbo was on the move again.

'That's about right, guv,' said Dave. 'That'll have given them time to shift enough of the legitimate load to get at the secret compartment, and be on the road again.'

'I wonder why Sharpe wasn't involved in the unloading,' I mused aloud, although he'd said previously that it wasn't a driver's job.

Twenty minutes later, the surveillance guys were on the air again to report another stop. Our suspect vehicle had pulled into another warehouse, this time in Broders Road, off Lambeth Road in Kennington, and was unloading. Once again, Sharpe had left the warehouse and gone for coffee.

'That'll be the wine they're unloading, I suppose,' volunteered Kate.

'Dave,' I said, 'call up a traffic car to get us to Chiswick before Jumbo arrives there.'

As ever, it was a hair-raising ride with the Black Rats, as we of the CID call the Metropolitan Police traffic units, but I take some comfort in knowing that its drivers are the finest in the world. And they proved it by getting us to Kerry Trucking at twenty-five past twelve.

Bernard Bligh was occupying his usual place on the loading platform and appeared to regard the arrival of a white traffic car with the same apprehension as he had shown on the previous occasion that one had appeared on his premises. But perhaps I was imputing guilty knowledge where none existed.

Five minutes later, our suspect vehicle pulled into the yard. Billy Sharpe jumped down from the cab, raised his arms in the air and stretched.

'All right, lads, you know what to do,' I said to the traffic officers, having briefed them during our journey to Chiswick.

'What the hell's going on now?' demanded Bligh.

'These officers,' I began, 'are here to inspect Sharpe's tachograph, Mr Bligh.'

'Can they do that?'

I laughed. 'You were a driver yourself once,' I said, 'and you know damned well they can.'

Bligh shrugged. 'But why are you so interested in that vehicle?'

'I think that your Billy Sharpe might be having you over,' I said, drawing Bligh to one side. 'It's possible he's been doing a bit of freelance carrying, and pocketing the profit.' Apart from the possibility that Sharpe had brought in firearms, I had no grounds for thinking that to be the case, but I was determined to get Bligh on our side. 'But my officers will soon know.'

'D'you reckon he's on the fiddle, then? I've always had my suspicions about that guy.' Bligh's expression was one of anger at the thought that one of his drivers was defrauding him; and he seemed even more annoyed that, as an experienced driver himself, he hadn't spotted it. 'Help yourselves, gents. You can take it apart, as far as I'm concerned.'

'Oh, we intend to,' I said, and walked across to Sharpe's rig. Bligh followed me.

One of the traffic officers, a PC called Jamison, got into the cab and spent a few minutes studying the information that the tachograph had recorded. Leaning out of the cab, he addressed the rig's driver.

'You made a stop at ten fifteen, Mr Sharpe,' said Jamison. 'What was that for?'

'Breakfast,' said Sharpe.

'Where was that?' I asked.

Sharpe paused long enough for me to sense that he was about to lie. 'Borough High Street.'

'And the load you brought back from France?' I asked. 'Where did you deliver that?'

'Folkestone,' said Sharpe.

'That's right,' put in Bligh.

'And what did that load consist of?' I asked Sharpe.

But it was Bligh who answered. 'Tyres.'

That was interesting. The tachograph showed that Sharpe hadn't stopped at Folkestone; in fact, he'd been nowhere near there, having gone straight on to the M20 from the A20. That raised the question of whether Sharpe was lying to Bligh as well as to us. But if he was lying only to us, that probably meant that Bligh was also involved in smuggling firearms. What's more, I'd be extremely surprised if Sharpe had collected a consignment of tyres from a wine merchant in Marseille.

'And then you stopped again at eleven fifteen,' said Jamison. 'Where was that?'

'Er, Victoria Embankment, I think.'

'You *think*?' Jamison studied Sharpe sceptically. 'Why?'

'Call of nature. What's this all about, anyway?'

'Just a routine check,' said Jamison with commendable aplomb.

'That'll be all the coffee he drank,' said Dave, in a sarcastic aside, as he busily noted all Sharpe's replies to Jamison's questions.

The running commentary from the surveillance team had told us that Sharpe had not stopped at either of the places in London he'd mentioned, but I wasn't about to say so.

'Well, that'll be all, Mr Bligh,' I said.

'As a matter of interest, Chief Inspector,' said Bligh, 'how does any of this help you find out who murdered Kerry?'

'Mr Bligh,' said Dave, 'we don't tell you how to run a haulage business, so I'd deem it a favour if you didn't try to tell us how to do our job.'

It was two o'clock by the time we returned to Curtis Green, but there was no time for lunch. We needed to act swiftly if we were to mount a search on the premises where Billy Sharpe had made his stops. From the time involved, I was fairly confident that the first stop of forty minutes had been for the purpose of unloading the firearms; it would have taken that long to clear enough space behind the cargo of wine to get at the secret panel. The second stop was certain to be where the wine was unloaded assuming, of course, that there had been any wine on board Sharpe's vehicle in the first place.

It was interesting that Bligh had said that Sharpe's load had consisted of tyres, and that seemed to imply that he knew nothing of the importation of wine, and had only learned about Kerry Wine Importers when we had mentioned it.

It was also interesting that Sharpe hadn't disputed Bligh's statement, and that led me to believe that wine importing was a private enterprise that had been set up by Kerry, and had been continued after her death. But who had taken it over? It had to be a legitimate business otherwise the customs people would have rumbled it by now, and Sharpe would've been nicked. The only fiddle I could think of was tax evasion. Not of import duty, but on the sale of the wine once it had arrived in the United Kingdom. But I don't know much about the levying of tax, except that I pay too much.

I had a feeling that we were getting farther away from solving Kerry Hammond's murder, but I couldn't help feeling that her death was somehow inextricably connected to the firearms and the wine.

I sent for Kate Ebdon and Len Driscoll, another of my DIs.

'Kate, get along to Westminster Magistrates' Court and swear out search warrants for both the Cantard Street and the Broders Road addresses. Suspicion of storing illegal firearms. Len, I want you to arrange for the local Territorial Support Group to stand by for a raid on both those addresses as soon as Kate's got the warrant.' A sudden thought occurred to me. 'And I suppose we'd better alert CO19. If there are firearms involved, and right now that seems to be a racing certainty, there might be some shooting, and it'd be as well to have the Firearms Unit standing by.'

'Good as done, guv,' said Driscoll.

'When d'you intend spinning these drums, guv?' asked Dave, once the two DIs had disappeared to complete their respective tasks. 'Today, or tomorrow morning?'

'By the time we've got the warrants and organized the attendance of the TSG and CO19 it'll have to be tomorrow, Dave. So, we'll go in bright and early tomorrow morning,' I said, and ignored Dave's groan. 'If I were an underworld armourer, I'd want to move those shooters ASAP. I think it's an odds-on chance that they're brought in to order for a particular job. In fact, they might already be on their way to the end users, but that's a chance we'll have to take. I just hope we won't be too late.'

'But if they're only brought in to order, guv,' said Dave, 'we might not find any firearms this time.'

'If that's the case, why would Sharpe have made a stop in Walworth and then lied about it? He might not always bring in firearms, but I'm certain that he did on this occasion.'

Kate Ebdon and Driscoll acted fast. It took Len Driscoll twenty minutes to put the TSG and CO19 on standby, and Kate was back with the warrants at half past three.

'Right, we're set to go,' I said to my team of eight that I'd nominated for the raids. 'Len, you take the Broders Road address where the wine was unloaded. But bear in mind that these guys might be playing a double bluff, and the firearms might be there.'

'Where d'you want me to go, guv?' asked Kate.

'You're with me and Dave.'

'D'you want us to go in at the same time as you're hitting Cantard Street, guv?' asked Len Driscoll.

'Yes, Len, five o'clock tomorrow morning, on the dot. We'll liaise by phone in case there are any problems.'

Finally I rang John Fielding and told him the arrangements we'd made for the raids.

'Thanks, Harry,' he said. 'I'll have a couple of my officers meet you at the Cantard Street address just before five tomorrow morning.' He paused, and I heard him rustling through paper. 'Their names are Jim Foley and Don Bridger.'

The Territorial Support Group was already in place when we reached Walworth at half past four on the Saturday morning. The inspector in charge had parked his carriers in a side street, out of sight of the target warehouse. And it was bloody cold; there was frost on the surrounding roofs and the first snowflakes had started to fall. All of which made me wonder why I'd ever become a policeman.

'Are you Mr Brock?' asked the TSG inspector, as I approached him.

'That's me,' I said.

'Inspector Taylor, sir. We're ready whenever you are.'

'What's your first name, Mr Taylor?' We detectives are never too bothered about formality.

'John, sir, but I'm usually known as Buck.'

I quickly introduced Kate Ebdon and Dave Poole, and then asked, 'How many men have you got in your unit, Buck?'

'It's the usual, sir: me, one and ten,' said Taylor. 'My other skipper and ten PCs are at Broders Road with your Mr Driscoll. But my lot aren't all men, sir,' he added. 'Four of them are women.'

'Will they be all right, these women, Buck?' I was satisfied that one inspector, one sergeant and ten PCs would be enough for our task, but I'm sufficiently old-fashioned enough to be concerned that police-women might get hurt in situations that could turn violent. It was not unknown for them to have been shot on previous occasions.

Taylor ran a hand round his chin. 'Let's put it this way, guv: I wouldn't argue with any of my girls. By the way, the CO19 firearms unit is tucked in behind my carriers with a skipper in charge.'

'Ask him to have a word, Buck.'

While I was waiting for the firearms sergeant, a couple of men approached. Wearing jeans and heavy duty Barbour jackets, they had fur hats and scarves. They looked as though they'd rather be someplace else.

'Chief Inspector Brock?'

'That's me.'

'Jim Foley, Customs Division, Border Agency, and this is my mate Don Bridger,' Foley said, indicating the man next to him. 'John Fielding asked us to make our number with you.'

I shook hands with each of the customs men and explained what we were about to do.

'It's possible there might be some shooting,' I said, 'so it might be as well if you hung back until my chaps have gone in, and then I'll give you a shout.'

'Don't worry, Mr Brock, I make it a rule never to be shot at before breakfast,' said Bridger, as he and Foley retreated to the safety of the area behind Buck Taylor's carriers.

'PS Dan Mason, CO19, sir.' The sergeant who appeared a couple of minutes later was wearing so much protective gear that he looked like a composite of the Michelin man and the Incredible Hulk. The reassuring part of his equipment was the Heckler and Koch carbine slung across his chest, and the Glock automatic pistol holstered at his belt.

'Come and have a look at the target, gents,' I said.

PS Mason and Inspector Taylor followed me to the corner of the street whence we had a good view of the warehouse. There were two large sliding doors with a wicket gate in the left-hand one. Fortunately, there were no windows that would enable the occupants of the building to see the street.

'That's the warehouse we're about to bust,' I said. 'I've reason to believe that it's occupied by a villains' armourer. There might be some shooting, Dan.'

'Sounds right.' Mason just nodded, as though such a situation was normal for him, which it probably was. 'By the way, sir, I've already checked out the venue myself. I like to suss out the ground before I take my guys in, so I wandered down yesterday evening and had a discreet look at it.'

'How d'you think we should approach it, Dan?' I always believed in leaving the planning of an operation like this to the professionals. That he had conducted a preparatory survey proved that they don't come much more professional than CO19, although there had been one or two occasions in the past when they'd made a bit of a pig's ear of things. I just hoped that this would not be one of those occasions.

'I intend to deploy my team on either side of the wicket gate, sir, and get one of the TSG lads to open it up with a rammer. Then me and my lads will go in fast.' Mason paused thoughtfully. 'But if they start shooting straight away, I'll have no alternative but to return fire.'

'Understood,' I said, hoping against hope that our search would proceed peacefully. 'Can you arrange for the rammer, Buck?' I asked Taylor.

'Yes, sir. By the way, ten minutes ago, I arranged with the local Traffic OCU to close the road. We don't want any of our villains to get knocked over if they do a runner, do we?' said Taylor. 'They might sue the Commissioner for pain and suffering,' he added cynically.

We returned to the side street where the other officers were waiting.

'Right,' I said, 'let's do it.'

The PC with the rammer, and PS Mason and his team of six, raced across the now silent and empty road until they were stationed immediately adjacent to the wicket gate. The remainder of the TSG serial quickly followed and fanned out on either side of the small door. And my team of detectives ranged themselves behind the uniforms.

'Right, lad, go for it.' Mason nodded to the PC known as 'the fourteen-pound keyholder'.

Swinging the rammer, the PC smashed in the door with a single blow. Within seconds, Sergeant Mason and company were inside the warehouse.

'Armed police. Get down on the floor. *Now!*' Mason's shouts were followed by sounds of scuffling. Ten minutes later, after satisfying himself that there was no one else in the warehouse, he appeared at the broken gate, now hanging drunkenly on its hinges. 'It's all clear, sir,' he said. 'There were only two men in the warehouse and they've been cuffed. It's safe to bring in the rest of the team.'

Buck Taylor, his sergeant and the ten PCs entered the warehouse, followed by me and my eight detectives.

Lying on the floor of the warehouse were two men, face down, their hands secured behind them with plastic handcuffs.

'All right, Mr Taylor, we'll have them on their feet, if you please.'

None too gently, the PCs of the TSG yanked the two prisoners upright.

'Well, well, well!' said Dave, as he walked across to one of the men. 'Look who we have here. None other than *Señor* Miguel Rodriguez, otherwise known as Michael Roberts, former owner of the Spanish Fly nightclub.'

'I still bloody own it, copper,' snarled Roberts. His hair was ruffled and he was now without his pointed sideburns.

'For the time being maybe, but I don't reckon the governor of Parkhurst will allow you to carry on running it from inside the nick, *señor*,' said Dave, laying particular emphasis on the *señor* bit. He knew that mention of the feared prison on the Isle of Wight usually succeeded in concentrating the mind of a villain.

'You can't prove a thing,' said Roberts, in an attempt to convince us that he was innocent of any wrongdoing, but I doubt that he even convinced himself.

'What can't we prove?' asked Dave.

Roberts maintained a sullen silence; probably his best option.

'Right, lads,' I began, addressing the TSG officers and my detectives. There was a sarcastic cough from one of the women PCs. 'And ladies,' I added hurriedly. 'I want a thorough search of the building. I'm looking for firearms. If you find any, or anything that looks like explosives, let Sergeant Mason know. He'll ensure that his chaps make them safe before you go any further.'

The ten PCs, led by their sergeant, fanned out and began a systematic search of the warehouse, directed by Inspector Taylor. My team followed them.

It was a large building and the search took nearly an hour, but the result proved to be a bonanza. The haul comprised ten Heckler and Koch carbines, twenty handguns of assorted makes and calibre, and a substantial quantity of ammunition.

'What were you going to do, *señor*?' asked Dave, moving closer to Roberts, 'start another civil war in Spain?'

'Don't know what you're talking about,' said Roberts.

I gave Kate Ebdon the task of overseeing the removal of the weaponry to Lambeth where it could be stored securely. And, just to be on the safe side, I asked PS Mason and his CO19 team to provide an escort. I didn't want our exhibits to be hijacked on the way. It would be extremely difficult to explain such an unfortunate occurrence to our esteemed commander.

'What d'you want done with this pair, sir?' asked Taylor, nodding towards our two prisoners.

'Take them to Paddington police station, Buck,' I said, after giving the matter a few moments thought. 'That'll be more secure than the local nick.' I wasn't too concerned that they might attempt to escape, but rather that other, as yet unknown, villains might attempt to get at them. At this stage, we didn't know quite how big a network of villainy we were dealing with, and I imagined there to be more people involved than the two we'd captured so far.

The two customs officers now appeared from within the warehouse.

'We've had a look at the firearms your people found, Mr Brock,' said Foley.

'Of interest to you?' I asked.

Foley smiled. 'Probably,' he said. 'My job now is to compile a report for our legal department. They'll decide what action is to be taken. *Eventually*.' There was an element of sarcasm in his last comment.

THIRTEEN

Although it seemed that we'd been at work all day, it was still only nine o'clock on that Saturday morning when my team and I arrived at Paddington nick. But detectives, constrained as they are by the Police and Criminal Evidence Act, can't keep office hours, and I could already visualize the rest of the weekend disappearing.

I told the custody sergeant to put Roberts in the interview room, and decided that Kate Ebdon would be best suited to assist me in interrogating him. I let her kick off.

'When we searched the warehouse at twenty-seven Cantard Street earlier today,' Kate began, 'a quantity of firearms was found.'

'Don't know anything about them,' said Roberts, making a statement that came as no surprise.

'Who is the other man who we arrested at the same time that we nicked you?'

'No idea.' Roberts lounged in his chair, fully relaxed. 'Never seen him before.'

'What were you doing there?'

'I'd gone to collect some wine for my nightclub.'

'We searched the place from top to bottom, mate,' said Kate, her Australian accent becoming a little more aggressive, 'and there wasn't any wine there.'

'So I made a mistake.'

'What d'you know about the wine business?'

'I sell it in my club.'

'Don't get bloody clever with me, sport,' said Kate. 'Did you ever buy wine from Kerry Hammond?'

Roberts laughed. 'No, she bought wine from me. That's what running a nightclub's all about, darling.'

Kate had had enough. Switching off the tape recorder, she stood up, placed her hands flat on the table and leaned very close to Roberts. 'The next time you call me "darling", Roberts, I'll have you off that chair and kick you straight in the balls. Have you got that, *mate*?'

Roberts sat up straight, and leaned back. He was obviously in no doubt that Kate meant what she said, was capable of carrying out her threat, and wouldn't hesitate to do so. As I've said before, it's extremely unwise to get on the wrong side of Kate.

Kate sat down and turned on the tape recorder again.

'Where were you on Christmas Eve, Roberts?' I asked, deciding to take a hand in the questioning.

'At the Spanish Fly.'

'Your bar manager, Fred Goddard,' I said, 'who masquerades as a Spaniard called Fernando, told me that you weren't there at all that evening. What's more, you did a runner straight after I saw you at the club two days after Christmas. So where were you?'

'No comment,' said Roberts, 'and I want a lawyer, and I want bail.'

'You can have as many lawyers as you like, but you won't be getting bail,' I said. 'Firstly, I'll be charging you with unlawful possession of firearms and conspiring illegally to import firearms. There's also a good chance that I'll charge you with murdering Kerry Hammond on the twenty-fourth of December last.'

'I had nothing to with that,' said Roberts, his face displaying the first sign of fear based on the misapprehension that he was about to be fitted up.

'You've already admitted to having an affair with her,' I said.

'So what?'

'I suggest that she found out about your sideline of smuggling guns and threatened to inform on you if you didn't cut her in.' I knew that Kerry Hammond was a rich woman, but I doubted that all her money had come from the haulage business that bore her name. I was fairly certain that Kerry was, or had been, the brains behind the operation, but it was a vain hope that Roberts was about to confirm that.

'I don't know what you're talking about,' said Roberts nervously, but I got the impression that I'd touched a nerve.

'So, where were you on Christmas Eve, Roberts?' asked Kate.

'With a bird.'

'Name?'

'I'm not telling you. She's married.'

'Really? Well, my friend, you're beginning to look quite tasty for the topping of Kerry Hammond. Unless you can come up with a name.'

Roberts capitulated. 'All right, she was a broad called Patricia Knight.'

'Does she have an address, this Patricia Knight?' asked Kate.

'Seventeen Coxtree Close, Chelsea,' said Roberts reluctantly. 'But for God's sake be discreet, otherwise her old man will kill me, and probably her too.'

'I'm the soul of discretion,' said Kate, as she scribbled the details in her pocket book. 'And where did you spend this evening of romantic shafting, mate?'

'I've got a bedroom at the club.'

'Who else uses it?'

'Only close friends, as and when,' said Roberts miserably.

'Are you telling me you run a knocking shop at your club?' Kate was being mischievous now. There was no way we'd have the time to investigate this comparatively trivial breach of the law.

'No, of course not,' protested Roberts.

We'd got nothing of consequence out of Roberts, which is exactly what I'd expected to get. I sent for a PC and told him to put Roberts back in his nice warm cell.

'Happy New Year, Mike,' said Kate, as we stood up to leave.

I went looking for Dave Poole, and eventually found him in the CID office.

'Anything on our other man, Dave?' I asked.

'I did a LiveScan followed by a LiveID on each of them, including Roberts, guv.'

'What on earth are you talking about, Dave?' I asked, completely mystified by Dave's excursion into the wonderful world of police technology.

'D'you remember the gizmo that Linda Mitchell used to check Kerry Hammond's prints at Heathrow?'

'Yes. What about it?'

'Well, you just put the suspect's fingers on something that looks like a mobile phone and bingo! You get a result within three minutes, *sir*.'

'Very impressive, Dave.' It didn't escape my notice that he was calling me 'sir' again. 'So, what did you learn from this wonderful gizmo?'

'His name's Patrick Hogan. Not only has he got form, but there's a warrant out for him. The Flying Squad want him for an armed robbery in Hillingdon last year. Apparently he's been lying low.'

'Not that low,' commented Kate. 'But I know that toerag. I thought I recognized him when we nicked him. I got him sent down for a five-stretch about seven years ago. I'm looking forward to having another chat with him.'

Patrick Hogan had all the distinctive features of a typical villain: late thirties, shaven head, muscular, tattoos and the obligatory earring. And Kate's years on the Flying Squad had taught her exactly how to deal with his type.

'Still at it, then, Pat?' Kate took a seat opposite Hogan, and smiled at him.

Recognition dawned on Hogan's face. 'Hello, Miss Ebdon. We can't keep meeting like this, you know. People'll start to talk.'

'It was your choice to be here, Pat,' said Kate, 'and what's more the Flying Squad's got a brief out for you. Post office blagging up Hillingdon way.'

'That was all a mistake, miss. I dunno anything about it and I weren't never there.'

'Case of mistaken identity, was it, Pat? Well, it's something you'll have to take up with the Sweeney. You should be all right, though; you know how compassionate the Squad can be. They're very considerate when it comes to rectifying genuine mistakes.'

'Yeah, thanks a bundle.' Hogan did not look happy at the prospect of another encounter with the Heavy Mob, as the Flying Squad was known to the criminal fraternity.

'Anyway, to get down to today's agenda, Pat, and all the shooters we found at Cantard Street. Your mate Roberts said he knows nothing about them. He's put it all down to you.'

'*He's done what?*' Hogan could not disguise his outrage at such a blatant betrayal.

'Oh yes, he reckons he knows nothing about the hardware. He claims he was only there to pick up some wine. It's a sort of variation on "I was only here for the beer".'

'What bloody wine? There weren't no wine there. That Roberts is a double-dealing miserable ratbag. What's he going on about? It's well down to him, miss, and no mistake. You can stand on me.'

'It's not looking good, Pat,' said Kate, shaking her head

sympathetically. 'Perhaps you ought to consider your position, as politicians say when they're in deep shtook.'

Hogan did indeed appear to consider his position. 'What's in it for me if I give you the SP, Miss Ebdon?' he asked eventually. 'I mean, can you make this Hillingdon blagging go away?'

Kate laughed. 'You know I can't make deals, Pat,' she said, 'but I could have a word with the Crown Prosecution Service if you come up with the goods about the firearms.'

'All right, so I was tied up in it, but Roberts is the man who does the business. He's the Mister Big, as you might say. He's well at it.'

'What, all on his own?'

'Nah, course not.'

'How about giving me a few names, then?'

'I hope you're going to make this worth my while, Miss Ebdon.' At first, Hogan seemed reluctant to furnish the identity of any of Roberts's fellow conspirators, but then he relented. 'There was a couple of blokes there last night. In the warehouse, I mean, but I haven't a clue who they was. As for the shooters, as far as I know Mike pushes 'em out to a geezer by the name of Pollard. Charlie Pollard.'

'Where's this Pollard's drum?' asked Kate.

'Down Bethnal Green way, I think. But I dunno for sure.'

'What's he look like, this Charlie Pollard?'

'Dunno, miss. I never clapped me peepers on him. Roberts says it's safer to keep things separate, like. In fact, I only ever heard Charlie's name mentioned the once, and I don't think I was meant to hear it, neither.'

At least that was something, but Kate decided to leave it for the moment. Going on to a different tack, she asked, 'What d'you know about a bird called Kerry Hammond, Pat?'

'Yeah, I reckon she was tied up in it, an' all. Leastways, Roberts let slip her name once, but I never met her neither. I think she was his fancy bit on the side.'

'So, you don't know for sure that she's involved.'

'Well, when I 'fronted Roberts about her, he done a bit of verbal tap dancing. Said something about her being a bird he bought wine from. But a nod's as good as a wink.' Hogan tapped the side of his nose with his forefinger. 'Know what I mean?'

'Did Roberts ever involve you with his wine business, Pat?'

'No, miss. I only ever heard him mention it that once, but even then, I reckon he was spinning me a fanny.'

'You knew, of course, that he owned a nightclub called the Spanish Fly in Mayfair where he was known as Miguel Rodriguez.'

'I never knew about that till I heard one of your coppers mention it when we was nicked. Strikes me Roberts has got his fingers in quite a few pies.'

Kate glanced at me. 'Anything else, guv?' she asked.

'Not at the moment, Kate,' I said, and turned to Hogan. 'You'll be charged with illegal possession of firearms, Pat. But, as DI Ebdon said, we'll have a word with the CPS about the Hillingdon job. No promises, though.'

'Cheers, Mr Brock,' said Hogan, apparently resigned to spending a few more years as a guest in one of Her Majesty's penal establishments.

The custody sergeant was all for granting bail to Roberts and Hogan. But I quickly persuaded him that there was a grave danger that, if released, either one of them, or both, might interfere with witnesses. Or that someone might interfere with them fatally in case they started singing like canaries. We needed to know who else was involved. Consequently, our two prisoners were kept in custody until appearing before the magistrate on Monday morning. I instructed Kate Ebdon to take them to court and object to bail.

'I checked Roberts's form after I took his fingerprints, guv,' said Dave, appearing as Kate and I left the interview room. 'He's got a previous.'

'What for?'

'Pyramid selling, and I don't mean flogging ancient Egyptian monuments.'

'I do know what pyramid selling is, Dave.' It was a fraud as old as the hills that involved its creator persuading gullible, greedy people to invest in a wondrous scheme that promised fantastic rewards. The trouble was that, unbeknown to the punters, the 'dividends' were paid out of the investments of subsequent idiots. Such a scheme, by its very nature, was destined to collapse, but usually after the scheme's architect had disappeared with the loot.

'He got seven years,' said Dave. 'Came out two years ago and set up the Spanish Fly nightclub, probably with some of the proceeds that he'd stashed away. He was made bankrupt at the time of the trial, but the bulk of the money was never recovered.'

'How the hell did he get a licence to run a club?'

Dave said nothing, but just rubbed forefinger and thumb together. It would not be the first time that someone had been bribed to overlook certain 'indiscretions' on the part of an applicant for a licence.

We got back to Curtis Green at one o'clock, and DI Len Driscoll was waiting.

'How did you get on at Broders Road, Len?' I asked.

'It was just like an Aladdin's Cave for piss artists, guv,' said Driscoll. 'There were cases of wine all over the place. The lads are still counting it all. I don't know whether it's legit, but I've asked customs to have a look. If it's bent, I'm damned if I know how they got so much into the country without being nicked.'

'I've a feeling that it actually is legit, Len,' I said. 'Any firearms?'

'No, nothing,' said Driscoll. 'How about you?'

'Ten H and Ks, twenty assorted handguns and matching ammo,' I said. 'Not a bad morning's work.'

We now had another name in the frame. According to Patrick Hogan, the mysterious Charlie Pollard was the receiver of the firearms that Michael Roberts and company had conspired to smuggle into the country. All we had to do now was find Pollard. Hogan had suggested that he lived somewhere in the Bethnal Green area, but that didn't help much. Apart from being a large area, Bethnal Green is densely populated by the unrighteous, and we were unlikely to receive any assistance from the inhabitants thereof. I was under no illusion but that many of them had criminal records and there is, of course, a strict code of honour among thieves. Until the chips are down, that is. With any luck this might be one of those occasions.

I gave the task of finding Charlie Pollard to Colin Wilberforce in the hope that he might discover the answer on his wonderful computer. But, after fifteen minutes of intense keyboard work, he was unable to produce any match that could possibly be the Charlie Pollard we were seeking.

I next asked Kate Ebdon to see what she could do. I'm a firm believer in old-fashioned methods, like informants, and I knew that Kate, an ex-Flying Squad officer, had snouts who were many and various. I had a few informants myself, but I hadn't contacted them for some time, or they me; it was years since I'd left the Flying Squad, and I suspected that most of them were either dead, doing time or had disappeared to some safe Brazilian haven.

However, despite having given Kate that job, I decided that there was something more immediately pressing for her to do.

'I think the time has come to arrest Billy Sharpe, Kate. You've got a list of all the home addresses of Kerry Trucking's employees, haven't you?'

'Yes, I have, guv. Bear with me for a moment; they're in my office.'

'On your way back, Kate, ask Len Driscoll to come in.'

When Kate returned, followed by Driscoll, she was holding the list Sheila Armitage had obtained from Carl Thorpe, the company secretary at the hauliers.

'Sharpe lives at Tunglass Road, Fulham, guv. Number sixteen.'

I decided that this was a job for DI Driscoll. 'Len, take Dave Poole with you – he knows what Sharpe looks like – and get out to this Tunglass Road address. Then, I want you to wait for a call from Kate. Kate, you take Charlie Flynn and go to Kerry Trucking. Find out if Sharpe is there. If he is, nick him. On the other hand, he might be doing a run somewhere. Should that be the case, find out when he'll be back. If he's away we'll have to catch him when he returns. However, if he's off duty, let Len know straight away so that he can pick him up at his home address. I don't want Bligh tipping off Sharpe that we're about to feel his collar. I've still got reservations about Mister Bligh.'

'No worries, guv,' said Kate.

'Once you get the go-ahead from Kate, Len, go into Sharpe's place and have him away. But both of you keep me posted.'

'Right, guv.' Len turned to Kate. 'Let me know when you've arrived at the haulage yard at Chiswick, Kate, so I know the SP.'

It was an hour before Kate rang in from Chiswick to say that Billy Sharpe had the weekend off prior to a trip to Germany on Monday.

She managed to convey the impression that she was disappointed not to be laying hands on Sharpe. Kate enjoys arresting villains.

'I didn't tell Bligh that he'd probably have to find another driver, guv,' she added with a chuckle. 'He seemed very interested in why we wanted to talk to him again, but I told him there was nothing to worry about. I gave him some nebulous fanny about tying up loose ends. I've given Len Driscoll the heads up and he should be going in about now. In the meantime, I'll have a quick word with this Patricia Knight that Roberts said he spent Christmas Eve with.'

Ten minutes later, Driscoll reported that Sharpe wasn't at home.

'His missus said he's gone to a football match at Craven Cottage, guv. Apparently, he's an avid Fulham supporter. There's no chance of finding him inside the ground, but with any luck we might feel his collar as he leaves.'

'Yes, but I'd suggest letting him get some way away before you nick him, Len. I don't want you starting a riot all by yourself if his mates turn nasty.'

'Of course not, sir,' said Driscoll curtly, and I realized that I'd offered him unnecessary advice; Len Driscoll knew what he was doing. 'The kick-off was at three, half an hour ago, so there's at least another hour of play, plus fifteen minutes for half-time, possibly more if they run to extra time. Fulham's playing Tottenham Hotspur and it's an FA Cup match, so I don't suppose our man will leave at half-time.'

'I'll take your word for it, Len.' Not being a football fanatic, I hadn't the vaguest idea why those two particular teams should be so irresistible to the spectators that they'd stay for the whole match.

FOURTEEN

Despite Kate Ebdon's comment that she was the soul of discretion, she had meant it to be sarcastic. But she could be diplomatic when the necessity arose.

There was a coffee bar just round the corner from Coxtree Close in Chelsea. Kate settled herself with a large latte, took out her mobile phone and rang the number that Roberts had given her.

Fortunately, a woman answered the phone.

'Hello?'

'Is that Patricia Knight?' asked Kate.

'Yes, it is. Who's that?'

'I'm a police officer, Mrs Knight. Detective Inspector Ebdon of New Scotland Yard.'

'What on earth d'you want?' There was an element of apprehension in the woman's cultured reply.

'A discreet word,' said Kate. 'Is your husband there?'

'Yes, he is. He's watching the football on television, but what has that to do with you?'

'Well, let's say that it would be better if he wasn't privy to our conversation, if you get my meaning.'

'Oh God!' exclaimed the woman, suddenly realizing why Kate was being so circumspect. 'Where are you?'

'I'm in Costas coffee bar, just round the corner. Can you meet me there?'

There was a pause. 'But what'll I tell my husband?'

'You'll think of something,' said Kate.

The woman who entered the crowded coffee bar five minutes later was about thirty, and nervous. She was attired in jeans tucked into knee-high boots, a faux fur jacket and a yellow pashmina wound around her neck. She took a few minutes buying herself a coffee and, after a quick glance round, walked across to where Kate, the only woman alone, was sitting.

'I'm Patricia Knight.'

'DI Ebdon, Mrs Knight.'

'What's this all about?' asked the woman, as she sat down opposite Kate.

'I won't beat about the bush, Mrs Knight,' said Kate, 'but are you having an affair with Michael Roberts?'

Patricia Knight looked mildly affronted. 'I've never heard of anyone called Michael Roberts, and I resent the implication that—'

'Perhaps you know him better as Miguel Rodriguez, Mrs Knight, and he runs the Spanish Fly nightclub in Mayfair, or did.'

Patricia stared at Kate. 'D'you mean he's not really Spanish?'

'No, he's not. And right now, he's in custody charged with serious offences. There's also a possibility that he'll be charged with murder.'

Patricia leaned back, her face white, and for a moment Kate thought she might faint. But then she recovered.

'What has any of this to do with me, Inspector?'

'When he was interviewed with regard to the murder of a woman – about your age, as a matter of fact – he claimed to have spent the evening of Christmas Eve with you in a bedroom at his club. Is that correct?'

There was a long pause before Patricia Knight replied. 'Yes, that's right, I did. Oh God, what'll happen if my husband finds out?'

'Roberts seemed to think your husband might murder you.' Kate smiled; but she had little time for adulterous wives.

Patricia Knight obviously didn't take the threat seriously. 'Will I have to go to court or anything like that?' she asked. 'I mean, will it get into the papers?'

'I shouldn't think so,' said Kate, 'but we might need a statement from you.' She handed the woman a card. 'Ring me on that number in a couple of days' time, and I'll let you know.'

'Thank you,' said Patricia, 'for being so discreet.'

'Incidentally, how did you manage to meet Roberts on Christmas Eve? What did you tell your husband?'

'He wasn't at home. He's an airline pilot, long haul, and he didn't get home until the afternoon of Christmas Day.' Patricia paused. 'You're Australian, aren't you?'

'Got it in one, mate,' said Kate.

DI Driscoll and DS Dave Poole had just parked their unmarked police car in Stevenage Road, home of Fulham Football Club, when they were approached by a policeman.

'You can't park here, mate,' said the PC, glaring at the car's driver.

'As a matter of fact, *Constable*, I've got this special parking permit,' said Dave Poole, and thrust his warrant card under the PC's nose.

'Oh, sorry, Skip,' said the policeman, and wandered away to badger some unfortunate who thought he could park his car right outside the main entrance to the ground.

It was just past five o'clock before the first of the home-going crowd began to emerge from the stadium.

'There he is, guv, that's Sharpe.' Dave pointed to a man who was in earnest conversation with another fan as the pair left one of the exits. They stopped outside the football club's shop and continued talking. Five minutes later, they split up, making their way along Stevenage Road in opposite directions.

Dave waited until Sharpe had turned into Harbord Street before starting the engine and slowly following him. When their quarry was almost at Fulham Palace Road, Dave accelerated and stopped alongside him.

'Billy Sharpe,' said Driscoll, as he leaped out of the car, 'I'm arresting you on suspicion of trafficking in illegal firearms.'

'Do what?' Sharpe was clearly stunned by the arrival of the police and the swiftness of his arrest, and looked around as though seeking assistance from other fans.

Driscoll opened the rear door of the car and bundled Sharpe into it before taking the seat next to him. 'You do not have to say anything, but it may harm your defence . . .' he began, and quickly reeled off the rest of the caution.

'I dunno what you're on about,' protested Sharpe as Driscoll handcuffed him. It was a lame and predictable response.

'You'll soon find out,' said Dave, as he drove off. 'Who won?'

'Spurs,' said Sharpe miserably.

'Not your day, is it,' said Dave, and glanced at Driscoll through the driving mirror. 'Charing Cross nick, guv?' he asked.

'That'll do nicely,' said Driscoll, and phoned Curtis Green to tell Wilberforce that Sharpe was on his way to the police station in Agar Street off the Strand.

I didn't have a lot to say to Sharpe; we had much of the evidence we needed to convict him, or so I hoped. He had lied about his stops on his drive up from Dover and that, to my mind, was good enough to confirm that he knew all about the gunrunning.

'What's this all about?' demanded Sharpe truculently.

'Yesterday, traffic officers inspected your tachograph when you returned to the yard at Kerry Trucking,' I began.

'So?'

'You stated that you had delivered tyres somewhere in Folkestone, but—'

'I did,' said Sharpe.

'Just listen,' I said. 'We know that you didn't go into Folkestone, and we know that you weren't carrying tyres. Furthermore, you claimed to have stopped at a quarter past ten in Borough High Street for breakfast, and at eleven fifteen on Victoria Embankment for a pee.'

'Yeah, well, I did.' Sharpe's response was unconvincing and he now appeared a little more apprehensive than when I'd started. It was slowly dawning on him that we knew he was lying, but he wasn't bright enough to work out how we knew.

'In fact your ten fifteen stop was in Cantard Street, Walworth,' I continued, 'and your eleven fifteen stop was at Broders Road, Kennington.'

'That's a lie.'

'I know all this, Billy, because you were followed right across France, and from Dover all the way to Chiswick,' I said, ignoring his pathetic attempt to distance himself from any involvement. 'We know exactly where you stopped, and we now know why. This morning we raided the premises at Cantard Street where we found a quantity of illegally imported firearms. During the course of that search, we arrested Michael Roberts, also known as Miguel Rodriguez, and we nicked Patrick Hogan as well. But, like you, they seem to be go-betweens.'

Sharpe had paled significantly, and was now sweating almost feverishly. But he remained silent, probably anticipating the clang of a prison cell door.

'I realize that you're just a pawn in all this, Billy,' I said, 'but unless we lay hands on the principals, you, Roberts and Hogan are likely to go down for the full whack.' That wasn't strictly true; they'd probably get a substantial sentence anyway, including Sharpe, particularly if the Crown Prosecution Service decided to deploy one of several anti-terrorism statutes available to it.

'But I was only driving the rig,' protested Sharpe. He had rapidly grasped the significance of the predicament in which he now found himself.

'I was only obeying orders,' muttered Dave, half to himself. 'That's the oldest excuse in the book, Billy. It's called the Nuremberg defence. So, who's the Mr Big?' he asked. 'Who's the guy at the top of the heap?'

'I don't know,' protested Sharpe. 'But if what you're saying about guns is true, it's heavy business, innit? They're the sort of people who'd bloody kill anyone they thought had grassed,' he complained. 'But I don't know nothing, so I can't tell you what I don't know.'

'I don't think you're being straight with us, Billy, keeping shtum,' said Dave, 'but you'll probably have twenty years to think about whether you've made the right decision,' he added casually, grossly exaggerating the length of gaol time to which Sharpe might be sentenced. 'Matter for you really.'

Sharpe spent some time pondering the prospect of emerging from prison just in time to draw his state pension. 'It's some geezer called Charlie Pollard, but I never met him,' he said eventually.

'And where does this Pollard live?' I asked. Patrick Hogan had already given us the name, and had told us that he thought Pollard lived in the Bethnal Green area. But no one seemed to have met this shadowy figure.

'Bethnal Green,' said Sharpe, somewhat reluctantly.

'It's a big place,' said Dave, who had been born there and knew the area thoroughly. 'Whereabouts?'

'I think it's in Argus Road.'

'How did you know that?'

'I heard Bligh let it slip one day. I was just outside the office and he was on the blower to someone.'

That was indeed a revelation. As I'd mentioned earlier, I'd harboured suspicions about Bernard Bligh from the outset and now Billy Sharpe had more or less confirmed them.

'You took over from a guy called Dixon, Gary Dixon, when he got the sack about three months ago,' said Dave.

'Did I? Never heard of him,' said Sharpe.

'Who gave you the job?'

'Mrs Hammond.'

'And did Mrs Hammond tell you about her little gunrunning operation?'

'No, I never knew nothing about guns. She said it was to do a special run from time to time to pick up wine.'

That might just be the truth. Sharpe had said that Marcel Lebrun's people had told him to go for a meal while they loaded the vehicle, and it was conceivable that they'd secreted the firearms behind the false panel during Sharpe's absence.

'Were you present when your vehicle was unloaded at Cantard Street, Billy?' asked Dave.

'No, they told me to push off and get some breakfast while they took care of it.'

That had been confirmed by the surveillance team that had followed Sharpe from Dover.

'If it was all legit, then, why did you lie about where you'd stopped?'

'Mrs Hammond told me I always had to do that because she didn't want Bligh knowing, seeing as how he wasn't in on the wine business.'

'But Mrs Hammond's dead,' said Dave. 'So who took over running the wine business after she was murdered?'

This time, Sharpe didn't hesitate. 'That bloke called Roberts you mentioned just now,' he said.

'So, now we come to the big question, Billy,' I said. 'Who murdered Mrs Hammond?'

'Well, you needn't look at me,' said Sharpe, combining relief with triumph in his voice. 'It weren't nothing to do with me.'

'Just for the record, Billy, where were you on Christmas Eve?' asked Dave.

Sharpe grinned. 'Having it off with a German bird I met in a nightclub during a stopover in Berlin. And if you want her name, it was Mia Steinbrück, and she was a bit of all right.'

'Address?' demanded Dave.

'She had a flat over some sort of Asian market shop in Dircksenstrasse,' said Sharpe triumphantly. 'I remember that because Mia went downstairs and bought the makings of a curry supper. Nothing like a bit of curry for getting a bird hotted up,' he added.

If Sharpe was telling the truth, I'd be able to check it with a *hauptkommissar* I knew in the Berlin police, but I was fairly

certain that Sharpe would not have been so specific if he had
been lying.

I'd told Sharpe that he was a pawn in Kerry Hammond's
operation, and it was beginning to look that way. He certainly
appeared not to know anything about the illegal importation of
firearms, and that we knew that he'd been sidelined during the
loading and unloading tended to confirm it. On the basis of our
conversation I got the impression that he was too thick to be
trusted with details of the operation, and Kerry had probably
come to the same conclusion. After all, the fewer people who
knew what was going on, the less the chance that the operation
would be compromised.

It was now half past seven and we needed to effect the arrests of
the mysterious Charlie Pollard, and of Bernard Bligh who clearly
knew more than he'd been telling.

Once more, I assembled a team.

I decided that Kate Ebdon, Dave Poole and I would go to Argus
Road, Bethnal Green. We didn't know which house was occupied
by Charlie Pollard, but a few resourceful local enquiries would
likely give us the information we required. The only possible hitch,
given that it was Saturday evening, was that Pollard might be out,
but it was a chance we'd have to take. On the other hand it was
on the cards that Pollard had already heard of the arrests of Roberts,
Hogan and Sharpe, and had done a runner. The intelligence grape-
vine of the underworld is extremely efficient when liberty is at
stake.

In the meantime, I assigned DI Driscoll to pick up Bernard Bligh
who, by now, was probably at home in Carmen Avenue, Hatton.

'If this guy Pollard is a villains' armourer, guv,' said Dave,
'shouldn't we have some armed support?'

'Not this time, Dave. We'll get tooled up ourselves.'

'But we need authority for that, and I somehow doubt that the
commander—'

'I've thought of that, Dave,' I said, 'but I've had an idea.'

'Good luck, sir!' said Dave.

I went into my office and telephoned the DAC at home.

'I've tried to get hold of the commander, sir,' I lied, 'but I think
he must be out.'

'That's all right, Harry,' said the DAC. 'What's the problem?'

I explained, as briefly as possible, what we were about to do and why.

There was no hesitation. 'Go ahead, Harry, but keep your heads down and try not to shoot any innocent bystanders.'

'Not much chance of finding any innocents in Bethnal Green, guv'nor,' I said.

'I'll sign the authorization on Monday, Harry,' said the DAC, 'And I'll send it over to your office first thing.'

That satisfied me. I knew that the DAC wouldn't renege on his undertaking if it all went pear shaped, unlike some senior officers I'd known.

I returned to the incident room and arranged for the issue of three Glock automatic pistols from our armoury.

It was past eight o'clock by the time we found ourselves in Argus Road, Bethnal Green. To my surprise, it proved to be a street of gentrified houses, but we still didn't know which of them was occupied by Charlie Pollard.

That problem, however, was solved by the ever-resourceful Dave Poole. Seeing a dreadlocked black man lolloping down to the road towards us, Dave alighted from the car.

'Hey, bro, which is Charlie Pollard's flop?'

'Number fifteen, bro,' said the man, without breaking step, and waved vaguely at a house somewhere behind him.

The three of us, Kate, Dave and I, walked down the road, and approached the front door of Charlie Pollard's house. As I rang the bell, Dave drew his Glock automatic and held it down by his side, out of sight.

The door was answered by an attractive young woman, attired in jeans and a sweater. I reckoned she was in her mid-twenties.

'Hello,' said the girl. 'Can I help you?'

For a brief moment, I wondered if we'd been misled into believing that Charlie Pollard, reputed armourer to the underworld, lived here.

'I'm looking for Charlie Pollard, miss,' I said.

'Who are you?'

'We're police officers,' I said.

The young woman leaned back while still holding on to the door. 'Charlie, there are some police officers here to talk to you,' she shouted. 'Have you been speeding again?' she added. Turning to face us, she smiled. 'Just coming.'

Dave moved alongside me, and I sensed that his grip on his Glock was tightening. I unbuttoned my jacket to give myself faster access to my pistol, should I need it.

'I'm Charlie Pollard. What's the problem?' asked the thirty-something blonde woman who appeared at the door.

FIFTEEN

'**Y**ou're Charlie Pollard?' Confronted by this shapely, attractive woman, I found it difficult to disguise my astonishment. Over the years, I'd met many women connected with the criminal world, but the only ones who looked like her were either West End villains' birds or high-class prostitutes. Instinctively, I felt that this woman didn't fit into either of those categories.

'Yes, I am. Is it something to do with my car? What exactly is it that you want?' An element of impatience crept into the woman's voice; my surprise at being wrong-footed had made me pause for too long.

'May we come in?' I asked.

'Of course.' There was no hesitation, and Charlie Pollard held the door wide open.

Dave turned away and discreetly re-holstered his Glock.

Although the room into which the woman conducted us was comfortably and tastefully furnished, it was apparent that it had not cost a great deal of money.

'I'm Detective Chief Inspector Brock of Scotland Yard,' I said, and introduced Kate and Dave.

'Please take a seat,' said Charlie. Her gaze lingered on Kate Ebdon longer than on Dave Poole who was the usual object of female admiration. 'You've met my friend Erica Foster, of course.'

Erica smiled in our direction, turned off the television, and squatted on a beanbag next to it.

'How well d'you know the Spanish Fly?' I asked.

'The what?' Charlie giggled and shot a sideways glance at Erica. 'Are you talking about the aphrodisiac?' she asked, and laughed openly.

'It's a nightclub in the West End,' I said, immediately sensing that this interview was going to be an uphill struggle.

'I'm sorry, but I've never heard of it.'

'Does the name Miguel Rodriguez, otherwise known as Michael Roberts, mean anything to you?'

'No. Should it?'

'Or Patrick Hogan, Billy Sharpe, Gary Dixon or Bernard Bligh?'

Charlie Pollard laughed again. 'What is this, twenty questions? Do I get to phone a friend?'

'Early this morning, Miss Pollard . . . it is *Miss* Pollard, isn't it?'

'Yes, it is, if that has anything to do with our conversation. But I'd rather you called me Charlie.'

'Were you christened Charlie, or is your name actually Charlotte?'

'I wasn't christened, but my given name is Charlie, and that's what's on my passport, and all my other documents.'

'Early this morning,' I said, 'we arrested Roberts and Hogan—'

'Look, Chief Inspector . . .' began Charlie patiently and paused. 'It is chief inspector, isn't it?'

'Yes, it is,' I said.

'None of those names means a thing to me and, to say the least, I'm puzzled as to why you're telling me all this.'

'They were arrested for being involved in the illegal importation of firearms. Eventually, one of them stated, under caution, that it was you he worked for, and you who received those weapons. This has subsequently been confirmed by a number of other people to whom we have spoken.'

Charlie Pollard stared at me with an expression combining perplexity with amusement, but nothing that conveyed guilt. 'Is this some kind of a joke?' she asked eventually.

'I can assure you, Miss Pollard, that it's no laughing matter.'

'I asked you to call me Charlie. Well, if you think I've got anything to do with guns, have a look round. Anywhere you like.' She circled a hand in the air, as if to encompass the entire house. 'But I'll say it again: I haven't the faintest idea what you're talking about, and I find the entire allegation preposterous. In fact, I really think it's time I talked to a solicitor.'

'Are you familiar with the name Kerry Hammond?' I asked, determined to finish what I'd come here to do.

'No, I'm not,' snapped Charlie. It was obvious that she was beginning to get annoyed with my persistent questioning.

'What do you do for a living, Charlie?' asked Kate.

'I'm a school teacher,' said Charlie with a smile, her gaze resting on Kate for longer than seemed necessary.

'And before you ask,' chimed in Erica Foster, 'I'm an accountant.'

To put it mildly, it was beginning to look as though I'd been the recipient of false information. The thing that intrigued me was why Charlie Pollard's name should have been fed to me as an arms dealer by more than one person. I was starting to think that I'd been made the butt of a villain's elaborate joke. I just couldn't wait to interview Messrs Roberts, Hogan and Sharpe again.

'I'm sorry that we bothered you, Charlie,' I said. 'We've clearly been misinformed.'

'Not at all, Chief Inspector. You've quite brightened up our Saturday evening. It'll be something to tell our friends over dinner.'

We piled into our car and drove off. I was not in the best of moods. Perhaps we'd got the wrong Charlie Pollard, and that there was actually a man of the same name in the area. But Billy Sharpe was adamant that Argus Road was the address he had heard Bernard Bligh mention on the telephone.

Erica Foster twitched a gap in the curtains, and peered out.

'They've gone, Charlie.'

'D'you think they suspected anything, lover?'

'Nah!' said Erica derisively. 'They're just a bunch of plods. Anyway, who cares about women having it off together? It's not illegal.'

'Maybe,' said Charlie, 'but I'd rather my boss didn't find out.'

'D'you mean the headmistress?' asked Erica, and they both laughed.

I had now been working since about five o'clock this morning. But still the day wasn't over. When we got back to Curtis Green, there was a message waiting to say that DI Driscoll had arrested Bernard Bligh and he was in custody at Charing Cross police station.

'Just the man I want to talk to,' I said. 'Dave, you're with me.'

'I've just been dragged from my home like a common criminal, and I want to know why I've been arrested.' Bligh, who was almost incandescent with rage, stood up as Dave and I entered the interview room.

'Sit down, Mr Bligh.' Dave and I sat down on the opposite side of the table. 'I've just been to number fifteen Argus Road, Bethnal Green, where I interviewed a suspect named Pollard.' At this stage,

I had no intention of revealing that Pollard was a woman, and a damned attractive one at that.

'Is that supposed to mean something to me?' asked Bligh, with a sneer.

'But you knew that that's where Pollard lives.'

'I know nothing of the sort,' retorted Bligh.

'So far,' I continued, 'we've arrested Michael Roberts, who runs the Spanish Fly nightclub under the name of Miguel Rodriguez, and Patrick Hogan, Billy Sharpe and Gary Dixon.'

'So what?'

'And you have been arrested for being concerned with them in smuggling firearms into the country.'

'That's bloody nonsense. I don't know a damned thing about any firearms. If that's what Dixon and Sharpe were up to, I don't know anything about it. And I've never heard of the other two you mentioned.' Bligh paused. 'Except that you mentioned Rodriguez' name to me some time ago, but I told you then that I didn't know him.'

'When Billy Sharpe was arrested, he was very quick to tell me that he'd overheard you on the telephone one day, and that during the course of your conversation you'd mentioned Pollard's address.'

'He's a lying little bastard.'

'That may be so, but on this occasion I believed him.'

'Pollard had certainly heard of you,' put in Dave, gilding the lily quite outrageously.

'Look, all right, so I knew about Pollard, but I didn't know she had anything to do with smuggling.'

It was, I supposed, a natural reaction to my allegation that he'd been conspiring with those we had in custody.

'You said "she",' Dave continued. 'You knew that Pollard was a woman, then.'

'How did you come to know of her?' I asked, taking back the questioning from Dave.

'She was one of Kerry's lesbian mates.'

'Are you saying that Kerry Hammond was bisexual?'

'Yes, that's exactly what I'm saying. Bloody disgusting, I call it. That woman was sex mad. She even tried it on with me. She'd go after anything in trousers or, better still, out of them. It was a way of life to her.'

'Just how much d'you know about Charlie Pollard, Mr Bligh?'

'Nothing more than I've told you.'

'Who were you telephoning when Sharpe overheard you?' asked Dave.

'Her husband. I thought it was time he knew what she was getting up to.'

That sounded like sheer spite and may have had something to do with the ownership of Kerry Trucking rather than gunrunning. Bligh had made no secret of the fact that he felt he should've taken over the company when Dick Lucas was killed. And he was even more annoyed that control of the haulage company had passed to Nick Hammond on Kerry's death.

'What was his reaction?'

'He said he knew about it, and he didn't care. To be perfectly honest, I think Nick Hammond's only interest was in getting a slice of the company. And now he's bloody well got it.'

'Are you suggesting that Hammond had something to do with his wife's murder?' I asked.

Bligh shrugged. 'Your guess is as good as mine, Chief Inspector, but I did hear that his estate agent's business was going downhill. I think I told you before that Kerry had put some money into it.'

But Bligh didn't know that Hammond's estate agency was merely a front for his more arcane occupation. Not that it mattered, one way or the other.

'How did you know that Pollard was Kerry's lover?' I asked.

'I guessed. Charlie Pollard rang the office one day and asked for Kerry when she wasn't there. She asked me to pass on a message.'

'What was the message?'

'She said that she and Kerry were spending a naughty week together at an all-girls' nudist colony in Switzerland, and that Kerry was not to forget her passport. Sounded a bit lame to me – Kerry's been abroad often enough not to forget her passport – and I wondered if this woman wanted me to know about Kerry's sexual habits.'

'How did you know Charlie Pollard's address?'

'I found it in Kerry's address book. She'd left it in her office.'

So, Kerry had more than one address book. The one we'd taken from her house in Barnes on the night of her murder did not contain an entry for Charlie Pollard.

'I suppose that address book isn't still in the office, is it?' I asked hopefully.

'Shouldn't think so. Kerry seemed in quite a panic about it when she turned up the next day. She said she thought she'd lost it.'

That was a blow, but not a surprise, given that it might've contained some other names that were connected to the firearms business. I made a mental note to visit Nick Hammond again, to see if he knew.

'I shall admit you to police bail, Mr Bligh,' I said, 'to return to this police station in one month, unless you hear otherwise.'

'What for? I had nothing to do with this business.' Bligh stood up. 'You'll be hearing from my solicitors about this,' he said angrily.

'I dare say,' I said, but it was a threat I'd heard many times before. And usually nothing ever came of it.

It was now ten o'clock and it had been a long day.

'Tomorrow morning, Dave, I want Gary Dixon brought in here. I think he knows more than he's told us so far.'

'It's Sunday tomorrow, guv,' said Dave.

'That's all right,' I said. 'I don't suppose he's a churchgoer.'

'Just as well I'm not, either,' muttered Dave.

At ten o'clock on Sunday morning, Dave and I joined Gary Dixon in the interview room at Charing Cross police station. He was clearly unhappy at being there, and that made three of us.

'D'you still maintain that you've no idea who assaulted you, Gary?' I began. 'Was it Roberts and Hogan?'

'I've told you already, I don't bloody well know.'

'Would it loosen your tongue if I told you that they're both in custody, and won't be getting bail?' asked Dave.

'What you nicked them for?'

'Unlawful possession of firearms, and sundry other offences,' continued Dave. 'We can easily add GBH with intent to the ever-lengthening list of charges.'

'I never saw their faces.' Dixon was obviously not risking it. But as a former prison inmate, he knew that he could probably be got at more easily in prison than out of it. And he seemed to be in little doubt that prison is where he'd end up.

'Did Kerry Hammond ever mention a woman called Charlie Pollard, Gary?' I asked.

'Yeah. Kerry was having it off with her. She liked doing it with a bird as well as with a bloke.'

'How did you know that?'

'She told me and said that it turned men on. I asked if I could watch, but she drew the line at that.'

'Did she ever mention anything about Pollard in connection with the business?'

'What business?'

'Kerry Trucking, of course.' I wasn't sure whether Dixon was being devious or obtuse.

'Nah, I don't think so. Oh, hang on a mo, though. Yeah, she did say something about Charlie Pollard having one of them self-storage places she sometimes used.'

'That Kerry sometimes used?'

'Yeah, that's what I said, weren't it?'

'Where was this lock-up, Gary?' asked Dave.

'Ah, now you're asking,' said Dixon, running a hand round his unshaven chin.

'That is indeed what I'm asking,' said Dave patiently.

'Yeah, got it. It's in Sastow Road, Bethnal Green.'

'And she told you that?' Dave was having some difficulty in believing that Kerry would've made such a careless admission.

'Yeah.'

'Did you ever go there?'

'Nah.'

'Right,' I said, 'off you go, Gary. And you're still on bail.'

'Bloody charming, that is,' muttered Dixon as he limped from the interview room.

At last, it looked as though we were getting somewhere with the firearms enquiry, but we were still not moving any closer to discovering Kerry Hammond's killer.

I knew that attempting to obtain a search warrant from a magistrate on a Sunday morning was a non-starter. Instead, I'd singled out the local detective superintendent at his home and told him that we suspected the existence of explosives at the lock-up in Sastow Road.

'It is a matter of some urgency, guv'nor,' I'd said, adding the requisite legal proviso to my application.

The superintendent had laughed. 'I'm retiring in a couple of weeks' time, Harry, and I couldn't care less about the legal niceties. So you don't have to give me a load of old moody.' And with that pithy comment, he cheerfully signed a written order to search.

It was midday by the time I arrived at Sastow Road, Bethnal Green. I had Kate Ebdon, Dave and Nicola Chance with me, and half a uniformed serial of the local Territorial Support Group.

There were one or two dodgy-looking individuals working in their respective stores, and our arrival seemed quite to upset their Sunday. I regretted that I didn't have the time to take a look at what they were up to because I'm sure it would've cleared up a few burglaries, blaggings and other assorted villainy.

We found the guy in charge, who showed us to the store that Charlie Pollard had hired, and one of the TSG lads took off the padlock with bolt cutters.

There was not much in the store, but what there was proved sufficient. Four boxes contained a total of twenty-four handguns in pristine condition, all of which were wrapped in oilskin.

I left the TSG sergeant and his team in charge of our find, and told him to arrange for an armed escort to take the weapons to Lambeth.

'And now,' I said, 'we will arrest Charlie Pollard.'

'Oh, not you again.' Charlie Pollard, barefooted and wearing a kaftan, answered the door. 'We're in the middle of having lunch,' she protested.

'Charlie Pollard,' I said, stepping into the hall, 'I am arresting you for the constructive possession of twenty-four automatic pistols. You do not have to say anything, but it may harm your defence if when questioned you do not mention now something you later rely on in court. Anything you do say will be given in evidence.'

Kate Ebdon stepped forward and laid a hand on Charlie's arm as a token of arrest.

'What the hell are you talking about?' screamed Charlie. 'I haven't got any pistols. Have you gone raving mad?' She attempted to shake Kate's hand away from her arm. 'Leave me alone,' she cried.

'Inspector Ebdon will escort you to your bedroom, Miss Pollard,' I said, 'and you can change into something more suitable.'

'Unless you want to come like that, ducky,' said Kate, waving a hand at the woman's kaftan.

'What on earth's happening?' demanded Erica Foster angrily, who'd appeared in the hall to see what all the fuss was about. 'We're having lunch.'

'I should stay out of this if you want to be a clever little sheila,' said Kate.

'I want a lawyer, and I want one now,' shouted Charlie and, breaking away from Kate's grasp, ran into the sitting room, presumably with the intention of making a phone call.

'You'll have every opportunity to send for a solicitor from the police station,' I said to the woman's retreating back.

'Well, I'm not coming, and that's that,' exclaimed Charlie.

Kate raced after Charlie and, seizing her in a crippling hammerlock and bar, forced her up against the wall by the door. 'Don't be a drongo, mate,' she said, putting her mouth close to Charlie's ear. 'You're coming with us, like it or not. But if you want to make a blue of it, I'll get my big sergeant here to pick you up and carry you out. Not that I couldn't do it myself, but I wouldn't give you the pleasure.'

Charlie Pollard twisted her head round to glance apprehensively at Dave. 'I'll go up and get changed,' she said.

'Good thinking,' said Kate, and followed the woman upstairs.

In the meantime, Dave and I sat down and waited.

'You've got it all wrong, you know. Charlie doesn't know anything about guns,' said Erica.

It was a comment that we ignored, mainly because I didn't think it was true.

Had Charlie Pollard not made such a fight of it, I might've believed her to be an innocent party in all this.

But that apart, now that I'd arrested her, she would have to be taken to a police station, and the nearest was at Victoria Park Square in Bethnal Green. I left Dave and Nicola behind to conduct a thorough search of the Argus Road house.

'We searched your store in Sastow Road earlier today,' I began, once Kate and I were settled in the interview room with Charlie Pollard.

'That place is nothing to do with me,' said Charlie with a churl-ishness that attempted to disguise her apprehension.

'But it's rented in your name,' said Kate. 'And in it, we found the twenty-four automatic pistols that Mr Brock mentioned earlier.'

'I don't care what he says you found,' said Charlie, 'but I've never been there.'

'If that's the case, why did you rent it?'

There was a long pause, during which time Charlie fiddled with her necklace. 'Because Kerry asked me to,' she said eventually.

'You do know Kerry Hammond, then,' I said. 'When I asked you previously, you said you didn't.'

Charlie shrugged. 'So I lied.'

'Did Kerry say why she wanted this storeroom?'

'She said she wanted to keep some old furniture there. She said she wasn't using it any more, but didn't want to get rid of it.'

'But Kerry Hammond lived in Barnes. Didn't it strike you as odd that she should want to keep furniture in a store that was some thirteen miles away?'

'I thought it was a bit strange and I wondered why she didn't rent it in her own name, but it was her business.' Charlie paused. 'But now I know. She wanted to keep guns in it.' Suddenly the full impact of Kerry Hammond's betrayal became apparent to Charlie Pollard. 'That bitch bloody well framed me,' she exclaimed furiously.

I was inclined to agree, but kept that opinion to myself until I'd discovered *why* Kerry should've wanted to frame Charlie. 'Did you ever visit the storeroom?' I asked.

'No, never.'

'What exactly was your relationship with Kerry Hammond?' asked Kate.

'We were lovers,' said Charlie. 'Why? Are you interested in a little get together?'

Kate just laughed. 'You said "were". Does that mean that the relationship ended before she died?'

'Died?' Charlie looked aghast. 'What d'you mean?'

'Kerry Hammond was murdered on Christmas Eve at Heathrow Airport,' I said.

'Oh my God, how awful,' said Charlie.

'When did you split up with her?

'In November. She said she'd found someone else.'

'I understand that you and Kerry went to a nudist colony in Switzerland on one occasion,' I said.

Charlie laughed nervously. 'Whatever gave you that idea?'

'A conversation you had some time ago with Bernard Bligh at Kerry Trucking.'

'Yes, well, it wasn't true. I was just trying to make trouble for her because she'd ditched me. I knew she was the boss of this big company, and I thought I'd put the bubble in to get back at her. But I'm sorry I did it, now that you tell me she's dead.'

There was little else to be gained by questioning the woman any further, at least at present.

'Very well, Miss Pollard, you'll be bailed to report to Charing Cross police station in one month, unless we send for you earlier. Meanwhile, further enquiries will be made in connection with the weapons we found at Sastow Road.'

'But I knew nothing about the guns,' protested Charlie. 'You've got to believe me. What would I want with guns? It was all to do with Kerry, the bitch.'

SIXTEEN

Nicholas Hammond was at home when Kate and I called at Elite Drive on the Sunday evening. He was casually dressed in rust-coloured trousers and a London Welsh rugby shirt, although I doubted he was a member of that prestigious club; he hadn't the physique. He was holding a copy of yesterday's *Guardian*; presumably he was catching up on old news in a paper I wasn't surprised to find that he read.

'Have you discovered who murdered my wife yet, Chief Inspector?' he asked, tucking the newspaper under his arm.

'Not yet,' I said, as Hammond showed us into his sitting room. 'But I have one or two questions to put to you.'

'Fire away.' Hammond waved a hand at the armchairs. 'Do sit down. May I get you a drink?' he enquired, as he took off his horn-rimmed spectacles. He made to slip them into the pocket of his shirt, only to realize that there was no pocket. He fiddled aimlessly with them before putting them on a table.

'No thanks. By the way, this is Detective Inspector Ebdon,' I said, indicating Kate.

'How d'you do, Inspector?' Hammond nodded briefly in Kate's direction.

'Ripper, thanks,' replied Kate who, despite years in England, had yet to grow accustomed to that quintessential English greeting.

Hammond looked surprised at Kate's response; he obviously had as much trouble with Australian vernacular as I did.

'Were you aware that your wife was conducting a lesbian affair with a woman called Charlie Pollard?' I could see no point in pussyfooting around the reason for our visit. Anyway, I wanted to check whether Bernard Bligh had in fact told Hammond of the relationship.

'Yes, I knew all about that. As a matter of fact, Bligh made a point of telephoning me one day to tell me about Kerry's affair with her. I don't know why he should have felt it necessary to inform me; spite of some sort, I suppose. I know he resented the

fact that Kerry had taken control of the business when her first
husband died, and I think he derived a measure of delight at knowing
something he thought I wasn't aware of. But I knew already, and
the Pollard woman wasn't the first. Before that she had a fling with
someone called Erica Foster.' Hammond was quite unembarrassed
by his disclosure, and ran a hand over the arm of his chair, as if
caressing it.

That was an interesting revelation. Charlie Pollard had told us
of her sexual relationship when we'd interviewed her, but had said
nothing about Hammond knowing. But perhaps she didn't know
that he knew. If she was as vindictive about Kerry as she'd implied,
I'd've thought she'd've told the husband rather than Bligh. That
Erica hadn't mentioned it either really came as no surprise.

'Didn't it concern you?'

'That she was bisexual? Not really, no.' Hammond spoke in an
offhand sort of way. 'To tell you the truth, Kerry and I didn't have
much of a marriage; in fact, it didn't take long for either of us to
realize that getting married had been a terrible mistake. As a consequence each of us tended to go our own way, if you take my
meaning.'

'Were you surprised that Kerry had left you the haulage business
in her will?' I asked.

'Very surprised, yes. Mind you, we'd never thought much about
dying and wills and things like that. As with most people of our
age it wasn't something that was uppermost in our minds; it was
all something that was going to happen in the distant future.'

'Tell me what you know about your late wife's relationship with
Charlie Pollard, Mr Hammond.'

'There's not much to tell. She told me about it one day after
we'd had a bit of a disagreement. "Threw it in my face," is the
common term, I think, but at the time I couldn't've cared less. For
some months, I'd been involved with a rather attractive girl who
worked in my department at . . . well, you know where.'

It was typical of a Security Service officer that, even though
he knew that I knew where he worked, he still found himself
unable to mention its title aloud.

'Talking of which, Mr Hammond,' I said, 'was your wife aware
of your clandestine occupation?'

'Good heavens no!' Hammond sounded genuinely shocked at the

very idea that he should have told his wife what he really did for a living. 'In the Service we tend not to tell even our nearest and dearest what we do.' He shot a glance at Kate, presumably wondering if she'd seen through his euphemism. Not that he seemed to care any more.

'Nearest and dearest' was an interesting phrase for Hammond to have used; his wife might have been his nearest, but from what he'd said earlier, she was certainly not his dearest. And presumably Kerry was persuaded to invest in his failing estate agency so that she wouldn't query where the money had come from if MI5 had injected capital. It seemed a complicated way to carry on, and a quite unnecessary one in my view.

'Are you still involved with this woman from your office?'

'Actually, my section head had a quiet word in my ear. He said that the Service strongly disapproved of extramarital relationships, especially with someone who worked in the same office. I'm afraid she was transferred elsewhere as a result of our rather obvious liaison. But we still meet whenever we can; most of the time she comes here, but occasionally we stay at a hotel.'

'Was that the woman called Natasha Ellis you introduced us to the last time we were here?'

'Yes, it was,' said Hammond promptly. 'She was going to stay the night on that occasion, but I suppose she took fright when you turned up. She probably thought it unseemly for anyone to suspect that she was sleeping with a recently widowed man. She's very discreet. Well, she has to be; she's married as well.'

Hammond didn't seem to care about revealing details of his sexual adventures or those of Kerry, but I was not altogether surprised by his openness. Over the years, I'd found that people will happily discuss their sex life with a complete stranger while jealously guarding it from friends and family.

'We've uncovered evidence that your late wife was involved in gunrunning, Mr Hammond,' said Kate, speaking for the first time.

'*What?*' Hammond's jaw dropped. 'You must be joking, surely?' Kate's statement, and the direct way in which she had made it, had clearly shocked him, and he passed a hand across his brow. The gesture was almost theatrical. 'How the hell could she have been doing that under my very nose?' As the spectre of terrorism entered his mind, I imagined that he was concerned that his wife had been engaged in something that was justifiably within the purview of his organization. Therefore, as a Security Service officer, he should have known about it. And secondly, he was probably contemplating the embarrassment it would cause him once that fact became known to his superiors. 'I suppose there's no doubt.'

'None whatsoever,' continued Kate, with more confidence than I felt. 'Furthermore, she involved Charlie Pollard in her enterprise.'

'Mind you, I'm beginning to think that Miss Pollard was unaware of this whole business,' I commented. That was true. The more I looked into the matter of the smuggled firearms, the more I was inclined to the view that Charlie Pollard had known nothing about the real reason for Kerry persuading her to hire the self-storage facility in Bethnal Green.

That Kerry Hammond had persuaded Charlie to rent the lock-up was an example of her deviousness. No doubt Kerry's thinking was that if the wheel came off – and it had – it would deflect suspicion from her. And perhaps, in her innocence, Charlie had just complied with Kerry's request without enquiring too deeply into what was, by any standards, a somewhat specious reason for wanting a store room miles away in Bethnal Green.

'D'you think that someone involved in this gunrunning was responsible for Kerry's murder, Chief Inspector?' The question was put wearily, and Hammond suddenly sounded very depressed at this latest revelation about his dead wife.

'It's possible,' I said cautiously. I was not about to tell him that several people were in custody in connection with the matter. I had yet to rule out the possibility that Hammond himself had had some hand in his wife's murder, despite his apparent indifference to her infidelity. Neither was I convinced that Natasha Ellis was the attractive woman from his department that he'd mentioned; MI5 officers tend to be secretive even when there's no need. Furthermore, it would not be first time that an outraged husband, upon discovering that his wife was a lesbian, had read into it some inadequacy on his part, and had murdered her; either from disgust or jealousy.

'I think it's more than possible,' said Hammond. 'In fact, I'd go so far as to suggest it's highly likely. From what little I know of gunrunning, there are some very unsavoury people involved in it.'

'Have you met Bernard Bligh?' I asked. 'I know you've spoken to him on the phone, but have ever met him in person?'

'Yes, at one of the firm's Christmas parties.'

That, at least, confirmed what Bligh had told me, and I was beginning to suspect that he genuinely knew nothing about the firearms racket in which Kerry had been involved. But that still didn't solve the question of the wine importation; there was something odd about that business, but right now it took second place in our investigation. Nevertheless, it prompted a thought.

'Did you know that Kerry was running a wine importation business, Mr Hammond?'

'No, I didn't.' Hammond raised his eyebrows at this further revelation.

'I don't suppose Bligh's too happy about Kerry leaving you the company in her will, either,' I said.

'He needn't worry,' said Hammond. 'I'm going to hand it over to him as soon as we can arrange for the solicitor to prepare the paperwork. What the hell would I do with a haulage firm? Apart from which, the Service doesn't allow me to have private interests. It's a case of choosing between the two and, quite frankly, I don't fancy giving up my job to learn a new trade at my stage of life.'

And with that view, I was inclined to agree. Hammond certainly wasn't cut out for the hurly-burly of the commercial world. Kate and I stood up. 'Thank you for your candour, Mr Hammond,' I said. 'Sadly, it doesn't get us very much further forward in our search for your wife's killer.' I paused at the front door. 'There is one other thing. We have your late wife's address book.'

'Oh? Where did you get that from?'

'It was in her luggage when we found her body at the airport,' I said. I had no intention of telling Hammond that I'd taken it from a desk drawer in his house on Christmas Day; that, after all, had been an illegal seizure. 'Do you know if she had another address book?'

'Yes, she did, as a matter of fact. I found it when I was going through our safe the other day. We keep things like passports and birth certificates in it. D'you think it'll be of interest?'

'I'd certainly like to examine it, Mr Hammond,' I said. 'It's just possible that it might contain the name of your wife's murderer.'

'Good grief,' exclaimed Hammond, 'I hadn't thought of that.' He left the room, returning minutes later with a leather-bound Filofax. 'There you are, Chief Inspector,' he said, handing it to me.

On Monday morning, I set Dave Poole and Colin Wilberforce the task of discovering everything they could about Charlie Pollard and Erica Foster. I'd been particularly interested in Hammond's statement that Foster, who was now living with Pollard, had once been in a relationship with Kerry Hammond.

'Kate, go out to the Dixons' address at Hardacre Street, pick up Sonia Dixon and bring her to Westminster magistrates' court. I want her to take a look at Michael Roberts.'

'What about her children, guv?'

'Take one of the women DCs. She can look after them until Sonia gets back.'

'That'll please Sheila,' said Kate, having decided to give DC Armitage the babysitting job.

'Good practice for the future,' I said, and received a frown that implied I'd been guilty of sexism.

That done, I rushed off to court with Roberts and Hogan, and secured an eight-day lay-down, as we detectives describe a remand in custody to the Crown Court.

As Roberts and Hogan were returned to the cells to await transport to Brixton, Kate Ebdon arrived with Sonia Dixon.

We escorted her to the cells beneath the court and I asked the gaoler to open the wicket of Roberts's cell.

'See if you recognize that man, Sonia,' I said.

Sonia Dixon needed only a brief glance. 'That's the man who called at the house looking for Gary,' she said, without hesitation.

'I thought as much,' I said. 'Take Mrs Dixon back to Ealing, Kate.'

'Is that it?' asked Sonia.

'Yes, and thanks for your assistance.'

Len Driscoll had sent a couple of detective officers to the Broders Road warehouse with a view to discovering the secrets of Kerry Hammond's wine importing business. The two officers were Detective Sergeant Lizanne Carpenter and Detective Constable John

Appleby. Lizanne, a recent arrival in HSCC from Hackney, was proving to be a very competent addition to the unit.

It was not the most popular of duties entailing, as it did, waiting around for something to happen. Something that, in their experience, might never occur.

Hunched in parkas, Carpenter and Appleby had spent most of the morning exchanging gossip about the Job, and drinking coffee out of vacuum flasks. But at about midday, just when they were starting to wonder what to do about lunch, the door of the warehouse opened.

The two men who entered were in their fifties, dressed casually in sweaters and jeans, and heavy topcoats.

'Good morning,' said Lizanne Carpenter, emerging from the small office at the end of the warehouse.

'Oh, hello, love,' said one of the men. 'We've come for three cases of Chablis and three of claret. We phoned the order in a couple of days ago.'

'Did you indeed?' said Lizanne, having now been joined by John Appleby. 'We're police officers. Who are you?'

'Er, I'm Tony Manning and this is Ted Piper. But what are you doing here?' They each looked a little surprised and somewhat apprehensive to find the police there.

'Investigating a suspected case of fraud involving this wine importer,' said Lizanne. 'What's your involvement?'

'We've got nothing to do with any fraud,' said Manning. 'We've always got our wine from here.'

'Who was your contact?'

'A Mrs Hammond.'

'And did you ever meet Mrs Hammond?'

'No, it was always done on the phone, and usually there was a bloke here to hand over what we'd ordered.'

'Any idea of his name?' asked Lizanne.

'No, sorry.'

'What's your line of business, Mr Manning?' asked Appleby, joining in the conversation.

Manning glanced at Piper before answering. 'We're civil servants, but we run the bar at a bowls club down near Bromley. In our spare time.'

'What did you expect to pay for today's order, Mr Manning?'

'I can't tell you the exact amount, but it works out to about three quid a bottle.'

'Is it all right to pick up our consignment, then?' asked Piper, speaking for the first time.

'I'm afraid not,' said Lizanne. 'The stock has been seized as possible evidence, and as Mrs Hammond is now dead, I don't suppose the business will continue.'

'Dead? But what do we do for our wine now?'

'You could try a supermarket,' suggested Appleby. 'However, until customs decide whether any offences have been committed the stock of this warehouse stays where it is.'

Manning turned to Piper. 'Well, that's that, I suppose, Ted. Sorry to have bothered you, miss,' he said to Lizanne.

By the time I got back to Curtis Green, I found that Dave Poole and Colin Wilberforce had been busy garnering a few routine facts. A search at the General Register Office revealed that Charlie Pollard had been born thirty-five years ago in Southampton, the daughter of Charles Pollard, at the time a second officer in the merchant navy, and his wife Clarissa. Erica Foster, born in Bromley, was twenty-six, her parents being Frederick Foster, a musician, and Mary. All of which was useless in terms of furthering our enquiries.

'I did a check with the Department of Education, sir,' said Colin Wilberforce, 'but they don't have any record of a Charlie Pollard. That means that she's not teaching in a state school or in the private sector, providing it's a private school that has to register.' As usual, he was making a thorough job of tying up the loose ends. 'As for Erica Foster, she's not a member of any of the recognized professional bodies for accountants, but that doesn't mean very much; anyone can call themselves an accountant.'

'Pollard and Foster are shown on the electoral roll as the only occupants of the Argus Road address, guv,' said Dave.

'Fascinating,' I said, 'but if Charlie Pollard's not a teacher, where does her money come from?'

'Not from the Department for Work and Pensions,' said Dave. 'I've checked. She doesn't receive any sort of benefit. Neither does Erica Foster.'

'Dig deeper,' I said, mildly irritated that Charlie Pollard appeared to have been deceiving us. 'I suppose she could be living on whatever Erica Foster brings in. Any information on where Erica works, Colin?'

'Not yet, sir,' said Wilberforce. 'But we do know that Charlie Pollard owns a new car. At least, it's only a year old.' He turned his computer screen so that I could see the DVLA entry.

'A Ford Mondeo, eh? They don't come cheap,' I said. 'She must garage it somewhere else; it wasn't outside the house on either of the occasions we were there. Although she did mention owning a car; she thought that's what we'd called about. Put the details on the PNC, Colin. You never know what they might turn up.'

Further discussion on the matter in hand was interrupted by a telephone call from *Capitaine* Henri Deshayes.

'I'm at the Gare du Nord, 'Arry, on my way to see you. I have some information about your smuggling investigation.' There was a pause. 'And I 'ave Gabrielle with me also.'

'How did you swing that, Henry?' I asked.

'Swing it? Swing what? What is this swinging, 'Arry?'

'How did you arrange it with your boss?' Although Henri spoke fluent English, I realized that he was not necessarily conversant with the more obscure vernacular.

'*D'accord!*' exclaimed Henri. 'The information is not for passing over the telephone, 'Arry. *Comprenez*?' I could visualize him tapping the side of his nose with a forefinger.

'I understand. What time are you arriving at St Pancras?'

'About 'alf past twelve your time.'

'Where are you staying?' I asked. Henri knew that neither Gail nor I had sufficient room to accommodate visitors.

'We 'ave booked an 'otel in London. It is all arranged. I was due a few days leave, so I thought it would be a good idea to combine business with pleasure.'

'I'll have someone there to meet you, Henry, and take you and Gabrielle to your hotel.'

'There is no need, 'Arry. We can get a taxi, but perhaps you and Gail will have dinner with us this evening.' And Henri gave us the address of his hotel.

My thoughts of a pleasant dinner with Henri Deshayes and his lovely wife were interrupted by Kate Ebdon.

'I've been through the address book that we got from Nick Hammond, guv, but there were only a couple of names that might be of interest. There were mobile phone numbers alongside the names, and I did a subscriber check.'

'Anyone we know, Kate?'

'You could say that. Frankie Saunders and Danny Elliott, and both have got form for robbery.'

'Very careless of Kerry to keep a list,' I said, although I wasn't surprised. Kerry Hammond didn't expect to be murdered, and she didn't anticipate that the police might have access to her address book. But criminals do the silliest of things, even educated ones like Kerry. And I was now firmly convinced that she had been a criminal. 'Anything in the book about Charlie Pollard, Kate?'

'Yes,' said Kate. 'She's got Pollard's address in here under C. Pollard, but the phone number is written backwards, silly cow.'

'Not as clever as she thought she was, then,' I said. 'Bligh obviously worked that out.'

'I presume you want Saunders and Elliott picked up?'

'Too right,' I said. 'Get a team organized and see if you can find them. Of course, if they'd heard about Roberts and Hogan being nicked, they might've taken it on their toes, but it's worth a try.'

'I don't suppose they're bright enough to make a connection, guv. Either that or they think they're fireproof.'

SEVENTEEN

To my astonishment, at two o'clock Kate reported that Saunders and Elliott were in custody at Charing Cross.

'Are you coming over, guv?'

'I'll be with you in ten,' I said, and told Wilberforce to tell Dave where I was going.

Kate was waiting in the front office of the police station when we arrived.

'I've got Saunders in the interview room, guv.'

'Right, let's go. And you can kick off.'

Frankie Saunders was forty-three years of age, and had the appearance of the conventional robber. He was muscular and belligerent.

'What's this all about?' he demanded.

Kate turned on the tape recorder and made a big thing of announcing the presence of Detective Chief Inspector Brock and Detective Inspector Ebdon of the Homicide and Serious Crime Command. That caused Saunders to sit up and take notice.

'You are in serious shtook,' said Kate, as we sat down opposite Saunders.

'Is that a fact? Well, p'raps you'd start off by telling me what I've been nicked for.'

'Gunrunning,' said Kate, 'and to make it quite clear, you're likely to be charged with conspiring with Kerry Hammond, deceased, and others now in custody, illegally to import firearms.'

'Dunno what you're on about.'

'Furthermore, you are also likely to be charged with the murder of the aforementioned Kerry Hammond on the twenty-fourth of December last.'

'Bloody leave it out,' protested Saunders, his face working in panic. 'I don't know nothing about no topping.'

'Well, you'd better start by telling us what you know about the shooters, and the murder might just go away.'

'I don't know nothing.'

'As a result of a raid on premises at Cantard Street, Walworth, on Saturday,' continued Kate, as though Saunders hadn't spoken, 'a quantity of firearms was discovered and Michael Roberts and Patrick Hogan have been arrested and charged.'

That piece of news appeared to unnerve Saunders. 'Well, it ain't nothing to do with me.'

'Fingerprints found at Cantard Street have been identified as yours and Danny Elliott's so, as you've nothing to say, you'll both be charged as principals in the conspiracy.'

Both Kate and I knew that a fingerprint examination of the warehouse had failed to prove the presence of either Saunders or Elliott, but Saunders didn't know that.

'All right, so I was there, but I was just helping to unload some gear. I never knew what it was.'

'Did you ever meet Charlie Pollard?' I asked.

'Nah! I heard his name mentioned once or twice, but I never met him.'

'Who mentioned Pollard?'

'It was Mike and—' Saunders stopped, realizing that he was on the point of saying too much.

'So you do know Roberts,' said Kate.

'Yeah, well, he asked me to give him a hand unloading some gear. But, like I said, I never knew what the stuff was.'

'D'you want me to tell you exactly where we found your fingerprints, Frankie?' Kate persisted with the fiction of the fingerprints.

Saunders slumped in his chair. 'All right, he asked me for a bit of help, but if I'd known what it was to start with, I'd've told him to get lost.'

'So, you did know it was firearms, and you were there when Roberts and Hogan opened the secret panel in the lorry.'

'It was a one-off,' said Saunders.

'How did he contact you?'

'In a boozer.'

'Of course he did,' said Kate acidly. 'It's where all the dodgy transactions are made. And Danny Elliott was there too, I suppose.'

'Yeah. What d'you reckon I'll get for this?'

'Difficult to say,' said Kate, 'but if I was in your position I wouldn't buy a five-year diary.'

I sent for a PC and asked him to put down Saunders and bring up Elliott.

Danny Elliott strolled into the interview room as though he hadn't a care in the world.

'Wass this all about, then?' he demanded, dropping into the vacant chair.

'Mike Roberts, Pat Hogan and Frankie Saunders have given you up,' said Kate, 'and unless you've got anything useful to say you'll be charged with conspiring with them illegally to import firearms.'

'I don't know nothing about no shooters,' protested Elliott.

'Furthermore, my chief here,' continued Kate, indicating me with a wave of her hand, 'is looking for whoever topped Kerry Hammond.'

'Who?' Elliott's relaxed and truculent attitude vanished. 'I don't know who you're talking about. Who's Kelly Hammond?'

'Nice try,' said Kate, 'but it's *Kerry*: K-E-R-R-Y, and I'm talking about the woman who masterminded the whole shebang, along with Charlie Pollard.'

'Never heard of 'em,' said Elliott, shifting his position slightly.

I thought that was probably true.

'As my inspector told you, Danny, you'll be charged with conspiracy,' I said.

I sent for the PC-gaoler and told him to settle Elliott in a cell for the night.

It was as well that I arrived early to collect Gail from her house in Kingston.

Aware that Gabrielle Deshayes was something of a fashion icon, Gail had taken a considerable amount of time selecting her outfit. After several false starts, and frequent reminders from me about the time, she'd eventually appeared in a dark green confection of heavy silk with a daring décolletage. Nipped in at the waist, the dress did everything to emphasize her perfect figure.

'You look gorgeous, darling,' I said.

'Thank you, kind sir,' said Gail, and sketched a curtsy.

Henri and Gabrielle, already seated at a table in the hotel restaurant, stood up to greet us as we arrived.

Gabrielle, the epitome of the chic Parisienne, was fetchingly attired in a white cashmere suit with black ribbon trims at the collar, the pockets and the cuffs. In true Chanel style, so Gail later told me, the straight skirt came to just below her knees, inevitably directing male attention to her shapely legs.

Henri and I were wearing suits, of course. Gail had once commented that it was all right for us men; we just had to throw on a suit. But at least we were wearing ties, something of a rarity these days.

There were handshakes and kisses all round, and Gail and Gabrielle started talking about the latest fashions in London and Paris even before the aperitifs were served.

There was a minor amusing diversion when the waiter, addressing Henri with a pseudo-French accent, was taken aback when Henri rattled off his order in his own native language. To adopt a sporting term, the waiter retired hurt.

'It was a very successful operation, 'Arry,' said Henri as he took a sip of his pastis. 'The *Police Judiciaire* in Marseille found a cache of firearms in Marcel Lebrun's warehouse, and arrested him and three others immediately after your man had left with his load. It seemed that for some time now, Lebrun had been crossing from Sète to Morocco to buy wine, but also to buy firearms at the same time. I don't know how the *douaniers* didn't catch 'im before.' He gave a Gallic shrug of the shoulders. 'Why go to Morocco for wine? France is full of it.'

'Did he use a commercial lorry for these runs, Henry?' I also wondered how Lebrun had avoided the usually vigilant French customs officers.

'*Non!*' Henri shook his head. 'It is not a commercial ferry, and I understand that Lebrun used a small van. 'E was clever to carry only very small amounts. The PJ found the van at the warehouse. It 'ad a very cleverly concealed compartment underneath.'

I told Henri about the arrests we'd made in London, but that we still had to find evidence implicating others, notably Charlie Pollard. I gave him further details about the murder of Kerry Hammond, too, and that she was probably the brains behind the gunrunning.

'Do you think her murder was connected with this business, 'Arry?'

'It's beginning to look like a strong possibility, Henry,' I said.

'As a matter of interest, did Lebrun supply others, apart from the people we arrested?'

'Maybe,' said Henri. 'There are many enquiries still to be made, and it could take a long time. The PJ in Marseille are looking into possible connections in Belgium and the Netherlands, but the worrying aspect is that Lebrun might also 'ave been selling guns to extremist groups in France itself, and possibly also to ETA in Spain. And there's always al-Qaeda.' He shrugged and spread his hands. And that means that the DCRI 'ave now become involved.'

'What's the DCRI, Henry?'

'*Direction Centrale du Renseignement Intérieur*,' said Henri. 'It is like your MI5, I think.'

'Oh, I see. If they're anything like our lot, they could take forever.' I just hoped that their operatives were not all like Nicholas Hammond, whose laid back attitude did not impress me.

Henri sighed. 'I think so, but that does not worry you, 'Arry. Your job is all . . . What's that expression you use? Done and dusted?'

I laughed. 'Not yet, Henry,' I said. 'Now, about tomorrow. Would you like to have a look over Scotland Yard?'

Henri gave me an apologetic smile and spread his hands in a typical Gallic gesture. 'I don't think so, 'Arry, if you don't mind. I am on leave, and one police headquarters is much like another, I think. If it's anything like our Quai des Orfèvres it's full of people running about with bits of paper. No, if you don't mind, I'll spend the day at the British Museum and 'aving a poke about in 'Arrods.'

'With Gabrielle?'

Henri laughed and glanced across at our two women; both were now deeply engrossed in a conversation about dancing. As I'd mentioned earlier, Gabrielle had once been a dancer at the *Folies-Bergères* and Gail had done her fair share of what she called 'hoofing'.

'I think I will leave the girls to go out together and raid the fashion shops, 'Arry. Just think yourself lucky that you are at work.'

Gail and I returned to her house in Kingston at just after eleven o'clock.

'I suppose you and Gabrielle are going shopping tomorrow, darling,' I said, as we relaxed in her middle-floor sitting room.

'Yes, I've promised to take her to Knightsbridge and Chelsea. There's a new boutique in King's Road I want to show her.' Gail gave me one of her fetching smiles. 'Are you sure you wouldn't like to come?' she asked impishly.

'There's nothing I'd like more,' I lied, 'but I'm in the middle of a complicated murder enquiry.'

'Oh, what a shame.' Gail pretended disappointment, although she knew I'd do anything to avoid one of her trips around the fashion emporia of London. 'How is it complicated?'

Gail had never asked me about my work before, at least not to the extent of being interested in the details.

'Well . . .' I said hesitantly, preferring to leave my work at the office, 'the female victim was found stabbed to death in a car park at Heathrow.'

'Ooh! Nasty. Was she good-looking?'

'Very, and very rich. She was involved with a haulage company.'

'You can't possibly mean she drove a lorry,' said Gail, wrinkling her nose in feigned horror.

'Of course not, you silly girl, she owned it. The difficulty, as far as I'm concerned, is that she appears to have had a quite a few men friends.'

'That should be easy, then. I expect one of her studs killed her.' Gail dismissed the problem of my dead socialite with a wave of one of her elegant hands.

'If only it was that simple,' I said. 'A glass of champagne to round the evening off?' I suggested, changing the subject.

'Why not?'

I was about to make my way downstairs to the kitchen when Gail stopped me.

'Where are you going?'

'To get the champagne and some glasses,' I said, wondering why she'd asked a question that appeared to have an obvious answer.

'I've had a fridge put in the bedroom,' said Gail.

'In the bedroom?' I stopped in the doorway. 'When did you do that?'

'This morning. A nice young man carried it all the way upstairs and installed it for me.'

'And what did you have to give him to persuade him to cart a damned great fridge up to your bedroom on the top floor?' I asked assuming an expression of mock severity.

'It's not a damned great fridge. In fact, it's only a teeny-weeny one. But he was a very nice young man. Very fanciable, if you know what I mean; muscles and a six-pack.' Gail shot me one of her sexiest smiles and then ran her tongue round her lips.

'So, what *did* you have to give him to persuade him?'

'A five-pound note. What on earth did you think I gave him?' Gail stood up. 'But I haven't taken any glasses upstairs yet. Be a darling and pop down to the kitchen and bring a couple up.'

By the time I reached the bedroom, armed with champagne flutes, Gail was languishing on top of the bed, her clothing scattered untidily across the floor. Consequently, we never did find out whether her new fridge had efficiently chilled the champagne. Not for an hour or two, anyway.

On my arrival at Curtis Green first thing on Tuesday morning, I was greeted by a mildly excited Colin Wilberforce. Colin was never more than *mildly* excited.

'It would appear that Charlie Pollard is a corporal in the army, sir.'

'How the hell did you find that out, Colin?'

'She was spotted by an ANPR unit near Regent's Park about an hour ago—'

'A what?' My staff were trying to blind me with science again.

'Automatic number plate recognition, *sir*,' said Dave, joining in the conversation. 'You must've seen one of those vans parked on the side of the road. They scan numbers into the PNC and it turns up anything of interest. It's usually driving offences though, things like no insurance or disqualified drivers.'

'However, sir,' Wilberforce continued, 'the ANPR unit picked up that Pollard's vehicle was of interest to HSCC and passed it to the traffic guys. They gave her a pull, and she produced an army ID as evidence of identity. Apparently, she's a corporal in the Royal Logistic Corps.'

'Brilliant!' I said. Once again, a routine check by traffic officers had produced information that assiduous searching by detectives had failed to discover.

'I wonder if Corporal Pollard has access to firearms,' suggested Dave. 'Maybe that's why she didn't tell us she was in the army.'

'If she does, I think it would just be coincidence,' I said. 'I don't think she knew anything about Kerry's smuggling operation. What d'you think, Colin?' I asked Wilberforce.

'It could be that she doesn't want her relationship with Erica Foster made known to the army, sir,' said Wilberforce. 'Perhaps she thought that we'd tell them if we made enquiries at her unit.'

'I don't see why that should worry her, Colin. The embargo on homosexuality in the army was lifted some years ago.'

'Maybe so, sir. But she might've thought it would prejudice the authorities against promoting her.'

'Possible, I suppose. Just because the rule book says it makes no difference doesn't necessarily mean that it doesn't make a difference in practice. Was Pollard in uniform, do we know?'

'No, sir. She was apparently in plain clothes. I think that these days most army personnel don't change into their uniform until they arrive at work.'

'There wasn't any military uniform or equipment at Argus Road, was there, Dave?'

'No, sir,' said Dave, his use of 'sir' confirming that I'd asked a question to which he'd earlier given me an answer. He'd already said that there was nothing of evidential interest in the house, and if there'd been any military accoutrements there, he'd've spotted them.

'Is Miss Ebdon here, Colin?'

'Yes, sir, she's in her office.'

I went next door and told Kate what Wilberforce had learned. 'Perhaps you'd find out from the Ministry of Defence where Charlie Pollard's stationed, and then I'll have a discreet word with her commanding officer. I'm worried about her having access to firearms.'

Kate wasted no time in trying to cut her way through the bureaucracy of the MOD; she'd jousted with them before. She went straight to the Assistant Provost Marshal of London District, a lieutenant-colonel of the Royal Military Police, and confronted him in his Whitehall office. Even so, it was not until midday on Wednesday that the APM came up with the details of where Charlie Pollard was stationed in central London.

After persuading a rather dim armed sentry that Dave and I really were bona fide police officers, we were eventually shown into the office of a major who told us he was Charlie Pollard's commanding officer.

'Good morning, gentlemen.' The major, positively oozing charm, crossed his office, hand outstretched. 'How may I help you?' he asked, as he shook hands. 'Do take a seat.'

'I understand that you have a corporal named Charlie Pollard on your strength, Major,' I said, once Dave and I had introduced ourselves.

'Yes, indeed. Pollard's a very capable young NCO, and she's a London District swimming champion. Does a good butterfly stroke, so I'm told. Is she in some sort of trouble? Some of our young soldiers do occasionally have a little too much to drink. It's all these nightclubs that youngsters seem to frequent, you know.' It seemed to have escaped the major that Pollard wasn't exactly a youngster; she was thirty-five.

'We're not here about drunken soldiers, Major,' said Dave. 'We're investigating a serious case of international gunrunning and the evidence points to Corporal Pollard's involvement.'

'Oh my God!' The major's bland composure evaporated in a second, the expression on his face indicating the onset of blind panic. 'Are you suggesting that Corporal Pollard's actively engaged in this gunrunning, Chief Inspector?' he asked, turning to me.

'Not necessarily, but our enquiries are far from being finalized.' In fact, I didn't think that Pollard had any involvement in the smuggling operation other than having been persuaded to hire the lock-up for the unlikely purpose of storing Kerry's furniture.

'Are they military weapons?' asked the major.

The police discipline code includes the offence of 'lack of supervision', a spectre that hangs over anyone holding a rank above that of constable. I presumed that there was something similar in the army. The major appeared to be mentally searching for any possible culpability on his part. I decided to put him out of his misery.

'As far as I can tell, Major, the firearms that we've so far seized have been imported rather than acquired from a source in the United Kingdom.'

'I can't tell you what a relief that is, Chief Inspector.' The major relaxed, and some of his previous equanimity returned. 'Nevertheless, I think I'll order a check of the armoury.'

'Does Corporal Pollard have access to the armoury, then?' asked Dave.

'No, she's a staff-car driver. Her usual duty is to drive a brigadier attached to the Ministry of Defence. She has no direct access to the armoury without the permission of the quartermaster, and he'd want to know why she was there and what she wanted.'

'Your staff-car drivers aren't routinely armed, then, Major.'

'Certainly not.'

'I'd be grateful if you didn't speak to Corporal Pollard about this matter, Major,' I said. 'It could have an adverse effect on our investigation.'

'Quite so,' murmured the major, 'but I take it that it won't prejudice your enquiry if I check the armoury.' He seemed desperate to do some stocktaking.

'Not at all.'

'Could I ask you to keep me informed of any developments, Chief Inspector? The question of a court martial might arise.'

'Of course,' I said, determined that he'd be told as little as possible and as late as possible.

EIGHTEEN

When Dave and I returned to Curtis Green, I found Kate almost bubbling over.

'Have you won the lottery, Kate?' I asked.

'No such luck,' said Kate, giving me a smile of self-satisfaction. 'However, I've got a bit of information that might just round off this job of ours.'

'Go on, Kate, cheer me up.'

'As you know, guv, we are still in the process of checking ownership of all the cars that were parked at Heathrow on Christmas Eve and Christmas Day. But once we'd discovered details of Charlie Pollard's car, I was able to short circuit the search.'

'Don't keep me in suspense, Kate.'

'At one minute to seven on Christmas Eve,' Kate continued, with an air of triumph, 'Pollard's car checked into the same car park where we found Kerry Hammond's body. It left again at twenty-five past seven. She was stupid enough to pay the parking charge with her own credit card. I obtained a printout from the car park authorities, and a confirmatory copy from the credit card company,' she added, placing copies on my desk.

'Well done, Kate, I said. 'It looks as though we've got her now.'

'D'you want me to go to the barracks and pick her up, guv?'

I thought about that, but only briefly. 'No, Kate, we'll wait until she gets home and nick her there. That way, we can feel Erica Foster's collar at the same time. I think it's likely that she's also involved in Kerry's murder.'

'Anything you want me to do, guv?' asked Dave.

'Yes, Dave. Go back to Pollard's unit and ask the bold major if you can search her locker, and her desk if she has one. If he argues the toss, tell him we'll get a search warrant, but I'm sure he'll cooperate.'

On reflection, I decided not to take a personal hand in the arrests

of Charlie Pollard and Erica Foster. Instead, I sent Kate Ebdon, DS
Tom Challis and DCs Sheila Armitage and Nicola Chance.

At seven o'clock, I received a telephone call from Kate to say that
both women were in custody at Charing Cross police station.

'Charlie Pollard's in Interview Room One, guv,' said Kate, when
I arrived. 'Both she and Erica Foster have been fingerprinted, photog-
raphed and had DNA samples taken. Checks are under way as I
speak.'

'Did they give any trouble, Kate?'

'Trouble?' scoffed Kate. 'It would've been very unwise of them
to risk it.'

'What did you tell them they were being arrested for?'

'I told them that it was in connection with the firearms smuggling, guv. I didn't mention Kerry's murder.'

'Right, Kate,' I said, 'let's do it.'

Charlie Pollard, attired in jeans and a cowl-necked green sweater,
gave me a sullen look as I entered the room.

'I told you before,' she began, 'that I know nothing about firearms
smuggling.'

'Why did you tell me you were a teacher, Charlie?' I asked, as
Kate and I sat down opposite the woman.

'I *am* a teacher.'

'Really? Where d'you teach? Which school?'

'Well, I'm not actually teaching at the moment.' Pollard rapidly
backtracked. 'But it's what I'm hoping to do.'

'That'll be when you leave the army, I suppose,' observed Kate.

'How did you know I'm in the army?' Charlie Pollard's surprise
showed how little she knew of police procedure, and she obviously
hadn't realized that traffic officers sometimes speak to detectives.
It was clear that we'd caught her on the back foot.

'Where were you on Christmas Eve, Charlie?' I asked, ignoring
her question.

'On Christmas Eve? What sort of question's that?' demanded
Charlie, recovering from the shock of discovering that we knew she
was in the army.

'Just answer the chief inspector,' snapped Kate.

Charlie glanced apprehensively at Kate. She knew from their
first meeting that to cross this abrasive Australian DI was a bad

idea. She was not the first female prisoner to arrive at that conclusion.

'At a party.'

'Where?' asked Kate.

'With some friends.'

Kate slid a writing pad across the table and placed a pen on top of it. 'Write down their names, and where the party was held.'

Charlie pushed the pad back again. 'I'm not going to implicate my friends,' she said.

'You were at Heathrow Airport, Charlie, weren't you?' said Kate.

'I don't know what you're talking about.' But the red flush that crept slowly up Charlie's face was indication enough that we'd caught her out.

'You parked your car there at one minute to seven on the afternoon of Christmas Eve, and left again at twenty-five past seven, just twenty-six minutes later. And it so happened that you parked in the same section of the car park where we found Kerry Hammond's body.'

'I deny it,' said a flustered Charlie.

'And you were stupid enough to pay the parking charge with your own credit card.' Kate laid copies of the two printouts on the table, turning them so that Charlie could read them. 'What have you got to say about that, Charlie? Change your mind about flying somewhere, did you?'

But before Charlie Pollard could answer, there was a knock at the interview room door, and Dave poked his head in.

'Might be as well if you stepped outside, guv,' he said. He was looking pleased with himself.

'What is it, Dave?' I asked, once we were in the corridor.

'I found this in Pollard's locker at her unit, guv,' said Dave, displaying an SA80 army bayonet in an evidence bag, 'and the major confirmed that she'd not been issued with it, so she'd obviously nicked it. It's been cleaned, but not very well. There appear to be minute traces of blood around the hilt. I'm sure the lab will be able to confirm it is blood, and, with any luck, match it to Kerry's DNA.'

'The icing on the cake, Dave,' I said.

'They'll probably find Charlie Pollard's fingerprints on it as well.

And talking of fingerprints, Linda Mitchell has checked Pollard's against those found in Kerry's car and came up with a match.'

'She would, Dave. We know that Charlie had a relationship with Kerry so she would probably claim that she was legitimately in Kerry's car at some time.'

We returned to the interview room and Kate told the tape recorder that I'd re-entered along with Dave. 'Chief Inspector Brock is showing Charlie Pollard an army bayonet marked Exhibit DP Seven,' she said, as I placed the plastic-shrouded weapon on the table.

'Earlier today Detective Sergeant Poole found this in your locker at your army unit, Miss Pollard,' I said.

Charlie stared at it transfixed. There was a long period of silence that we were shrewd enough not to break.

'Kerry Hammond was a bitch,' said Charlie eventually. It was not the first time she'd used that unflattering term to describe her erstwhile lover.

'You do not have to say anything, but it may harm your defence . . .' began Kate, and she went on to finish the caution.

'Although Detective Inspector Ebdon has told you that need not say anything further,' I said to Charlie, 'you may, if you wish, make a statement about this matter. In which case, you may either write it yourself, or the inspector will write it down and ask you to sign it when you've finished.'

'Oh, I'll tell you about it,' said Charlie vehemently, 'and you can write down every word of it. It was a *crime passionnel*.'

So that was to be her plea. I forbore from pointing out that a crime of passion has no standing as a defence in English law, apart from which I didn't think that the murder of Kerry Hammond would've fallen into that category anyway.

'We had a wonderful relationship, and that woman promised me everything,' continued Charlie. 'More fool me to believe her,' she added bitterly. 'I should've known she'd betray me in the end.'

'Would you care to say when it started?' asked Kate, looking up from the statement form on which she was recording what Charlie was saying.

'We began our relationship about a year ago, but I can't remember the exact date,' said Charlie, making no secret of her sexual orientation. 'We met in a lesbian club near Tottenham Court Road,' she added, and furnished the exact address.

'Yes, go on.' Kate was writing very quickly now.

'Kerry told me that she'd been seeing Erica for some time, but had broken up with her. It wasn't long before Kerry and I became very close; in fact, we were in love with each other.' The words tumbled out as Charlie breathlessly continued her narrative. 'She told me that she had let Erica go, and was leaving her husband – Nick, I think his name was – and that she wanted shot of the business she was running. Clearing the decks is what she called it. She said she wanted me to leave the army and set up home with her in the south of France, away from all the hustle and bustle of London and its God-awful weather. She described the villa she owned in St-Tropez; it all sounded idyllic. She said there was a swimming pool there, too.' She paused and gazed wistfully into the middle distance. 'Too bloody good to be true, if I'd thought about it.'

That was interesting, I thought. St-Tropez was less than two hours' drive to Marcel Lebrun's base at St-Circe. But at the time that Kerry Trucking's solicitor had mentioned the location of the villa, I wasn't aware that Lebrun's winery and illegal armoury were that close. However, that was probably irrelevant.

'A bit slower, Charlie, please,' said Kate, hurrying to keep up with the woman's torrent of words.

'Kerry told me that she was going to leave me everything in her will, but as she was young and fit I didn't pay much attention to that. More to the point, she said that she'd pay two thousand pounds a month into my bank account.' Charlie paused. 'But that never came about either. Then one night, I bumped into Erica Foster in the same club, and she said she knew I was sleeping with Kerry. But she went on to say that she was still sleeping with her too.'

'". . . still sleeping with her too",' repeated Kate slowly, as she continued to record Charlie's statement.

'I had a hell of a row with Erica about it – in fact, we almost came to blows – and I told her that she should leave Kerry alone. I told her that Kerry belonged to me now, and that we were lovers, and that we were going to live together in the south of France once Kerry had left her husband. And I also told Erica that Kerry was leaving me everything in her will.' Charlie looked up at the high window of the interview room, an expression of betrayal on her face.

'Hang on a tick,' said Kate, her pen rapidly recording the last sentence.

'It was then that I found out the truth about Kerry,' Pollard went on, looking back at Kate once more. 'Erica laughed, and told me not to be a little fool. She said that Kerry had also promised to leave *her* everything in her will, and that she'd met another woman at the club who'd known Kerry before either of us had met her, and she'd been told the same thing. More fool me to have believed that damned woman.'

'Please try not to go so fast, Charlie,' said Kate, who was having some difficulty with keeping up.

Charlie waited until Kate finished writing and had looked up again.

'It was then that the blindingly obvious hit me, and I realized that Kerry was using us, Erica and me, and probably a few others, too; especially the other girl who Erica had mentioned. She didn't give a damn who she upset so long as *she* got what she wanted. And she set me up to take the fall for her gunrunning business. After that, Erica and I became close, and she moved in with me.' There was a long pause while Charlie seemed to give great thought to what she was going say next. 'We came to the conclusion, Erica and me, that one or other of us was going to benefit from Kerry's will, and we decided that whichever way it was, we'd share it.'

Although Charlie had provided us with a motive, I thought that she would hold back from actually admitting to the murder, but, to my surprise, she didn't.

'Kerry had told me that she was going to New York with her husband for one last time, and that while she was there she'd tell him that she was finishing with him, and was going to make a life with me.' Charlie had started repeating herself now. 'Well, that didn't ring true. If she was going to leave her husband, why go to New York with him? Why not dump him on this side of the pond? Anyway, I got her to tell me which flight she was on and when she'd be at the airport. And I asked her when she'd be coming back so that I could meet her.'

'Slow down a minute,' said Kate, as she rapidly recorded the last of Charlie's sentences.

'It was easy.' Charlie waited until Kate had lifted her pen, and then continued. 'Erica and I drove to the airport and waited in Wayfarer Road until Kerry went past in her car, and then we followed her into the car park. I'm a good driver,' she said, 'I do it for a living. Kerry was surprised when I pulled up beside where she'd parked, and I think she was shocked to see Erica with me when we got into her car. I sat in the passenger seat next to her, and Erica got in the back. We were determined to have it out with her, and I asked her which one of us she was in love with. She just laughed and told us both not to be silly little cows, and that it was just a fling we'd had. Then she said she wasn't really going to leave her husband. I saw red at that, and I pulled out my bayonet and stabbed her. And she bloody deserved it, setting me up to take the fall for her gunrunning,' she said vehemently. 'Then Erica and I went home to Bethnal Green and opened a bottle of champagne.'

Even for a case-hardened detective like me, that sounded pretty cold-blooded. Charlie Pollard might be claiming that her murder of Kerry Hammond was a *crime passionnel*, but her condemnation of Kerry for setting her up tended to negate that. Furthermore, the fact that she had taken a bayonet with her when she was going to meet Kerry implied a premeditated act of violence. And that, I thought, would be good enough to sway even the most sceptical of juries.

There was one thing that didn't seem right about all this. Charlie Pollard claimed that she had been sitting beside Kerry when she stabbed her, and we knew that she had been stabbed several times. So, how did she do it when she was sitting in the passenger seat?

But Charlie Pollard provided the answer when she took Kate's pen to sign her statement. *She signed it with her left hand.* And we knew she was strong; the major had told us she was a champion swimmer.

We left it at that, and I told the custody sergeant to return Charlie Pollard to her cell pending our interview with Erica Foster.

'Get someone to photocopy that statement as quickly as possible, Kate,' I said, 'and then we'll tackle Erica.'

'By the way, guv,' said Kate, 'there's no scientific evidence to put Erica Foster in Kerry's car, or even that she was at the airport at all.'

'No,' I said, 'I half suspected that, although the lack of trace evidence doesn't necessarily mean that she *wasn't* in the car. Anyway, it is winter and she was probably wearing gloves.'

Erica Foster had been wise enough to ask for the duty solicitor to be present. 'It's nine o'clock, Chief Inspector,' he said, as we entered the same interview room where we had earlier spoken to Charlie Pollard. 'I would suggest that it's a little late to start questioning my client. The guidelines in the Police and Criminal Evidence Act—'

'I'm well aware of the PACE guidelines,' I said, interrupting him, 'but all I intend to do now is to serve a statement on Miss Foster. Charlie Pollard has made this statement admitting to the murder of Mrs Kerry Hammond. It also implicates your client in that murder, but I've no intention of interviewing Miss Foster at this stage, unless she wishes it.'

'Very well.' The solicitor opened his briefcase and took out a legal pad. He placed a fountain pen on the pad and spent a few moments polishing his spectacles with a pocket handkerchief. That little charade completed, he sat back with an air of expectancy. It was a typical lawyer's ploy, and one that had been tried on me many times before, but he was wasting his time.

Kate handed Erica Foster a copy of Charlie's statement, and gave another one to the solicitor. A quarter of an hour passed while they each read Charlie's damning allegation. And then they read it again.

Eventually, Erica Foster tossed the statement aside and looked up. 'This is absolute rubbish,' she protested. 'I was nowhere near Heathrow Airport on Christmas Eve. Why on earth is Charlie trying to drag me into this?' She sounded genuinely crestfallen that her lover should have turned traitor on her. 'This bit about the will is nonsense though. Kerry said nothing about leaving her estate to me, but I wouldn't have believed her if she had said it. I suppose this whole statement is really about Charlie getting back at me because I'd carried on seeing Kerry after Charlie took up with her.'

'So, if you were not at the airport, Miss Foster, where were you on Christmas Eve?' I asked.

'Charlie and I had arranged to go to a Christmas fancy dress party at the lesbian club near Tottenham Court Road that evening, but at the last minute Charlie cried off. She said she wasn't feeling well and was going to bed, so I went on my own.'

'What time did you leave Bethnal Green?'

Erica thought about that for a moment or two. 'It must've been about twelve o'clock, I suppose. Charlie and I had arranged to have lunch with a friend of ours.'

'Who was that?' asked Kate.

'Sally Hyde. She's got a flat in Limehouse.'

'What's her address?'

'Six Bugle Street, flat four,' said Erica promptly.

'And Sally Hyde will be able to verify your story, will she?'

'Eventually,' said Erica. 'She went on holiday to Thailand straight after Christmas. She won't be back until the end of January. The three of us were going to share a taxi and go on from Limehouse to Tottenham Court Road, but in the event it finished up just being Sally and I who went.'

'What time did you get to this fancy dress party?'

'About six, I suppose. We didn't leave Limehouse until around five, perhaps a little later. It was a boozy lunch, you see,' said Erica with a shy smile, 'and then we showered to sober up and changed into our costumes. Yes, it must've been about six by the time we got to the club.'

'Is there someone at this club who can verify your story, Miss Foster?' I asked.

Erica laughed. 'About fifty or sixty of the girls who were there, I should think. The party went on all night, but I left at about eleven o'clock and got a cab back to Bethnal Green.' She paused. 'I suppose I was lucky to get one at that time of night on Christmas Eve,' she added thoughtfully. 'The driver said he was on his way home, but when I said I wanted to go to Bethnal Green, he said he lived out that way and was prepared to take me. I certainly didn't fancy walking five miles in a silly costume, high heels, fishnets and a short duffle coat.'

'Have you any idea where Miss Pollard was during this time, Miss Foster?' asked Kate.

'I'd assumed she was at home in Argus Road, but now you tell me that she was at Heathrow. When I left, she'd said she was going to bed, and when I got home that's where she was. But she seemed to have recovered from whatever was wrong with her, because the moment I got in beside her, she started making love to me. Really wild, she was. Much wilder than I'd ever known her before.'

'You didn't share a bottle of champagne, then?'

'Good God no! I'd had more than enough to drink by then.'

'Well, Chief Inspector?' The solicitor laid down his pen and raised a questioning eyebrow.

'I shall admit Miss Foster to police bail while enquiries are made to verify her alibi.'

'But it must be obvious to you that she wasn't implicated in this affair.' The lawyer assumed one of his best mystified expressions.

'That might be your view,' I said, 'but I'm sure you understand that in the circumstance I can't accept her word without corroboration.'

The solicitor gave a nod of defeat; he'd tried and failed. 'Yes, I understand,' he said.

'There is one other thing, Miss Foster,' I said, as Kate and I stood up to leave. 'Charlie mentioned a woman that she said had also been promised that Kerry would leave everything to her. Said she was a former partner of Kerry's and a friend of yours.'

'What about her?'

'Is it true?'

'Well, it's true that she's a mutual friend of Kerry's and mine. We'd met her at the club.'

'What's her name?'

'Donna Wilcox. But, as I said just now, Kerry said nothing about leaving me anything in her will, and I very much doubt that she said anything like it to Donna.'

Kate paused at the door. 'When we first saw you, Miss Foster, 'you said that you were an accountant. Where d'you work?'

Erica smiled. 'I'm not really an accountant,' she said, 'but it sounds better than what I really do.

'And that is?'

'I work on the counter in a building society in the West End.'

NINETEEN

Although not advertised as a lesbian club, it was obvious to anyone entering that those not of the 'sisterhood' would feel out of place. But as Kate Ebdon and Sheila Armitage had often visited such places in the course of duty, they were not too worried about that.

'Hello, darlings,' said a short-haired woman in a catsuit. 'I haven't seen you in here before.'

'Just thank your lucky stars you haven't,' said Kate. 'What's your name?'

'You can call me Kitten. Everyone does.' She placed her hands on her hips, pushed out a leg and pouted in what she believed to be a fetching manner.

'I don't think so,' said Kate, producing her warrant card. 'I'm Detective Inspector Ebdon. What's your real name?'

'Jill Clark,' said Kitten. There was a hint of regret at having to admit to so prosaic a name.

'Is there anyone here who knows Erica Foster?' asked Kate, addressing the group of women who by now had gathered around her.

'I do,' said a thin mousey-haired woman with tattooed arms. 'In fact, most of us know her. Why? What's she done?'

'Nothing that need concern you,' said Kate, 'but can any of you tell me if she was here on Christmas Eve?'

'Yes, she was,' said the cat-suited one who'd called herself Kitten. 'We had a fancy dress party, and Erica came in a sexy pirate's outfit. Very revealing.'

'That's right, she was definitely here.' said an overweight, but nevertheless rather voluptuous blonde, a statement to which several of the others added murmurs of assent.

'And what's your name?' asked Sheila Armitage.

'Donna Wilcox.

'When did she arrive, Miss Wilcox?'

'It must've been about six o'clock,' said the blonde.

'It went on all night,' said the woman in the catsuit, 'but Erica pushed off just before midnight. About eleven, I suppose. She said that her girlfriend wasn't well, and she wanted to make sure she was OK.'

'Did she mention this girlfriend's name?' asked Kate.

'Yes, it was Charlie Pollard,' said Donna Wilcox. 'We were sorry she couldn't make it. We all know her, and Charlie could always be relied on to go the extra mile, if you know what I mean,' she added, winking broadly.

'Did Erica come with anyone else?' asked Sheila Armitage.

'Yes,' said Kitten. 'She came with another of our friends, Sally Hyde.'

'Does the name Kerry Hammond mean anything to any of you?' Kate asked.

'Not to me,' said Kitten. She glanced round at the group of women. 'Girls?'

No one seemed to know Kerry, even though Charlie Pollard had insisted that she'd met Kerry in this very same club.

But then Donna Wilcox spoke. 'I knew her,' she said.

Kate drew her to one side. 'How well did you know her?'

'We had a fling,' said Donna, 'but nothing serious. It lasted a month, I suppose, and then we split.'

'And did Kerry promise to leave you everything in her will?'

Donna Wilcox laughed. 'Yes, she did as a matter of fact, but I took that with a pinch of salt. It was the sort of stupid thing she'd say in a moment of passion. She even talked about setting up home with me in St-Tropez, but I didn't pay any attention to that, either. We just had a few good times in the sack and then moved on.'

'Well, that's that, I suppose,' I said, when Kate reported to me on the Thursday morning. 'I'll put it in the report to the Crown Prosecution Service, but I can't see them being prepared to charge Erica Foster with anything.'

'But what about the question of the smuggled firearms, guv?' asked Kate.

'Frankly, Kate' I said, 'I don't think that Charlie Pollard knew anything about them, much less that Erica Foster did.'

And so it proved to be; the CPS decided that there was no case for Erica Foster to answer. But Charlie Pollard was charged with Kerry Hammond's murder and had appeared at the City of Westminster magistrates Court on the morning following her confession. A remand in custody had followed, as surely as night follows day. Sometimes.

However, before Charlie Pollard's appearance at the Old Bailey, we had to attend there for the trial of Michael Roberts, Patrick Hogan, Frankie Saunders and Danny Elliott. They faced a string of offences under the Firearms Act and several other related statutes that the Crown Prosecution Service had dredged up. It came as no surprise that the CPS declined to prosecute either Gary Dixon or Billy Sharpe, the argument being that there was no proof that either of them knew the contents of the vehicles they were driving. The CPS lawyer muttered something about there being a less than fifty per cent chance of a conviction. Personally, I'd've had a go, but these days it's out of our hands.

The trial of the others, who Dave had christened the 'Walworth Four', was short. The evidence was overwhelming and the outcome was never in any real doubt, even though English juries can be extraordinarily fickle at times.

The upshot was that Roberts got fifteen years and Hogan ten. Saunders and Elliott were sent down for four apiece. Dave cynically observed that he was surprised that they hadn't been given community service. Although Hogan had been charged with his part in the Hillingdon post office robbery, it was adjourned *sine die*, a decision that must've upset the Flying Squad. They don't like having 'unsolveds' on their books.

I was about to leave the Old Bailey when an usher caught up with me.

'DCI Brock?'

'That's me.'

'That bloke who just got sent down, Michael Roberts, guv'nor.'

'What about him?'

'He's asking to see you,' said the usher.

Dave and I descended the familiar staircase to the cells. A prison officer nodded in recognition, and opened up Roberts's cell.

'What d'you want to see me about, Mike?' I asked.

'Bloody Gary Dixon, Mr Brock. I was well pissed off when he got away.'

'There wasn't any evidence that he knew what he was carrying.'

'Of course he bloody knew,' scoffed Roberts, 'and I'll tell you something else an' all. That little toe rag tried to put the arm on Kerry. He rang her on Christmas Eve and said that a grand a month wasn't enough, and he wanted five, the saucy little bastard.'

'Now you tell me, Mike,' I complained.

'Yeah, well, we've got our own way of dealing with the likes of Dixon. Straight after he'd rung Kerry, she gave me a bell, and Pat Hogan and me sorted him. But it took us a long time to find the little bastard.'

'So it was you,' I said, at last having confirmation of what I'd suspected.

'Yeah.' Roberts grinned. 'Want to tack it on the end of my fifteen?'

'I'm not bothered, Mike, but you can tell me who you were knocking out the shooters to.'

'I can't do that, Mr Brock,' said Roberts. 'You see, now I'm likely to be banged up for a while, I've let my private health insurance lapse.'

And we never did discover who was supplied with these firearms, despite a protracted enquiry. I suppose we might find out one day, but none of the Walworth Four would give him up. In the circumstances, I suppose it was wise of them. As Michael Roberts had hinted, Her Majesty's prisons can be unforgiving places for a grass.

The other aspect of our investigation that came to nought was Kerry Wine Importers. After exhaustive enquiries by customs it was decided that no offences had been committed. I could only assume that any fraud that might've existed was the use of Kerry Trucking's vehicles to bring the wine to England without paying for the carriage. But that, in my view, merely amounted to one half of Kerry Hammond's empire fiddling the other half. And that, presumably, was some aspect of either company law or tax law in which I had no desire to become involved.

But, despite my original thoughts, that wasn't the end of it. Several days before Pollard's trial began, a Fraud Squad detective constable called Baker appeared in my office.

'I've been looking into the affairs of the Spanish Fly nightclub and Kerry Wine Importers, guv,' he announced.

'What, all by yourself?'

'Of course,' said Baker. 'If it's a multimillion job, you get a sergeant. And it has to be an international scam of epic proportions before you get an inspector.'

Things had clearly changed since I was on the Fraud Squad.

'Did you learn anything?' I asked.

'Money laundering, guv, both of them, but it'll be months, possibly even years, before we get a result.'

But that didn't concern me, thank God.

Some weeks later, at the beginning of March, Charlie Pollard appeared at the Central Criminal Court at Old Bailey charged with the murder of Kerry Hammond.

'By the way, guv,' said Kate, as we entered that forbidding building, 'I eventually interviewed Sally Hyde, the woman with whom Erica Foster said she'd spent most of Christmas Eve. She confirmed that the two of them did have lunch at her flat in Limehouse, and that they then went on to Tottenham Court Road, arriving at around six o'clock. She also said that Erica left the club at about eleven.'

'I didn't doubt that she would confirm Erica's story,' I said. 'What I don't understand is why Charlie Pollard was at such pains to implicate her. Erica must've done something far more serious than just carrying on with Kerry, surely?'

'I don't think so,' said Kate. 'Catfights – even verbal ones – can turn very nasty, and I think that Erica was right when she suggested that, because she and Kerry were still seeing each other, Charlie was trying to exact revenge on her.'

'Perhaps you're right, Kate,' I said, as we entered Court One. I'd never professed to understand sexual relationships between women, or the underlying tensions that seem to be implicit in such affairs. But to me, it still remained a mystery why Charlie Pollard should've been so vindictive as to attempt to implicate her friend in a murder.

The usual sombre opening to a trial for murder began as the clerk stood up and put the single indictment to the accused.

'Charlie Pollard, you are charged in that on the twenty-fourth of December last at Heathrow Airport in the County of London you did murder Kerry Hammond, against the peace. How say you upon this indictment: are you guilty or not guilty?'

The figure of Charlie Pollard, flanked by two female prison officers, now looked smaller than it had done in real life. But, cynic that I am, I took the view that this was not real life; it was a tragicomedy cloaked with the panoply of justice.

'Not guilty,' said Charlie, in little more than a whisper.

'You may sit down,' said the judge, who enjoyed the splendid title of Common Serjeant of London. 'Bring in the jury.'

It was the signal for the prosecution witnesses to leave the court-room. We returned to the splendour of the vast echoing Grand Hall, and sat down on one of the benches, knowing what form the next part of the performance would take.

About now there would be the usual arguments until counsel arrived at a mutual acceptance of the jurors. Prosecuting counsel's opening address would follow, during which she would set out what she would seek to prove, or disprove. After she had finished, the trial proper would at last begin. I knew that I had at least an hour to kill, and I picked up an abandoned copy of *The Times*. After several unsuccessful attempts at the crossword, I gave up.

Eventually, an usher opened the door. 'Detective Chief Inspector Brock,' he bellowed in stentorian tones, even though I was only six feet away from him. Another usher at the far end of the hall repeated the summons.

'You don't have to shout,' I said, standing up. 'I'm not deaf.'

'Sorry, guv,' said the usher. 'I thought you might be outside having a crafty smoke.'

I stepped into the witness box and took the oath. For a moment or two, I studied the jury of nine women and three men, and wondered if the women would be sympathetic or hostile to a lesbian charged with the murder of her ex-lover. I was cynical enough to ponder whether any of them were lesbians themselves, and whether that would make a difference.

My evidence was fairly straightforward and would be difficult to challenge, but, although I say it myself, I was fairly skilled at this sort of thing.

Prosecuting counsel asked the usual routine questions, and, having satisfied herself that she'd got the answers she needed in order to prove her case, she sat down.

Defence counsel stood up to cross-examine, and went through the usual pantomime of adjusting his gown, his spectacles, and carefully perusing his brief. But I hadn't left many gaps in my evidence into which he would be able to drive a wedge of doubt. He asked one or two run-of-the-mill questions about the circumstances under which Charlie Pollard had made her written confession, and then he, too, sat down.

The judge asked Crown counsel if she wished to re-examine.

'No, My Lord,' she said, bobbing briefly.

The usual procession of prosecution witnesses followed me into the box. Henry Mortlock gave his evidence of the cause of death and the manner in which it was inflicted. As usual it was concise and left no excuses for defence counsel to pick holes in it. Linda Mitchell's testimony of the scientific evidence was, as ever, clear, succinct and indisputable.

Testimonies were given by each member of my team who had played some relevant part in the investigation, together with anyone else whom prosecuting counsel thought might help to nail down what was already, in my view, an irrefutable case.

Even so, for a murder trial, it was remarkably short: five days. As I had thought from the outset, the evidence that Charlie Pollard had taken a bayonet with her when she went to the airport to meet Kerry Hammond was the clincher. Nor was there any doubt that it was the murder weapon; an expert from the forensic science laboratory stated that he had found traces of Kerry Hammond's blood on the bayonet.

After taking a mere ninety minutes to weigh the evidence, the jury returned the inevitable verdict of guilty.

A month later, we were back at the Bailey to hear the sentence. Thankfully, His Lordship didn't deliver one of the lengthy homilies that those familiar with major murder trials had come to expect from judges. Sentencing Charlie to life imprisonment, he imposed a tariff of fifteen years before she could be considered for parole. I thought it was remarkably lenient in the circumstances.

There then followed another little scene in this command performance. As Charlie Pollard was put down, I was approached by an army officer, a major from the Army Legal Corps, who had been in court during both the trial and the sentencing hearing.

'Chief Inspector, I am required to interview the prisoner in accordance with military law.'

'May I ask why, Major?'

'I have to serve her with notice of dismissal from the army,' said the major. 'It's a formality, of course. Even so, she has the right of appeal.'

We descended to the cells beneath the court.

'Corporal Pollard,' began the major, 'I have to inform you that, following your conviction, you are reduced to the rank of private. Furthermore, you are discharged with ignominy from the army.' He handed her an official document before adding, 'You have the right of appeal, should you so wish it.'

Charlie Pollard took the sheet of paper and without even a glance at it, tossed it on the floor. 'You can stuff your fucking appeal, *Major, sir*,' she said, and raised a single finger in his direction.

'I'll take that as a no, then,' commented the major drily.

It had taken ten minutes to complete that little drama and Charlie Pollard's reaction was hardly surprising. She knew that an appeal would be pointless.

However, the cynic in me imagined that she was quite looking forward to her sojourn in Holloway prison and, doubtless, at any other women's prison to which she was eventually transferred.

Dave and I finally left the depressing surroundings of the Old Bailey, and in the street outside, we breathed the air of the real world.

'*Nor Hell a fury, like a woman scorn'd*,' quoted Dave, hands in pockets, as he gazed hopefully at the Magpie and Stump public house opposite. 'I'll bet William Congreve didn't have a couple of lesbians in mind when he penned those words, guv,' he said. 'Fancy a pint?'